Do you ⬚⬚⬚ what it takes?

Picture this: I'm sitting in my apartment in Washington, D.C., wearing my red power suit. Pretty mature, huh? Now picture this: I just put on a wig and also practiced applying a fake mustache from my disguise kit. (I don't want you to worry that I've become too serious and sophisticated now that I'm working in the nation's capital.)

I know you'll be relieved to hear that I'm totally in my element at the Spy Museum!

Today I watched a Spy Museum movie about the good and bad reasons people become spies. Good reasons: patriotism and a passion for intrigue. Bad reasons: greed and egotism. The movie also talked about the risks of getting caught spying on a foreign government—little things like deportation, jail, and death.

"Do YOU have what it takes to be a spy?" the movie asked.

My answer: a resounding YES.

Other Books You May Enjoy

GILDA JOYCE
The Dead Drop

GILDA JOYCE
The Dead Drop

JENNIFER ALLISON

SLEUTH
PUFFIN
An Imprint of Penguin Group (USA) Inc.

PUFFIN BOOKS

Published by the Penguin Group

Penguin Young Readers Group, 345 Hudson Street, New York, New York 10014, U.S.A.

Penguin Group (Canada), 90 Eglinton Avenue East, Suite 700, Toronto, Ontario, Canada M4P 2Y3
(a division of Pearson Penguin Canada Inc.)

Penguin Books Ltd, 80 Strand, London WC2R 0RL, England

Penguin Ireland, 25 St Stephen's Green, Dublin 2, Ireland (a division of Penguin Books Ltd)

Penguin Group (Australia), 250 Camberwell Road, Camberwell, Victoria 3124, Australia
(a division of Pearson Australia Group Pty Ltd)

Penguin Books India Pvt Ltd, 11 Community Centre, Panchsheel Park, New Delhi - 110 017, India

Penguin Group (NZ), 67 Apollo Drive, Rosedale, North Shore 0632, New Zealand
(a division of Pearson New Zealand Ltd.)

Penguin Books (South Africa) (Pty) Ltd, 24 Sturdee Avenue,
Rosebank, Johannesburg 2196, South Africa

Registered Offices: Penguin Books Ltd, 80 Strand, London WC2R 0RL, England

First published in the United States of America by Dutton Children's Books,
a division of Penguin Young Readers Group, 2009

This Sleuth edition published by Puffin Books, a division of Penguin Young Readers Group, 2010

1 3 5 7 9 10 8 6 4 2

THE LIBRARY OF CONGRESS HAS CATALOGED THE DUTTON EDITION AS FOLLOWS:

Allison, Jennifer.

Gilda Joyce: the dead letter drop

p. cm.

Summary: Almost-fifteen-year-old psychic investigator Gilda Joyce interns for the summer at
the International Spy Museum in Washington, D.C., and solves a mystery involving national security.

ISBN: 978-0-525-47980-2 (hc)

[1. International Spy Museum (Washington, D.C.)—Fiction. 2. Spies—Fiction. 3. Psychic ability—Fiction.
4. Mystery and detective stories. 5. Washington, D.C.—Fiction.]

PZ7.A4428 Gh 2009

[Fic]—22

Puffin Books ISBN 978-0-14-241638-9

Printed in the United States of America

To my friends at the International Spy Museum with appreciation,
and to anyone whoever dreamed of becoming a spy.

CONTENTS

GILDA JOYCE
The Dead Drop

PROLOGUE

Packing List for Washington, D.C.,
Internship and Spy Activities

- Jackie Kennedy-inspired pink taffeta dress with
  matching pillbox hat (awesome vintage clothing
  store find!)

- Jackie Kennedy accessories: short white gloves,
  multistrand pearls, oversize white sunglasses,
  white clutch purse

- White stiletto pumps (because my feet can
  take it)

- Rollers and curling iron for bouncy bobs and
  flippy flips

- Ponytail hairpiece for 1960s-style "spy hair"

- Leggings and boots (to approximate 1960s Diana
  Riggs Avengers-style catsuit)

- Nancy Reagan-style fire engine red "first lady"
  power suit with quarterback-sized shoulder pads

- Red-sequined evening gown for dinner parties

- Agent 99-style light blue trench coat (wear on rainy days with collar up and vinyl knee-high stretch boots)

- Jogging suit for early morning workouts near the U.S. Capitol Building (opportunity to rub elbows with winded senators)

- Ordinary tourist clothes, including yellow sundress and flip-flops

- Nondescript government-employee-style black skirt and white blouse (to blend in with the crowd during surveillance activities)

- 1960s "spy chic" minidress found at excellent garage sale

- Liquid "spyliner" and false eyelashes for creating sultry spy eyes

- Hairspray for big spy hair

- Disguise kit: wig, makeup, fake mustache and beard (for extreme disguises), spirit gum, thick eyeglasses

- Water bottle needed to brave scorching temperatures

- Map of Washington, D.C.

- Tourist guidebook

- Polaroid camera for ghost hunting

- Professional guidebooks: <u>Haunted</u> <u>Government</u>:
  <u>The</u> <u>Famous</u> <u>Ghosts</u> <u>of</u> <u>Washington</u>, <u>D.C.</u>, and
  "<u>Spy</u> <u>Savvy</u>": <u>A</u> <u>Tradecraft</u> <u>Handbook</u>

- Notebooks, pens, and my beloved typewriter!

1

The Arrival

Gilda exited Reagan National Airport and made her way toward a line of people waiting for taxis. The air was thick with humidity and, as she dragged her heavy suitcase behind her, she found herself wishing she hadn't worn her Jackie Kennedy outfit for traveling. How did women stand wearing panty hose and high heels every day back in the old days?

You're a spy and you're actually here in Washington, D.C.! she told herself. *Stop griping about a little hot air!*

Gilda climbed into the taxi and was relieved to feel a cold blast of air-conditioning as the cab zoomed onto the highway.

"You coming home to D.C. or just visiting?" The driver peered at her through his rearview mirror, eyeing her pillbox hat with curiosity.

"I'm actually in D.C. to study spy tradecraft." Gilda knew that a true spy would never actually give away this information; she would stick with a "cover" identity and purpose. *I'm going to visit my sick grandmother,* she might say, or *I'm here to study church music at the National Cathedral.* But Gilda simply couldn't resist telling *someone* about the adventure that lay before her—a summer job at the International Spy Museum, where she planned to learn intriguing secrets while improving her own spy skills by picking up tips from the experts.

"A spy!" The cab driver grinned. "You workin' for the CIA?"

"Not exactly." Gilda hoped she actually looked old enough to be working for the Central Intelligence Agency, since this would make the grown-up tidiness of her Jackie Kennedy outfit and hairsprayed hair well worth the effort. At the very least, she needed to look older than her age of fourteen years and eleven months, because she had told the Spy Museum that she was *already* fifteen after learning that this was the youngest age they would consider for summer interns. Gilda figured that fourteen going on fifteen was close enough, considering her passion for spying.

"Lotta people ride in my cab are spies," the cab driver continued.

"Really?" Gilda knew from studying her *Spy Savvy* handbook that Washington, D.C., was "the spy capital of the world"—a place where people from around the globe came in hopes of obtaining secret information from the U.S. government.

"I overhear everything in this taxi." The driver exited the highway and drove through a lush, tree-dense neighborhood where grand foreign embassy buildings lined the street. "In fact," he said, "maybe I should be a spy."

Maybe he is a spy, Gilda thought, remembering how her *Spy Savvy* handbook had warned that "nothing is exactly what it seems" when you're operating in the world of espionage. "Don't expect the spies around you to announce themselves," the book warned. "A bus driver, delivery person, or even a homeless person on the street could actually be a spy in disguise—perfectly positioned to conduct surveillance or await a handoff of secret information without anyone noticing."

The driver pulled into the entranceway of an enormous old apartment building surrounded by magnolia trees: Cathedral Towers Apartment Homes. Gilda's stomach fluttered. *This is it,* she thought. *My new home for the summer.* She felt nervous, realizing she would actually be on her own in a new city. Gilda had traveled away from her family a couple of times before, but this would be her first experience in Washington, D.C. Not only was she in an unfamiliar city, she would be sharing an apartment with a much older roommate as well—a young woman who had just graduated from college. It would also be her first experience figuring out a subway system, making all of her own meals, and going to a real job. Gilda had flippantly assured her mother she could handle it, but suddenly she didn't feel quite so confident.

"Good luck with your spying," said the cabdriver, giving her a wink as he pulled her suitcase from the trunk of his cab.

"Thanks," said Gilda, handing him some wadded dollar bills and almost wishing he would stick around to make conversation, even though he was a complete stranger. "Same to you."

The lobby of Cathedral Towers reminded Gilda of an elegant hotel in an old Hollywood movie. For a moment, she thought she must have gotten the wrong address; she hadn't expected anything quite so sophisticated compared to her surroundings back home in Ferndale, Michigan. High ceilings with ornate moldings soared above. A silent grand piano sat upon a plush area rug, surrounded by velvet benches and chairs. Large abstract oil paintings in earth tones decorated the walls, and tranquil music piped into the room.

A young woman wearing a pantsuit carried a very official-looking briefcase through the lobby, her high heels clicking across the gleaming floor. She hurriedly pushed through the front doorway without smiling at Gilda or even looking in her direction.

Gilda sensed an aloof emptiness in the building. *This place is impressive, but it kind of gives me the feeling you get when everyone else is at school and you've been home sick for a week,* she thought. *It's kind of a lonely feeling.*

"Can I help you?" A pale, fleshy woman peered at Gilda from the reception desk, her mouth stained with peach-colored lipstick and her graying hair slicked back in a severe bun.

"Hi—I'm Gilda Joyce, and I'm moving in today."

The woman appeared displeased with this piece of information. She grumpily pulled a large book from beneath the desk and flipped through the pages, scanning a list of names and dates with a false fingernail and shaking her head. "There's no record of a move-in request today."

"There must be. I'm moving in to share an apartment with Caitlin Merrill, and she was supposed to leave me a key. I just spoke with her yesterday."

"In that case, Ms. Merrill neglected to log a move-in request for you Miss—"

"The name is Joyce. Gilda Joyce." Gilda was beginning to feel as if she were a real CIA agent trying to cross the border of a hostile country. For some reason, she suddenly wished she had made up a false name. "And you are?"

The desk attendant pursed her lips, reluctant to give out her own name. "Ms. Potts," she said coldly.

Gilda had a sudden urge to call her mother for help—an urge she did her best to squelch. *If I'm going to be on my own in a city, I'm going to have to learn to take charge.* "Ms. Potts," Gilda said, doing her best to sound authoritative, "I must have the key to my apartment, or I shall have to call a building manager."

Ms. Potts gazed very directly into Gilda's eyes. "Miss Joyce, you *are* talking to the building manager. And I will welcome you with open arms once your name is properly in the move-in request book."

"Then, Ms. Potts, let us inscribe the name Gilda Joyce into yon Move-In Request Book herewith." Gilda wasn't quite sure why she had begun to speak in such a ridiculously pompous tone, but it seemed to suit Ms. Potts's own attitude.

"I can't just write your name here because you *want* me to. The move-in request has to be made at least twenty-four hours in advance of the requested move-in time."

I know her type, Gilda thought. *She's the kind of person who doesn't want to give you something you want simply because she knows you need it.*

"Ms. Potts," said Gilda, attempting a different strategy, "I'm sure this is not the sort of welcome foreign diplomats typically receive to the nation's capital." Gilda realized this was a risky fib, but it seemed worth a try. *If I'm going to be a spy, I may as well practice using a cover identity while I'm here,* she thought.

At the mention of "foreign diplomats," Ms. Potts's eyes widened slightly, registering the tiniest flash of fear. What if she had made a mistake and offended one of her truly important tenants? *But her name isn't in the move-in request book*, Ms. Potts reminded herself. *We must follow procedures.*

Gilda and Ms. Potts locked eyes like poker players, each trying to determine whether the other was bluffing, whether the other would back down. Gilda had a fleeting memory of her father complaining about "Washington bureaucrats."

Realizing that Ms. Potts was stubborn enough to stand there all day without budging from her position, Gilda decided she had no choice but to call her new roommate for help. "Excuse me, Ms. Potts. I'll speak to Caitlin Merrill about this."

Gilda turned away from the desk and dialed Caitlin's number.

"National Criminal Justice Association," a chirpy voice answered. "Caitlin Merrill speaking."

"Hi, Caitlin; this is your new roommate, Gilda, and I have a little problem here." Gilda explained her predicament.

"Ms. Potts loves to act as if we live in the FBI building or something. Pass me over to her, okay?"

Gilda handed the phone to Ms. Potts, who flipped through her beloved move-in request book while listening to Caitlin. Gilda thought she saw the ghost of a smile on her peach-stained lips as she listened to Caitlin's bright, chatty voice. Gilda watched as Ms. Potts scribbled the name Gilda Joyce into the timetable and pulled a key from a hook on the wall. "All right, darlin'," Ms. Potts said to Caitlin into the phone. "She's all set." Ms. Potts handed the cell phone back to Gilda with a gesture of disdain.

Gilda was seriously impressed with her new roommate. "How did you do that?" she whispered into the phone as Ms. Potts turned to find some paperwork in one of her files.

"I bribed her with chocolate. Ms. Potts likes me because I'm the only person in the building who at least pretends to be nice to her."

I guess I could learn a couple things from my new roommate, Gilda thought.

"That's politics in D.C., right? Oh, and I'm really sorry about the mess when you get up to the apartment. I was going to clean, but I've been so busy this week."

"Don't worry; I like it messy," said Gilda, whose room at home was notoriously unkempt.

"Not *too* messy, I hope."

"Not gross-messy, just kind of neat-messy."

Caitlin laughed. "I should be home pretty soon; I've just got to proofread one more brief for this week's newsletter, and I'm outta here."

Ms. Potts slid a key across the desk toward Gilda. "Remember," she warned, "if you ever need to use our freight elevator, you must sign up more than twenty-four hours in advance."

"I shall never forget that, Ms. Potts." Gilda headed toward the elevator to make her way up to the fourth floor.

2

The Roommate

Gilda felt instantly happy when she opened the door to her new apartment. It was definitely a girl's apartment: sunny, comfortable, and also slightly messy, just as Caitlin had promised. Art posters from museums including the Smithsonian and the Corcoran decorated the walls, and quirky mismatched furniture filled the room—an enormous brown couch, an antique armoire, a Tiffany lamp, and chairs of different shapes and colors that Caitlin had acquired as hand-me-downs from relatives or flea market purchases. CDs were scattered across the windowsills amid several wilting potted plants.

Gilda enjoyed testing her profiling skills to see if she could accurately anticipate personalities based on the objects people kept lying around, and Caitlin's absence gave her a perfect opportunity to get to know a little about her roommate before meeting her in person. Gilda wandered around the living room, noticing that the windowsills displayed an assortment of candid photographs of college-age young people with broad, goofy smiles and arms around one another's shoulders. Peering at the pictures, Gilda decided that Caitlin must be popular and very social. *She has a lot of friends*, Gilda thought. For a moment, she imagined returning to school and posting pictures in her locker of herself clowning around with Caitlin's entourage. *I wonder if she'll introduce me to her friends, or if she'll think it's too uncool to hang out with a high school kid.*

Gilda looked at the titles of the books on Caitlin's shelf and noticed a law school entrance exam workbook and several books with titles like *Turbo Dating* that appeared to be about finding either a boyfriend or a husband. She was particularly intrigued by a book on handwriting analysis and made a mental note to study it later.

Gilda peeked into one of the bedrooms and felt pleased when she found an unmade bed, a pile of law school study guides, and a tornado of shoes, socks, panty hose, suit jackets, and skirts that appeared to have been taken off in a great hurry and abandoned exactly where they fell. *I wish Mom could see this,* Gilda thought. *She'd see I'm not the only person who has a messy bedroom.*

Gilda carried her suitcase into the second bedroom and discovered a striking contrast with the rest of the apartment: a bed with a white, lacy bedspread; a cream-colored dresser; a small vanity table with a mirror; and off-white walls that were almost completely bare except for a few tranquil watercolor paintings of Washington, D.C., settings—the National Cathedral, the Washington Monument, the Tidal Basin surrounded by cherry blossoms. It was the sort of room that was both pretty and impersonal enough to be a guest room in a bed-and-breakfast.

Caitlin's usual roommate was gone for the summer; Gilda

was renting her room at the suggestion of a Spy Museum employee who volunteered to help Gilda find housing. Gilda snooped around the room, trying to get a sense of the absent roommate's identity. While Caitlin's belongings were strewn everywhere, yielding obvious clues, this girl had left scarcely a trace of herself behind. There were no incriminating journals, letters, books, or receipts. Aside from the fact that she was clearly very neat, clean, and feminine, the room conveyed little evidence of her personality and interests. *I wonder if she and Caitlin get along,* Gilda mused.

Gilda noticed that her bedroom window gave her a clear view into the apartment windows on a parallel wing of the building overlooking a small courtyard. *A promising people-watching opportunity!* she thought happily. At the moment, however, she couldn't see anything interesting: the apartments in view were all concealed by closed blinds or curtains.

Gilda unpacked her suitcase, then carefully placed her manual typewriter on the vanity table. Catching a glimpse of herself in the mirror, she noticed that her Jackie Kennedy–style flip hairstyle was drooping after a day of travel and afternoon humidity. She found a comb in her cluttered handbag and energetically backcombed sections of hair, then spritzed the gravity-defying 'do with a cloud of hairspray. "The goal is big hair that doesn't move in a windstorm," she had read in an article about "spy chic" of the 1960s. "A minidress, knee-high boots, perfectly molded curls piled high, and dramatically upswept eyeliner and false eyelashes complete your spy look."

Gilda had just begun to type a journal entry when she heard a key turning in the apartment door. A moment later, Caitlin

Merrill appeared in her bedroom doorway, wearing a slim black pantsuit and carrying a backpack over her shoulder. "Hey!" Her face was shiny with perspiration.

Caitlin's expression tensed as she absorbed the visual impression of her new roommate for the summer: a freckle-nosed teenager with a hairsprayed flip—a girl who wore a pink dress and sat typing at a manual typewriter.

"I'm Gilda." Gilda stood up and extended a hand to Caitlin in what she hoped was the right gesture to greet her new roommate. "Nice to meet you."

Caitlin shook Gilda's hand and stared at her with boldly inquisitive blue eyes, her long brown lashes layered with mascara—the only makeup she wore. She eyed Gilda's typewriter. "Do you always travel with a typewriter?"

Gilda was so used to keeping her typewriter on hand whenever possible, she sometimes forgot that her choice of writing tools seemed odd to other people. "I'm a writer, so I just like to have it with me in case I get any ideas for new projects."

"Wouldn't a laptop be easier to carry when you're traveling?"

Gilda knew that Caitlin had a point, but her love for her typewriter had nothing to do with convenience; it was simply the way she preferred to write. "It's kind of a long story," she said. "The typewriter was a gift from my dad. Something he owned when he was a kid. I guess I just feel better when it's around."

"Your dad's a writer, too?"

"He wanted to be, but it never really worked out for him. He died a few years ago."

Caitlin shifted her weight, clearly wishing that she hadn't brought up the subject of the typewriter. "Sorry to hear that."

"I guess the typewriter just makes me feel more creative or something." Gilda sensed it was best not to tell her new roommate that her typewriter was almost magical to her: it was a machine, but it was also something akin to an invisible friend to whom she confided all of her problems and dreams—a friend who seemed to help her solve mysteries.

Apparently deciding that it was safe to make herself comfortable in her new roommate's living quarters, Caitlin walked over to the bed, dropped her shoulder bag on the floor, and flopped down. Supporting her weight on her elbows, she regarded Gilda through narrowed eyes. "How old are you, anyway?"

"Fifteen." Gilda reasoned that it would be best to keep the details of her cover identity consistent just in case Caitlin talked to any of her new colleagues at the Spy Museum.

"Fifteen?! When that lady at the Spy Museum said an intern needed an apartment, I didn't realize they meant a mere child. I guess it's my job to be your substitute mom this summer."

"I'm actually totally independent." Gilda felt glad she hadn't told Caitlin she was actually fourteen. "I traveled all over England by myself this year." Gilda didn't mention that the trip had actually been chaperoned by Wendy's piano teacher.

"Still," said Caitlin, "I'll feel responsible. I'm twenty-two years old, Gilda."

"Practically old enough to be my grandmother," Gilda joked.

"In some circles," Caitlin added, playing along.

"Anyway, a lot of people tell me I'm old for my age, so you don't have to worry about me." Gilda had also once been told that she acted "young for her age," but there was no way she was going to tell Caitlin about that.

Caitlin stood up and peered over Gilda's shoulder at the journal entry Gilda had been typing. She frowned. "You're writing a letter to your dad?"

"Oh, it's just a story I'm making up." In truth, Gilda often kept a diary in the form of letters to her dad, but she realized that her new roommate might not understand her penchant for writing to a dead person. Gilda quickly rolled the paper out of the typewriter. She also didn't want Caitlin to see what she had written about hoping to be included in escapades with Caitlin's college buddies and the list of famous D.C. ghosts she hoped to investigate, including the ghost of Abraham Lincoln.

"I'd like to write a book someday." Caitlin flopped back down on Gilda's bed. "Maybe I'll write a comedy about my dating experiences in this city since I graduated from college."

"Like what?"

"Let's see." Caitlin counted off examples on her fingers. "Like people who post pictures of themselves on Internet dating sites that don't reveal the fact that they're actually about three hundred pounds heavier and thirty years older in real life. Like guys who tell you they only have ten minutes to meet you for lunch because they have 'another lunch date' lined up before they have to get back to work at the Senate office building. Like a guy who actually *hired* someone to pretend to be his friend and tell the girls standing around the bar how great he is. It's just crazy around here, Gilda." Caitlin clearly enjoyed talking about the "crazy" frustrations of her dating life, and Gilda suspected that she was secretly pleased with the experiences.

I wonder if hanging out with Caitlin is going to require going on dates with three-hundred-pound men who work as staffers in the House and Senate buildings, Gilda wondered. *On the positive side, I read in my* Spy Savvy *handbook that spying is primarily a social skill. I bet Caitlin is in the perfect position to get lots of information when she's out meeting all those people.*

Caitlin peered into Gilda's mirror and attempted to reshape her limp, dirty-blond hair with her fingers. "Hey, since I'm home from work so early, what do you say we go grab something to eat and do some sightseeing? You can see the Washington Monument and the Lincoln Memorial and all that touristy stuff on the mall."

"Sounds great."

Caitlin stared at Gilda's high-heeled pumps. "Those shoes are cute, but they're going to hurt your feet."

"I'm used to it," said Gilda.

"I wish I could dress fancy like you, but I wear sneakers with my suits any chance I get." Caitlin took off her suit jacket. "I'm just going to throw on a pair of jeans and then we'll go."

Gilda stood up in her high heels and decided that on second thought, it made more sense to change into one of her less interesting "blend-into-the-crowd" tourist disguises. *I have a better chance of picking up some secret information on the National Mall if people assume I'm just an ordinary kid from the backwoods of Michigan,* she thought. *After all, I'm in D.C. now, so you never know what I might overhear.*

3

The Psychic Spy

In a secret room inside a Washington, D.C., apartment complex, a man readied himself to steal secrets from a foreign government. He was about to spy on people thousands of miles away from his own location, but to do this, he would use no satellites, telescopes, or secret cameras. He would use only one tool—his mind.

Barefoot, he reclined on a soft chair. Wires connected several machines to his body to monitor his pulse, brainwaves, and other vital signs. He closed his eyes, preparing himself to receive instructions about his target from his supervisor, who observed and monitored him from a few feet away. His instructions might be coordinates for a specific geographical location or nothing more than a name used to track down a person of interest. On other occasions, he was simply tested to see if he could perceive details of random distant objects without ever seeing or touching them.

Most often, he was disturbingly accurate.

His body relaxed and he felt himself become weightless. After floating for a few moments, he felt himself plunging down very quickly into a fine mist, as if he were skydiving through endless clouds. In fact, his body was completely motionless; only his mind moved through space and time in search of his target—in search of secret information.

Finally, he reached a clear place where he expected to find her—the girl who would help him. The girl always led him to the information he was seeking; she was his most secret source of intelligence—his "trick of the trade."

The girl was dead.

But this time, something was wrong, almost as if some interference from another person's mind was blocking his own perception. The girl was nowhere to be found.

Someone else turned up instead.

The psychic spy was used to seeing frightening visions, but the face that appeared was upsetting in a way he couldn't understand. It was a woman's face with dark eyes and blood-stained crimson lips: strangely, the blood had dried in the shape of an asymmetrical red-black star. The face that didn't belong there; it had no connection to anything he expected to see.

"I need to stop," the psychic spy called out to his supervisor—a man sitting across the room who wore a yellow bow tie and took notes steadily. "Something's wrong."

"Keep looking for your target," his supervisor replied. "You can't stop now."

4

A D.C. Tour Guide
for Math-Camp Shut-Ins

Dear Wendy,

Here I am in Washington, D.C.--writing you a
letter at 11:00 P.M. in my new apartment! It's
late and I need to get some sleep before my first
day of work at the Spy Museum, but I promised you
I'd write you on my first day here, so here 'tis:

General summary: things are awesome so far. The
only thing missing is my best friend (that's you,
in case you've forgotten about me already).

How are things going at math camp? Have you
learned to multiply fractions yet? ⇦joke--haha.

Remember how we were trying to guess what my
roommate would be like, and we agreed she sounded
"perky" when you listened in on my phone conversation with her? Well, we were right! Except she's
not quite as girlie as we expected. For example,
I don't think she even owns a comb or even any
makeup. As we were walking around the city, she
kept combing her fingers through her hair, twist-

ing it up in a bun, and trying to keep it in place with a ballpoint pen (which didn't work). She's really nice, and I think we're going to be friends. However, she seems concerned that she's going to have to be my babysitter all summer.(We know how wrong she is about that!)

Caitlin took me on a tour of the national monuments today. Since I know you haven't had a chance to visit D.C. yet, I thought I'd write you a little tour guide to keep in your files for future reference.

WASHINGTON, D.C.--
A TOUR GUIDE FOR MATH-CAMP SHUT-INS
By Gilda Joyce

THE D.C. METRO SYSTEM:
The Metro system is the subway system of our nation's capital. It's also a great people-watching venue! If you have nothing else planned, just ride the Metro from one side of the city to the other, and you'll get a sense of who the American people really are.

In the middle of the afternoon, there are two basic types of people on the train: people wearing shorts and baseball caps, who smile and look out the window as if the train is a fun ride at an amusement park (because they're on vacation),

and people wearing suits, who view the ride as a
tedious journey from one point to another. I was
dressed like a tourist at that point (and yes,
I DID wear the Jackie Kennedy get-up on the plane
even though you thought I wouldn't have the nerve
or the stamina!) but I tried to look bored, as if I
was on break from my work at the Senate building.

Here and there, standing out like little
islands, you see the true Americans, who look
totally different from everyone else.

PEOPLE-WATCHING HIGHLIGHTS:

1. Standing next to me was a guy with the body
   of a sumo wrestler and a tall spiky Mohawk.
   His arms were covered with tattoos like pat-
   terned shirtsleeves. The surprising thing was
   the way he gazed down at the baby carriage he
   was pushing, smiling and making gooey faces at
   an infant dressed in the frilliest pink outfit
   you've ever seen.
2. A nun in full habit sat on the Metro stitching
   embroidery, surrounded by mustachioed men
   wearing security clearance badges and dark
   suits. It's unusual enough to see a nun in that
   get-up in the middle of the summer, but I also
   got the feeling she was surrounded by a bunch
   of FBI agents who were planning to arrest her
   as soon as she stepped off the train.

HIGHLIGHTS FROM THE NATIONAL MALL:

First of all, Wendy, the National Mall is NOT a giant shopping mall. (I know; I was disappointed, too.) It's more like a big open space devoted to monuments of important people and events in American history. It also serves as a running track where portly government employees shuffle their sagging bodies to and fro during their lunch hours.

The most important thing about the National Mall is the feeling of vast, open space. "We can afford to take up a lot of space," the National Mall seems to announce to visitors from foreign lands. "We've got plenty of it! And furthermore," the Mall declares to old ladies tottering from their air-conditioned tour buses, "If you're too weak to climb all these steps and too squeamish to use a Porta-Potty, you can just turn around and go home right now."

THE WASHINGTON MONUMENT:

If you want to think about big, inspirational ideas (for you that might mean a division problem with a really long remainder), just go sit at the foot of the Washington Monument, which is basically a giant arrow pointing up to the sky. It's very uplifting, and you also have the feeling that it just might fall over on top of you since it's

so much taller and more important than the antlike
people walking around it. (Slight disappointment:
Caitlin didn't want to wait in line to ride the
elevator up to the top.)

THE LINCOLN MEMORIAL:
The Lincoln Memorial contains a truly giant statue
of President Lincoln sitting on a big throne and
gazing at the U.S. Capitol building. Something
about the sheer giantness of this statue (yes,
Wendy, giantness should be a word) and the serious
look on his face makes even the most sweaty, hyper
kids fall silent when they enter the memorial.

Did I ever tell you Lincoln is my favorite
president from history? Why?, you ask?
1. Our nation's tallest president (so far)
2. Liked the theatre (although getting shot to
   death while watching a "funny" play is a big
   price to pay)
3. Just about the best writer we've ever had as a
   president
4. Psychic abilities! (Lincoln had a premonition
   of his own death--a dream in which mourning
   people gathered around a coffin in the White
   House. When he asked what was going on, someone
   said, "The President is dead." Very spooky.)
5. Numerous sightings of his ghost by foreign dig-
   nitaries visiting the White House
6. He knew what it's like to lose a close fam-

ily member. (Lincoln's mom died when Lincoln was only nine years old and Willie, Lincoln's twelve-year-old son, died while Lincoln was serving his term in the White House. Sad!) President Lincoln was thoughtful and sometimes moody--a man of deep thoughts. Not the cheerleader type!

SIGNING OFF FOR NOW--I'll write more tomorrow!

5

The Spy Museum

I just realized you're dressed very nineteen-eighties." Caitlin stood behind Gilda on the long, steep escalator descending into the Dupont Circle Metro Station.

Gilda didn't respond; she focused on quelling a feeling of vertigo as she looked down into the underground station. She was also intrigued by a Walt Whitman poem engraved into the granite wall encircling the escalator:

I sit by the restless all the dark night—some are so young;
Some suffer so much—I recall the experience sweet and sad. . . .

Gilda wasn't quite sure what the words meant, but she liked the haunting, poignant sound of the words—the eerie feeling of reading a poem while being lowered into the ground. She pulled out her reporter's notebook and jotted a note to capture the feeling:

So many buildings and monuments in this city are engraved with poetic messages that make you think about the
suffering of people in times past. It reminds me of walking

29

through a graveyard: it's beautiful and interesting but also lonely and a little spooky, too.

"Earth to Gilda," said Caitlin. "You look very eighties!"

"Oh, thanks." Gilda decided to interpret this as a compliment even if it wasn't intended as such. She had read somewhere that you should dress for the job you want rather than the job you have, and after much deliberation between her Nancy Reagan–style red power suit and her *Avengers*-style spy jumpsuit with boots, she had settled on the power suit combined with a red pair of cat's-eye sunglasses for her first day on the job at the Spy Museum. "I believe in dressing for success," she added.

"The Spy Museum might have a pretty casual office environment, especially in the summer," Caitlin continued. "My supervisor at the NCJA walks around in flip-flops half the time."

"Sounds like he aspires to go sit on the beach."

"I respect him for being so honest about himself."

"At the Spy Museum, it's all about showing that you can 'live your cover'." *"LIVE your cover identity"* was a guideline Gilda had read in her *Spy Savvy* handbook. It wasn't enough to simply *look* whatever role you were playing as a spy; you had to fully experience it in your everyday life. "Right now, my 'cover identity' is that I'm an experienced young professional who knows how to use a copy machine."

Caitlin laughed. "I'm sure they don't expect you to know everything before you even get there, Gilda."

After Gilda and Caitlin boarded the Metro, Gilda took out her reporter's notebook to quickly scribble a letter to Wendy:

Dear Wendy:

Here I am on the underground train on my way to work! The people on the train right now during morning rush hour look a lot different from how they did yesterday in the middle of the afternoon. For one thing, there are a lot more glum-looking, white-haired men wearing ties who sit behind newspapers with their shoulders slumped. Here I am, all ready to eavesdrop on incriminating conversations, and it's as if everyone's still half asleep.

"This is my stop," Caitlin announced as the train reached the Judiciary Square station. "You know where you're going, right, Gilda? You get off at the Gallery Place stop, then just walk down F Street to the Spy Museum."

"Got it." Gilda felt another flutter of nerves. "I'll see you after work."

"Make sure you have that gourmet dinner waiting for me when I get home."

"Don't worry," said Gilda, playing along, "I'll have the toast all buttered."

"And don't burn it this time," Caitlin joked. "I mean it."

"I promise I'll get it right this time." Witnessing this banter, people regarded Gilda and Caitlin with curiosity. A man slipped into Caitlin's seat as she got up to leave.

"Good luck!" Caitlin disappeared through the train doors.

31

"Nice sunglasses," said the man who had just sat down next to Gilda.

"Oh—thanks." Gilda prepared herself for the possibility that some weirdo had just seated himself next to her—something she had frequently experienced on Detroit city buses.

"They make you look more interesting than the average government employee."

Gilda couldn't help feeling flattered to hear this even as she felt wary of attention from a strange man. She glanced in his direction and saw that there was something almost handsome about his middle-aged, suntanned face and mirthful blue eyes. It was a likable face. She also wondered if she should conceal the true details of her identity just in case this man was actually a charming serial killer who might decide to follow her to the Spy Museum. "I'm actually starting a job on Capitol Hill today," she fibbed.

"Capitol Hill! Now that is impressive. What kind of job?"

"The House, the Senate—you name it."

"Sounds demanding, but I can tell it won't be any problem for you."

"Nothing I can't handle." Gilda was now enjoying the fantasy that her job involved passing important legislation.

"And where is such an impressive young lady as yourself from? You don't look local."

"California. San Francisco, to be specific."

"A wonderful city! Well, we're approaching my stop here, Ms.—"

"Stunn." It was the surname of a fictional character Gilda

had once created for a story, and it was the first alias that came to mind at the moment. "Penelope Stunn."

"What a charming name!" He extended a hand, and Gilda shook it. "I'm Jake Clarke."

Jake Clarke sounds like a fake name, Gilda thought. On the other hand, there was something maddeningly familiar about the name; she felt she had heard it somewhere before.

As Jake Clarke stood up to move toward the door of the train, Gilda realized that they were actually at the Gallery Place Metro—her stop as well. She hurriedly ran to the door and managed to jump off the train just before the sliding doors shut and the train pulled away.

In the quiet hours before the Spy Museum opened, security guards wearing white shirts and bow ties joked with one another as tourists began to gather in a line outside the door.

A guard let Gilda into the Spy Museum lobby, and Gilda was delighted to discover that her new work environment was both stylish and mysterious. Ominous quotations about espionage were projected onto the walls, and video screens featuring clips from famous spy cases were suspended all around. Flashing neon lights framed the doorway leading into the museum exhibits.

"You the new intern?" the museum guard asked.

"Yes—I'm Gilda Joyce."

"Just go up those stairs, honey, and look for a lady named April Shepherd. She takes care of our interns and does all those educational programs for the kids. If she's not in her office, go down to the Ultra Room or the Garbo Room, and you'll find her."

"Okay, thanks." Gilda was intrigued with the sound of the "Ultra Room" and "Garbo Room" and eager to explore her new surroundings.

"Just look for a crazy lady with curly red hair," added a man with dreadlocks who sat at the information desk grinning.

"You're so bad, Keith."

"Oh, right; I keep forgetting. Nobody here is crazy."

"Nobody except you."

As Gilda ascended the stairs, she passed an enormous, greenish statue of a bearded man that was bound with heavy ropes and suspended from the ceiling. Something about the violent, humiliating manner in which the statue was being hoisted made Gilda think of a lynching. She read a placard explaining that the statue was a replica of a famous statue of a man named Feliks Dzerzhinsky, "the father of the KGB."

RUSSIANS TOPPLED THE STATUE WHEN THE SOVIET UNION FELL, the sign explained.

Gilda knew that the KGB stood for the spy agency of the Soviet Union during the Cold War—an arm of the Soviet government that had also spied extensively on the Russian people and crushed free speech. Anyone who publicly voiced opinions contrary to those of the government was quietly sent to a Soviet prison.

At the top of the steps, Gilda turned down a hallway, her high heels clicking over a floor that looked as if it were made of tiny lights embedded within tin foil and glass.

"Sweetie, if you can do poo-poo in the potty today, you can

have a treat!" A woman who wore her curly, strawberry-blond

hair tied back with a colorful printed scarf walked quickly toward Gilda, speaking into her BlackBerry. Gilda immediately knew that this must be April Shepherd, her supervisor. "Okay—bye-bye, honey!"

"Sounds like you know how to motivate your staff," Gilda blurted as April approached.

April regarded Gilda with a surprised, frozen smile, clearly not sure who Gilda was.

"I'm Gilda Joyce." Gilda extended her hand.

"Oh! Gilda!" April's eyes moved to the red cat's-eye sunglasses perched on top of Gilda's head as she shook Gilda's hand. "You caught me talking to my toddler. He's turning three next month, and I'm trying to get him potty trained for preschool. I've tried every kind of reward—M&M's, television shows, toys, you name it."

"My friend Wendy told her two-year-old brother that if he didn't start pooping in the toilet, all the poop was going to come back as a big monster sometime when he least expected it." Gilda suddenly realized that in her attempt to make a friendly impression on her new boss, she had managed to say the word *poop* at least twice in one sentence.

April considered the story about Wendy with bemused horror. "I guess fear can be a good motivator for some kids, but it doesn't work for my little Gabriel. Did that work for your friend's little brother?"

"He actually got kind of curious to meet the poop monster."

"Well, then!" April seemed eager to change the subject. "Let's get you settled!"

35

April took Gilda to the human resources department, where Gilda was thrilled to receive her very own key card allowing her access to elevators and other parts of the museum building that were off-limits to ordinary tourists. She had noticed people walking down the street and riding the Metro displaying photo IDs worn as if they were special badges of honor—symbols placing them in an elite inner circle of people with special access to secret information. *I'm a real employee in Washington, D.C.,* Gilda thought, hanging the key card around her neck. *I have special access to the Spy Museum.*

"Now I'll take you further behind the scenes—to all the staff offices." April led Gilda through aqua-colored hallways decorated with black-and-white photos, past offices where employees tapped away at their computers, past a break room where museum guards and other employees sipped coffee near an open box of doughnuts. The offices were ordinary enough, but Gilda sensed a unique buzz of excitement and anticipation in the air that reminded her of being backstage in a theater before showtime. *This is the perfect place for me to work,* Gilda thought.

"Now I'll introduce you to some of your colleagues."

Gilda followed April into a crowded room divided into cubicles. Gilda had the impression of multiple projects and a creative overload just barely under control: everywhere she looked, books, papers, and random personal objects burst from files and careened in tall stacks. Floor-to-ceiling bookshelves encased behind glass doors lined the walls.

Sitting in one of the cubicles, a bespectacled young man wearing a black T-shirt advertising an obscure rock band scribbl[ed] notes as he talked on the phone. Two women sat on the carpeted floor, hurriedly stuffing papers into folders.

"How's that paper-stuffing going?" April asked the women.

"Good." They looked up at Gilda, subtly eyeing her business suit from head to toe, their hands still moving from papers to folders.

"We like to keep our employees sitting on the floor as much as possible," said April.

"She isn't kidding," said one of the women, who wore sweatpants and sneakers. She was strikingly tan.

"This is Gilda—our new intern," said April, placing a hand on Gilda's shoulder. "She's from Michigan. Gilda, this is Janet, who does just about everything, and Marla, our events coordinator, who's doing me a huge favor by stuffing envelopes to meet an educational-program deadline."

Marla had a young, sporty look, and Janet looked completely opposite: her plump face was smooth and unlined, but her dowdy blond hairstyle, frumpy cardigan, and reading glasses suspended from a chain gave her an almost matronly demeanor. *Janet has what I like to call a "young elderly" look where she could be either twenty-nine or forty-five,* Gilda thought.

"Aren't you glad you came all this way just to sit on the floor and stick things in folders?" Marla joked.

"It beats sitting home and watching the weeds grow," Gilda replied, secretly feeling a little worried that she would in fact spend the summer stuffing envelopes.

"Based on the bio you submitted, I'm sure you don't spend much time sitting around." April turned to Janet and Marla. "Did the two of you see Gilda's bio?" She picked up a piece of paper that was lying on top of a stack of books and waved it in front of their faces.

<u>NEW SUMMER INTERN!</u>

Fifteen-year-old Gilda Joyce joins us this week all the way from the Detroit area. Gilda impressed us with the diversity and uniqueness of her academic and extracurricular interests, which include: "solving mysteries, writing novels, ghost hunting, people-watching (spying, of course!), flea-market and garage-sale shopping, street fashion, and cooking for comfort."

Be sure to stop by and say hello to Gilda!

"Oh, yeah. It was cute," said Marla. Janet made no response and merely continued stuffing envelopes.

Gilda wasn't too concerned about the less-than-enthusiastic response from Janet and Marla because she was suddenly very interested in the phone conversation the man wearing the black T-shirt was having. "The artifacts might be of interest," he said, "although we do already have a lipstick gun in the museum, as you know."

Gilda's ears perked up at the mention of the Spy Museum's "lipstick gun." On the museum's website, she had read about the small silver handgun disguised as a tube of lipstick that could fire a single bullet. Along with objects including an umbrella that shot poison pellets, the lipstick gun was one of the Spy Museum's more whimsical, if deadly, examples of Cold War secret weaponry.

Gilda felt a familiar ticklish sensation in her left ear. She wished she could somehow tap into the man's phone conversation so she could hear what the person at the other end of the line was saying.

"I'm sorry." Gilda realized that April was staring at her and waiting for her to respond to a question. "What were you saying?"

"Uh-oh. Usually it takes the interns at least a couple weeks to get attention-deficit disorder."

"At which point we move them over to the marketing department," Marla joked.

"Can you keep your staff members under control, April?" The man in the black T-shirt hung up the phone, stood up, and stretched. He was strikingly tall and thin. "Some of us have work to do." He reached across a cluttered desk to shake Gilda's hand. "Hi—I'm Matthew Morrow."

"Sorry," said April, "I forgot to introduce you."

"Saving the best for last, huh?" Matthew joked.

Janet burst into laughter and then reddened.

There was something odd about that little outburst, Gilda thought.

"Matthew is our resident historian," said April. "He's written a book about espionage and he taught at Harvard for a couple years."

I always assumed that real historians probably look really old and dust-covered, as if they've been sitting around in an attic forever, Gilda thought. *But this guy looks like a totally normal person in his twenties.*

"Who were you talking to just now on the phone?" April asked.

"Wouldn't you like to know."

"There aren't any secrets around here, Matthew."

"That's right," said Marla from her spot on the floor. "She has ways of finding out things."

"Well, if you must know, I was speaking with a former KGB officer who defected to the U.S. during the Cold War."

"Interesting!" April turned to Gilda to explain. "'Defecting' means he was a spy who switched sides from the Soviet Union to America during the Cold War."

"Oh, you don't have to tell me about defecting and switching sides," said Gilda. "For example, this year there were these two groups of girls at school who hated each other. This one girl was in the more popular group, but then she defected over to the *other* group and told them all this secret stuff about the first group. Then the two groups kept glaring at each other across the lunchroom and planting false rumors and stuff, although they never actually got into an all-out fight. It was just like the Cold War."

Matthew regarded Gilda with a deadpan expression. "I see I'm not the only historian on staff anymore."

"I actually think she summed up the Cold War pretty well," said April. "Just throw in the threat of nuclear war and it was basically the high school lunchroom."

"Anyway," Matthew continued, "the man's name is Boris Volkov, and he said he recently discovered a couple objects in his attic that we might want to see for our collections."

"Was one of them a lipstick gun?" Gilda felt her cheeks turn pink as both Matthew and April stared at her.

"Impressive eavesdropping," said Matthew.

"No kidding," April laughed. "She's perfect for this place."

Gilda realized she really wanted to go with Matthew to visit this ex-KGB agent and see whatever it was he had "discovered in his attic." She sensed, though, that people wouldn't like it if she simply asked if she could go. After all, she had only just arrived at the museum, and it was her first day of work.

"Speaking of former spies," said April, glancing at her watch, "Gilda still needs to meet Jasper. Follow me, Gilda."

"Nice to meet you, Matthew." Gilda followed April from the office reluctantly, wishing she could ask Matthew a few more questions.

"Jasper is the executive director of the museum and a former CIA senior intelligence officer." April led Gilda into a large corner office where an expansive desk and a leather-covered armchair filled a room lined with bright windows—a striking contrast with the cluttered cubicles of the room where Matthew, April, Marla, and Janet worked together.

Gilda suddenly felt mortified as a suntanned man with salt-and-pepper hair rose from the desk to greet her. *It was the man from the Metro—Jasper Clarke!* "But—" Gilda stammered, "you said your name was Jake!"

"All my friends call me Jake. *You* said your name was Penelope Stunn from California."

April was amused. "Well, this seems like a match made in heaven."

Gilda couldn't believe she had already been caught fibbing to the executive director of the Spy Museum. "I guess I was practicing 'living my cover identity' to get into the mood for my first day of work," Gilda explained.

April cackled. "Seems like you might have a real spy recruit here, Jasper."

"Indeed."

Gilda was relieved that April found the exchange funny, but she was unnerved by Jasper Clarke, who regarded her with very blue eyes that seemed to look *through* her. His poised demeanor suggested the social graces of a man who had been to hundreds of cocktail parties in as many cities—someone who could converse with just about anyone on just about any topic. He also struck Gilda as someone who was constantly processing secrets in some part of his mind—taking speedy inventory, noticing a million details at once, and filing away data to draw upon if it became relevant later.

"Actually, I apologize," said Jasper. "I should have introduced myself and told you exactly who I was when I overheard you talking to your roommate."

Gilda felt a queasy mixture of embarrassment and vulnerability, realizing that he had been watching her—that he had known all along exactly who she was from the first moment she had attempted to fool him.

"That's terrible, Jasper. You let Gilda think you were just some weird guy on the Metro?"

"Old habits die hard."

"Jasper likes to see how much information he can get from other people without telling anything about himself."

"Ah," said Jasper, pointing a finger in the air. "But Gilda didn't tell me anything about herself. Only lies."

"Excellent work, Agent Gilda," said April with a wry smile.

This is the first time I've ever been praised for lying, Gilda thought. She was surprised to feel as disconcerted as she felt relieved.

Jasper picked up his briefcase and began stuffing some folders inside. "I'm actually just on my way to a meeting, but, Gilda, I hope you'll have a wonderful experience here at the Spy Museum." He extended his hand again and Gilda shook it. "No hard feelings, right?"

"Right."

"Has Gilda checked out the permanent exhibit yet?"

"That's where she's headed next."

"Well—enjoy!"

As Gilda left Jasper Clarke's office, she felt excited to discover more of her surroundings at the museum, but also uneasy. *With these people, I've met my match,* she thought.

6

The Life of a Spy

Dear Wendy:

I just finished my first day of work. Picture
this: I'm sitting in my apartment in Washington,
D.C., wearing my red power suit. Pretty mature,
huh? Now picture this: I just put on a wig and
also practiced applying a fake mustache from my
disguise kit. (I don't want you to worry that I've
become too serious and sophisticated now that I'm
working in the nation's capital.)

I know you'll be relieved to hear that I'm totally in my element at the Spy Museum!

Today I watched a Spy Museum movie about the
good and bad reasons people become spies. Good
reasons: patriotism and a passion for intrigue.
Bad reasons: greed and egotism. The movie also
talked about the risks of getting caught spying on
a foreign government--little things like deportation, jail, and death.

"Do YOU have what it takes to be a spy?" the
movie asked.

My answer: a resounding YES. However, it's also true that I'm not a "perfect" spy.

My strengths as a spy:

I'm naturally curious and even nosy.

I pay attention to details.

I don't mind being an outsider (well, half the time I don't mind).

I'm a "people person." (Please stop sniggering.)

People underestimate me: they assume I'm not a threat, and this gives me more time to investigate them.

I'm used to keeping secrets from my family. (Best friends are another story altogether.)

I'm courageous. (Hey, I didn't say I don't get scared.)

Psychic abilities!

My weaknesses as a spy (keep snide comments to yourself, please):

Spies are supposed to "blend in with the scenery," and my penchant for fashion makes me stand out in a crowd.

My need to tell my best friend (that's you, in case you've forgotten) everything could become a liability.

I have little interest in technology and no experience with surveillance equipment.

Lack of decoding expertise. (By the way, when I toured the Spy Museum, I learned how the Nazis used a code-making machine called ENIGMA during World War II: it resembles a sinister-looking typewriter. Anyway, a bunch of mathematicians managed to decipher this very complex machine-made code during the war. Let's hear it for the math kids! Maybe you can ask if you can learn some decoding techniques at math camp, okay? That might be more useful than all of these pointless long-division problems you keep doing--or maybe it's calculus, but whatever.)

Since you aren't here to explore this place with me, I'm sending you another installment of my Washington, D.C., virtual travel service! Aren't you excited?

"WHO KNEW?" GILDA JOYCE HIGHLIGHTS, FAVORITES & "JUST PLAIN WEIRD" OBJECTS AT THE INTERNATIONAL SPY MUSEUM

The Lipstick Gun (the "Kiss of Death"): This was created by the KGB (the intelligence agency for the Soviet Union during the Cold War in case you're clueless). There's something spooky about looking into what you think is a lipstick and instead seeing a little hole from which a bullet might fire.

<u>"Sisterhood of Spies" Exhibit:</u> Listen, there's A LOT they don't teach us in school. Who knew that there were so many female spies throughout history--women who went around hiding secret notes in their bonnets, sausage curls, petticoats, and china dolls?

<u>The Jefferson wheel cipher:</u> Who knew that Thomas Jefferson, one of the Founding Fathers of our nation, also invented a way to encode and decode messages? (And why is it that presidents don't invent things anymore? I guess they're way too busy to carve things out of wood.) The wheel cipher Jefferson made looks like a little wooden rolling pin, but it's actually made of twenty-six round wooden pieces, each engraved with letters of the alphabet and threaded onto an iron spindle. When you turn the wheels, you can scramble and unscramble words in lots of different ways. Great for passing secret notes during math class!

<u>Rectal tool concealment kit:</u> This is exactly what the name says. It's basically a container concealing a bunch of tools--lock picks, drills to be stored "where the sun don't shine," as my Grandma Joyce would put it. It was for very serious spies who were in imminent danger of being captured--kind of an emergency escape kit. I don't see why you're laughing. I'm sure the people who

had to use it didn't find the idea of spies going around with tools concealed in their butts the
least bit funny.

MOLES, SIGNAL SITES, AND "DEAD DROPS": No, a
"mole" isn't a nearly blind furry animal that bur-
rows underground, and it isn't a beauty mark on
your skin. In the spy world (or "intelligence community," as they like to call it in this town),
a "mole" is a person who has access to important
secrets--probably someone working for the military, the CIA, or the FBI. But this person is also
secretly working for an enemy organization, and
informing them of classified information, often
in exchange for money. Because it's too risky for
moles (and other spies, for that matter) to meet
their contacts in person, they use code names and
"dead drops" to communicate with their foreign
contacts without being seen associating with them
in person.

DEAD DROPS: It's usually too dangerous for spy
handlers (like CIA officers working overseas) to
meet directly with their "assets"--the people
who are willing to give them secret information.
After all, if spotted together, they might be
arrested or even killed. Instead, they use "dead
drops"--agreed-upon locations where they will drop
off messages and packages of information for each

other to pick up without meeting in person. They use "concealment devices" to hide the information they drop off: an empty soda can or a twig can be left out in the open while hiding classified information. Spies usually have "signal sites"--maybe a chalk mark on a mailbox or sign--to alert one another that a communication "drop" has been made.

<u>SPY CITY</u>: Even though the Cold War is officially over, the Russians and Americans (among others) are apparently spying on each other as much as ever. Kind of makes you wonder what's going on right outside the Spy Museum!

Looking up from her typewriter, Gilda peered out the window to check for any interesting activity in the apartments across the courtyard. She was pleased to discover that at this hour of the day, she could actually see directly into a few apartments.

In one window, a tall man wearing a business suit talked into his cell phone as he paced through his living room. Gilda had seen this man in the elevator, and he seemed to be one of the few people in the building who greeted her with a friendly "Hello!" She didn't know his name, but she thought of him as "The Politician" because of his fierce, broad smile. In another window, a young man who had the disheveled look of a college student studying for final exams thoughtfully picked his nose while he stirred something in a pot on his kitchen stove.

Gilda gasped when she glanced up at a window on the next floor. A mousy woman wearing glasses stared directly at Gilda.

How long has she been watching me? The woman didn't avert her gaze. She didn't wave. Something about her stare seemed inexplicably hostile.

Feeling her pulse race, Gilda jumped up and pulled the blinds shut.

Why was it so unnerving to discover her looking at me? Gilda wondered. *After all, I'm sitting here looking at other people, too. I guess it's funny how I love people-watching, but I hate the idea of someone spying on* me.

Gilda cautiously opened the blinds, forcing herself to take another look. But when she looked back at the window, the woman was gone.

7

CIA Project MINDSCAPE

The psychic spy emerged from his trance. It always took several minutes for him to reorient himself—to feel connected with his immediate environment and the people around him. Just minutes before, he had transported his mind from a condominium building in Washington, D.C., to the bowels of a government building in Iran, where he had searched for evidence of a clandestine military program. During the past few weeks, his mind had traveled the globe—Russia, Syria, North Korea, Afghanistan—while his body reclined in a leather easy chair.

He had been secretly hired by the government as part of its top-secret "remote viewing" program—an attempt to access foreign intelligence through psychic techniques. The official CIA program had been terminated years ago amid public ridicule at the notion of "out-of-body" spying, but the psychic spy had been more recently recruited as part of a newer, top-secret program headed by a CIA intelligence officer named Loomis Trench. Project MINDSCAPE was an effort to continue researching and exploring the possibilities of using psychics to spy on people and places that were formerly inaccessible.

The room from which the psychic spy worked was spare—almost clinical. It contained little more than his reclining chair, charts, a computer, and notebooks. Loomis, the spy's supervisor, was a longtime CIA intelligence officer with a penchant for wearing dark suits and bow ties. He took detailed notes of the objects, people, and even documents the psychic spy observed while in his trance state. Sometimes a military doctor came to monitor the psychic spy's pulse, brainwaves, and other vital statistics, but most often it was just the two men—the psychic spy searching for targets around the world, his CIA observer taking notes and passing the information along to higher-ups in the CIA and military.

At first, the project was a success: the psychic was amazingly accurate in his remote viewing sessions, and Loomis was excited about such an intriguing and seemingly magical way to gather information.

Sometimes Loomis scrutinized the psychic very intently, as if trying to see into the man's brain—trying to learn the secret of psychic knowledge. "Someday we'll develop a pill or an injection that gives anyone in the military power to do what you do," he said. He regarded the psychic with a fixed stare—with something close to envy.

"Perhaps," said the psychic, feeling annoyed at the comment. "And that will be either a wonderful day or a very frightening day."

"So how do you do it?"

"Do what?"

"What's the trick? Why can't I do what you do?" More than

anything, Loomis wished he had psychic powers to know things that others didn't—to know what others were thinking—particularly what others were thinking about *him*.

"For me, it's like channeling a spirit," said the psychic. "I make contact with an entity who takes me to the locations we want to view." The psychic spy did not mention something important—a potential problem. Recently, his spirit guide had been failing to turn up as she always had in the past. He didn't mention the inexplicable visions that had begun to muddy his field of vision, confusing his ability to search for the targets Loomis gave him. He assumed some form of counterespionage must be the problem. *Maybe some other psychic spy from a hostile country or terrorist organization is attempting to thwart my remote viewing sessions,* he thought. At any rate, the last thing he wanted to reveal was his greatest fear—that he was losing his precious psychic skills.

His supervisor held a report in his hand. "According to this report, the targets you viewed last time didn't check out at all when our men on the ground went to investigate. They were disappointed because your first sessions were so accurate."

The psychic spy felt his skin grow cold. His field of vision narrowed: objects around him flattened and blurred slightly as they sometimes did preceding one of his migraine headaches. "Nothing checked out?" His voice shook. *I'm wasting their time,* he told himself. "If my readings aren't yielding anything useful," he said, "then maybe we should go our separate ways. Far be it from me to waste taxpayers' money."

"Oh, no. No, no, no, no, no! It's not a waste at all." His

supervisor peered at him earnestly through rectangular glasses; his eyes were the color of evening fog. "On the contrary, our work together is incredibly useful. No—we mustn't stop. Now—let's move on to the next target."

The psychic spy leaned back in his chair and did his best to relax his body and release his fears—to allow himself to focus on the target. He had the usual floating sensation that preceded his ability to view a distant place, but he was disturbed by the stray images that emerged. He abruptly pulled himself out of his trance when *that face* appeared again: the cold white skin, the dead stare of those eyes, and—most disturbing—the star-shaped blood stain.

"Something wrong?" Loomis asked.

"No—not really. I just need to start over." For the first time in his life, the psychic spy felt he couldn't be honest. He was under pressure to find a specific target and he couldn't let his country down. *The face is irrelevant,* he told himself. *It's a distraction.*

The psychic spy closed his eyes, slowed his heartbeat and breathing. Gradually, his brainwaves changed and he felt as if his body were floating, moving swiftly through the misty realm from which he would attempt to perceive objects and people around the globe. He knew he was drawing closer to his target—a suspected terrorist training camp in a mountainous region.

But as the mist cleared, he didn't see mountains. *I'm in the wrong place*, he told himself. He found himself in an apartment building, but he saw no signs of weaponry or combat training. For a moment, his spirits lifted, because he spied a girl in the apartment—a girl who resembled his spirit guide. *She came back,* he told himself. *She's back to help me.* But confusion and disappointment returned when he realized this girl was not his spirit guide at all: this girl sat at a typewriter and wore cat's-eye sunglasses.

8

The Acquisition

Gilda sat at her desk in a corner of the cluttered office space she now shared with Matthew Morrow, April, Janet, and Marla. The last employee to use the desk was now on maternity leave: she had left a photograph of herself wearing a purple wig, dark sunglasses, and displaying a cheesy grin along with a group of kids who appeared to be about ten or eleven years old. Gilda guessed it was a picture from one of the "spy camps" that took place at the museum during the summer.

After wiping a film of dust from the desk and arranging her belongings, Gilda leaned back in her chair and took a bite of the "disguise dog" she had purchased at the Spy City Café—a hot dog loaded with spicy chili. She loved the feeling of sitting in a real office and having her own desk—a desk far more inspiring than the desks at school with their tiny, insufficient writing tables attached. She had her own telephone, stapler, Spy Museum coffee cup, and hanging file folders filled with museum program brochures. She also liked sitting near Matthew Morrow because she got the feeling he was the kind of person who *knew* things about espionage—things he might be willing to teach her if she could convince him she wasn't just an ordinary high school intern.

"Did they give you the test yet?" Matthew leaned back in his chair and stared at his computer screen as he spoke.

"What test?"

"You know, the museum test."

Gilda spun around in her swivel chair to face Matthew, who still tapped away on his computer. "April didn't tell me about any test."

"You're kidding me. You haven't taken the test yet?!"

"He's teasing you," said Janet, who seemed to perennially sit on the floor, now busy cutting cipher wheels from construction paper and affixing the decoder rings together with metal clips. "You have such a deadpan sense of humor, Matthew; nobody can ever tell when you're joking."

"I'm not joking. I wouldn't joke about the test." His eyes twinkled but he didn't smile.

Welcoming an opportunity to strike up a conversation with Matthew, Gilda decided to play along. "So what is this test about?"

"Oh, just a few questions to find out whether new interns are paying attention." He turned around in his chair to face Gilda.

"I've been paying attention."

"Then you should be prepared."

"You're awful, Matthew," said Janet, clearly enjoying the exchange.

"I just like to see what the new interns learn when they go

through the museum for the first time. It helps me find out if we're being effective in our educational outreach."

"So lay it on me," said Gilda. "I'm ready."

"Okay—what's the CIA?"

"Don't make me laugh. The Central Intelligence Agency, of course. Their job is to find out foreign secrets, and they have agents all over the world."

"And what about the FBI?"

"The Federal Bureau of Investigation focuses on criminal activity inside the U.S. They also dabble in counterespionage."

"'Counterespionage' is a pretty big word."

"I've used bigger."

"What do you mean by it?"

"Well, duh. Catching foreign spies inside U.S. borders and then trying to 'flip' them so they work for us and spy on their countries of origin instead."

"Nice work. I guess you were paying attention in the museum."

"I knew most of that stuff before I even got here."

Janet and Matt exchanged a brief glance and Gilda thought she saw Janet roll her eyes. *They think I'm bragging,* she thought.

"Well if those are such easy questions," said Matt, "what about the KGB?"

"You mean the spy organization of the former Soviet Union? What about it?"

"What does 'KGB' stand for?"

Gilda wasn't sure about this. "Kids Gone Bad?"

Janet snorted. Matthew's mouth twitched as if a small chuckle might be lurking somewhere, but he only fixed Gilda with an unblinking stare. "It stands for *Komitet Gosudarstvennoi Bezopasnosti,* which is Russian for 'Committee for State Security'."

"That was my next guess."

"Two out of three isn't too bad," said Janet.

"She *should* do better. We don't usually have interns listing 'solving mysteries' as one of their extracurricular activities." He spoke with a wry grin.

He thinks I made that up, Gilda thought, feeling disappointed. *He doesn't believe I could solve a real mystery.*

"Just let me know if you ever need my help with any of your work," said Gilda, doing her best to control her impulse to tell Matthew what she thought of his impromptu "test for interns."

"I could use some fresh coffee over here for starters."

"You're such a jerk sometimes, Matthew." Janet's harsh words were contradicted by the tidy smile on her face.

"Isn't getting coffee something our interns are supposed to do?"

"It's no problem." Gilda jumped up and picked up a pink mug labeled SPY GIRL that sat on her desk. "I was just about to pour myself a cup, too."

"It's weird how high school kids all drink coffee these days," said Janet. "I never liked it back when I was a kid."

"I've been drinking coffee since I was in preschool," Gilda fibbed.

"Doesn't that stunt your growth?"

"It oils your brain." Gilda bounced past Matt and whisked his coffee mug from his desk. In the break area, she poured two cups of coffee and added a generous portion of nondairy creamer to both. She noticed that some office employee had affixed a mailing label with the words *Fake Lard* to the coffee creamer.

As she stirred the cloudy brown liquid with a plastic stick, Gilda wondered how she could make Matthew Morrow see that she was qualified to participate in more exciting activities than stirring coffee. *Maybe I should just go ahead and ask him,* she thought.

Gilda marched back to Matthew's desk with new determination. She found Matthew standing up and gathering his belongings.

"Here's your coffee."

"Oh—thanks." He put it down without even tasting it. "I just remembered I'd better get going to my meeting in Georgetown."

"Is it with that KGB guy?"

"Very good guess. You're right."

"Could you use some help from an intern?"

"I think I've got it covered."

"It's just—I would *love* to see what goes on at that meeting," said Gilda. "It must be so fascinating."

"It's not like we're going to go stake out his house."

"Still—it's not every day you meet a Russian spy."

"He's not a Russian spy anymore; he's been on our side for some time now."

"I know. I'd just love to meet him and learn how you find all these cool things for the museum."

Matthew thought for a moment and shrugged his shoulders. "All right, then—why not. Let's go."

"Oh, yay! Let me grab my bag." As Gilda hurried to her desk to grab her handbag, she noticed a faint grimace crossing Janet's face, as if she had just bitten into something bitter. "April isn't going to like it," Janet muttered.

Sitting next to Matthew Morrow in a taxi heading toward Georgetown, Gilda couldn't help imagining that she and Matthew were partners like the FBI agents Mulder and Scully on one of her favorite shows, *The X-Files*.

"So what made you want to spend your summer at the Spy Museum?" Matthew asked.

"It sounded really cool," said Gilda, immediately wishing she had come up with a more interesting response. "I mean, I thought it would be a really good opportunity to improve my tradecraft."

"Your tradecraft?"

"You know. My spying skills."

"Sounds like you're really serious about becoming a spy."

"Well, I kind of already *am* a spy."

"Spies don't usually announce themselves as spies."

"I figured it's okay if we're both in the same field."

"I'm not a spy; I'm a historian of spying."

"Same diff."

"It's not the same at all."

"I know; I was just kidding. So—what made you want to become a historian of spying?"

"Well, just think about all the untold details of history—all the events that happened because someone behind the scenes gave someone else secret information. Not to mention all the events that turned on the handling of inconclusive classified information, like the Iraq war."

Matthew looked out the window at the embassy mansions along Massachusetts Avenue. "Besides, I like having fun at work. I used to be a teaching assistant at a university but this is way better."

Gilda watched a sleek black car glide into the guarded entrance to the Russian Embassy.

"People who live in this neighborhood say they still get bad TV reception because of all the surveillance activity that still goes on around the Russian Embassy," Matthew explained, following her gaze. "Not to mention the tunnel leading from the basement of a house in this neighborhood; the U.S. secretly built it when we were trying to listen in on the Russians' conversations."

Gilda was curious about the Russian Embassy, and she was also curious about Matthew. She knew he wasn't married, and she had overheard Marla and April in the ladies' room having a whispered conversation about a mutual friend who "broke his heart," even though "he won't admit he can't get over it." At the same time, Gilda found herself wondering whether Matthew and her roommate Caitlin might make a good couple. She imagined herself introducing the two of them. They would both be impressed with her for knowing such smart, successful young urbanites, and grateful to her for bringing them together. The three of them would become best friends. With this matchmaking scheme in mind, Gilda decided to learn more about Matthew's hobbies. "So Matthew—what do you do when you're not quizzing interns at the Spy Museum?"

"Not much," said Matthew. "I work on some writing projects and I run at least ten miles a day. I'm probably addicted to the endorphins."

"So what are you running from?" Gilda made a mental note to look up the meaning of "endorphins."

"I'm not running *from* anything. I just love that feeling of getting up really early and running—knowing I'm out there on the move while everyone else is still asleep in their beds. It kind of makes me feel like I have an edge on the day. It helps me think."

"What do you think about?"

"You ask a lot of questions, you know that?"

"I'm just gathering information, like any good spy."

The taxi crept more slowly as it descended a hill, past a graveyard perched on a hillside, then past little shops and restaurants.

"We're close to Georgetown now," said Matthew.

They climbed out of the air-conditioned cab and walked down R Street past rows of stately Victorian houses with arched entryways, towers, bay windows, and perfectly pruned gardens. The atmosphere was oppressively hot and there was a reserved stillness all around that made Gilda feel as if she were trespassing on private property—as if she had walked into a formal tea party without being invited. The houses and tall trees surrounding them reminded Gilda of elegant, judgmental ladies who *knew* things: they had seen and many heard secrets. *Oh, the stories we would tell if only we could talk,* they seemed to whisper.

"So what's the deal with this guy?" Gilda asked.

"Like I told you, he used to be a Soviet spy back in the Cold War days. His name is Boris Volkov, and he was based in the

Russian Embassy here in D.C. during the eighties. He switched sides and defected to the U.S. after he realized that the Soviet Union was collapsing. He's actually helped us out with a bunch of exhibits and even donated some important artifacts to the museum. He likes to keep a pretty low profile, though; we don't see that much of him."

"Interesting. Very interesting," said Gilda. She felt a distinct tickle in her left ear.

"You've got that 'pretending to be a sleuth' look."

"And you've got that 'pretending to be a historian look'."

Matthew stopped in front of a stately yellow house. "I think this is the place."

"So anyway," said Gilda, "our friend Boris suddenly has some spy artifacts to show us."

"That's right. He said he has something his wife recently found when she was cleaning the attic."

They walked up the path and approached an entranceway decorated with panels of stained glass surrounding a door. Matthew rang the doorbell, and a moment later, Gilda found herself gazing into the wide, eager smile of a stocky, balding man with a round, almost babyish face.

"Matthew! Good to see you!" Boris patted Matthew on the shoulder with a large hand that somehow reminded Gilda of a bear paw as he shook Matthew's hand firmly.

Then Boris turned his attention to Gilda. "And who might this lovely young lady be?"

"This is Gilda Joyce—one of our new interns. She's from Michigan."

Boris gripped Gilda's hand, and she felt a surprising strength and roughness in his touch that belied his pudgy exterior. "Such a pleasure to meet you. Come in, come in!" Gilda noticed that Boris's gaze darted over her shoulder for a split second, as if he were in the habit of checking to see who might be walking down the street. *As if he's afraid of being followed,* Gilda thought. His open friendliness was tempered by a subtly guarded alertness. *I bet once you're a spy, it's hard to ever stop thinking and acting like a spy,* Gilda thought.

Boris led them into an eclectic sitting room that suggested many years of entertaining guests who ate hors d'oeuvres and drank wine long into the night. Gilda and Matthew sank into a comfortable couch and Gilda looked around, surveying the contrasting patterns, and shades of gold and deep red that surrounded her. Her eye fell on the orange-red flow of a painting that hung over the fireplace—an image of a couple seated next to each other at a dimly lit café. A candle flickered on a table set with wineglasses, and the man leaned toward the woman to whisper some furtive secret. Two long evening shadows loomed ominously behind the couple.

"Can I offer you something to drink?" Boris clasped his hands together and leaned toward them. Gilda noticed a wide wedding band on one finger. It looked tight, as if his finger had grown fat after he had put it on. "Some lemonade? Perhaps a vodka tonic for Matthew?" Boris grinned at Matthew and put his arm around his shoulder jovially. "This man, he does not drink my vodka."

"Not at eleven in the morning, I don't."

Who knew KGB officers were such a barrel of laughs? Gilda thought.

Boris turned to Gilda. "I want you to know that every day, this man is waking up at sunrise with the crows to prance through the streets. Every day, he is running around the city like a squirrel."

Matthew grinned sheepishly, but he clearly didn't like the direction the conversation was taking.

Boris placed his hands on Matthew's shoulders and regarded him with ironic intensity. "This is no way to get a woman, Matthew."

"How do you know I don't have a girlfriend?"

"I am professional," said Boris, patting Matthew's arm. "I know these things."

"Look, aren't we here to take a look at your artifacts? There's a lot going on in the office today and we need to get back soon."

"I see you are in great hurry."

"I'm not in a hurry," said Gilda, who found Boris instantly likable. "I have all day."

Matthew shot her an annoyed glance.

"Excuse me for a moment," said Boris. "I go to unlock the safe."

"So no girlfriend, huh?" Gilda whispered when she thought Boris was out of earshot.

"That's a story I'd rather not get into right now," said Matthew.

A moment later Boris returned, inexplicably dressed in a beige trench coat. For some reason, he had also tied a colorful silk scarf around his neck.

Was he batty, or were the scarf and trench coat themselves artifacts—things that had been owned by spies?

Matthew beamed with excitement. "Is that what I'm hoping it is?"

"That all depends on what you are hoping, Matthew," said Boris, almost flirtatiously.

"I've never seen one of these made in the form of jewelry before!"

"It is quite something, isn't it? I think it suits me."

Gilda realized they were focusing on something pinned to Boris's scarf—a brooch made of dark red glass, set in the shape of a five-pointed star.

"Does it work the way I think it does?"

"I've already taken five pictures of you."

"What is it?" Gilda asked. "Is there a hidden camera in that brooch?"

"Look closely, Gilda."

Gilda stared at the dark center of the brooch.

"I just took a picture of you." Boris removed the brooch, and Gilda saw that the piece of jewelry actually concealed the lens of a tiny camera that Boris had kept hidden behind his trench coat and scarf.

"You see," said Boris, "this cable connects the camera to a little switch the spy keeps in her pocket to open the camera lens. While you make pleasant conversation over a glass of wine or shop at the market, nobody knows that you're secretly taking pictures of their whereabouts or maybe even secret documents."

"It's a Minox camera," said Matthew, gazing at the contraption lovingly. "The gold standard of Cold War spying. Gilda, you probably remember seeing the 'buttonhole camera' in the museum—the same basic principle, but instead of jewelry, a button on an overcoat would open up to reveal a camera lens, and the person wearing it would squeeze a shutter cable in the coat's pocket to snap a secret picture."

"The problem with these old Minox cameras," said Boris, "was that you have to wear an overcoat. No place to hide them if you are wearing bikini, right, Matthew?"

"Now they can hide a video camera in a pair of sunglasses or a ballpoint pen," said Matthew, ignoring Boris's talk of spying while dressed in a bikini. "They can make it so small, we'd miss it if it were stuck right on the wall next to us."

"We are always being watched," said Boris with an air of resignation.

"So," said Gilda, "I assume this brooch was worn by a female spy, right?"

"Oh, yes. I don't think it does much for my complexion," Boris joked. "It was in fact used by the KGB in Moscow during the nineteen-eighties."

"Cool! A female KGB agent!" Gilda took the brooch and camera cable from Matthew. She stared at the red-black star shape and felt suddenly queasy. She felt a tickle in her ear—a strong vibration that seemed to come from the object. "Did you know her—the KGB agent who wore this?"

"Oh, no. She was nobody I knew." Something in Boris's manner seemed to close. Gilda detected a sudden clipped tone in his voice—a slight chill in his magnanimous demeanor. *He doesn't want me to ask more questions about who the KGB spy lady was,* Gilda thought. *I bet he knows something pretty interesting about her.*

"*How* did you acquire these?" Matthew asked. Gilda detected the faintest hint of accusation in his voice.

"Well, as you know, Matthew, I had many connections in the KGB. When I left Moscow for the last time, knowing that I would most likely never return, I took some souvenirs with me, thinking they may someday have some historic value. As you know, I donated many objects to your Spy Museum, but I thought these last two items had been lost or stolen. Then, this summer, my wife has a bad dream and in the middle of the night, she decides to clean the attic. She tiell me she find an old briefcase and she is going to throw it away. Always, she wants to throw everything away. I say, 'no, no!' My wife, she say to me, 'I want these things out of the house.' She has an idea that they are bad luck."

"Why?"

"Because she's irrational—a crazy woman." Boris rubbed his nose as he spoke.

Either he has allergies, or he's nervous for some reason, Gilda thought. She also reflected that it was possible that Boris's wife was completely rational in her belief that the artifacts were "bad luck." Gilda had heard plenty of stories about objects that were "cursed" in some way—diamonds, paintings, and other valuables that left trails of misfortune as they passed through the hands of various owners

"Now, for the other object," said Boris. "You won't believe your eyes." Boris punched in a combination and turned a little key in a lock. The briefcase popped open on the coffee table.

Gilda peered inside eagerly. The briefcase was empty except for a red velvet bag tied shut with a silk cord.

Boris carefully opened the bag and removed what appeared

at first to be a gold tube of lipstick. He removed the cap to reveal a crimson tip, which he pointed in Matthew's direction.

Matthew laughed nervously. "Be careful where you point that thing."

It wasn't a lipstick at all, but a tiny handgun in disguise—a handgun very much like the Kiss of Death that was already on display in the Spy Museum, except that this one was slightly more elegant and deceptive because it was smaller and gold-plated.

"Wow," said Gilda. "It's another lipstick gun!" Why did Boris have a lipstick handgun and a woman's brooch used to conceal a hidden camera? He said he took the objects from Moscow as souvenirs and claimed that he had misplaced them in the attic, but maybe there was a bigger secret—a reason he had wanted to keep them hidden.

"Mr. Volkov," Gilda ventured.

"Please. Call me Boris."

"This is an odd question, but back when you were working for the KGB, did you ever disguise yourself as a woman to get information or avoid being discovered?"

Boris burst into hearty laughter.

"Gilda doesn't realize that most of your time was spent talking to people at cocktail parties and bars, and then trying to get *other* people to do the sneaking around," Matthew interjected.

"Gilda, I never had this opportunity to become a woman. But—you are very smart girl. Why? By far the most effective disguise you can pick—if done very well—is to change your gender. Say somebody is looking for you. They expect to see young lady and instead, they see a boy. How can that be you? It cannot be."

Gilda made a mental note of this for the next time she needed to disguise herself. *I'd have to get a lot better at applying a false mustache and beard,* she thought.

"But did I ever pretend to apply lipstick with this pistol? The answer is no."

"Did you ever shoot anyone with it?"

"Gilda, please." Matthew shot her a warning glance.

"No—I did not."

"How do you think this gun compares to the one we have on display in the museum?" Matthew asked.

"This one is even more valuable. It dates from the nineteen-seventies or eighties; it's gold-plated and slightly smaller so it looks more like a real lipstick, which would of course buy the spy a little more time to take her shot.

"Here." Boris handed the lipstick gun to Gilda. "Want to take a look?"

"Is it loaded?"

"Of course. It comes with only one bullet, so you would have to be a very good shot if you ever had to use it."

The gun felt heavy in Gilda's hand. As she held it, she felt a cold sensation radiating upward through her arm, as if an icy emotion had just been injected into her veins. It was all Gilda could do to keep from dropping the gun on the floor.

"On second thought, I don't want you holding that hand-gun," said Matthew, quickly taking the gun and placing it back in the briefcase. "The last thing I need is having to make a phone call to April and Jasper to explain why our newest intern is on her way to jail or the hospital."

Boris let out another belly laugh. "I'm sure we can trust this one, Matthew. She's got a good head on her shoulders." He placed an avuncular arm around Gilda's shoulders and gave her a squeeze.

I can see how he might have been successful as a spy, Gilda thought. *He butters people up, and then they probably spill the beans about a bunch of secrets.*

"Now, I hate to say good-bye," said Boris, checking his wristwatch, "but I am late for an engagement."

"Well, thank you for sharing these artifacts with the Spy Museum, Boris. We know you could sell them to a private collector if you weren't so generous."

The midday heat scalded the back of Gilda's neck as she and Matthew walked down the sidewalk toward Wisconsin Avenue. Matthew carried the small briefcase containing the lipstick gun and spy camera.

"So—what do you think of Boris?" Gilda asked.

"I think we got some amazing additions to the museum. Jasper is going to be thrilled when he finds out we have these artifacts to add to the displays. When I get back, I'll set up a meeting with our designer and get busy writing the signs for the display—"

"But what about Boris? What do you think of *him*?"

"He's an interesting guy."

"Very interesting." Gilda found Boris likable and intriguing, but something also made her suspicious. Something about the entire exchange had aroused what she liked to think of as her "psychic radar."

"Matthew, how do we know that he's switched sides for good?"

"What are you talking about?"

"You know. How can we really be sure he isn't secretly spying for the Russians? Like in the Spy Museum, I read about that guy Yuri Nosenko who defected, but they locked him up and kept questioning him because they thought he might be a Soviet dangle or a mole."

"I see you've been studying your spy terms."

"I've been talking this way forever."

"I think we can be sure he's switched sides for good. For one thing, he can't exactly go back to Russia again; if anything, he's worried that some undercover Russian agent might slip him some poison as punishment for his past disloyalty to the homeland."

"I guess you're right."

"I'm definitely right."

Still, Gilda had the sense that something was amiss, although she couldn't put her finger on exactly what that something might be.

On the taxi ride back to the Spy Museum, Gilda felt a heightened awareness of the leather briefcase sitting on the seat next to her, almost as if *someone* were riding in the car along with them.

Maybe this is how some people feel about carrying weapons, Gilda thought. *Maybe there's an energy in having an actual weapon close to you, as if you have an invisible bodyguard. But this isn't a good feeling. Something about this feels ominous—and weirdly sad.*

9

Spy Camp

Where have you two been?!" April stood barefoot on the carpeted office floor, munching on a handful of M&M's. Janet smirked.

From the way she's talking, you'd think we'd both just snuck off to see a Disney movie during work hours or something, Gilda thought.

"Gilda came with me to check out a couple new acquisitions for the museum," said Matthew. "Some pretty interesting stuff."

"Matthew," said April, glancing in Gilda's direction and obviously wanting her to leave the room, "can I talk with you in private for a minute?"

Uh-oh, Gilda thought. *He'll never take me anywhere interesting again if he gets in trouble for it.* "It's my fault," Gilda blurted. "I kind of begged him to take me along."

"Look, Gilda, I'm glad you got to go. It's just that, as Matthew knows, we have our Spy Camp and Midnight Spy Slumber Party right around the corner, and everyone needs to stay on task to get ready for that."

Gilda liked the intriguing sound of "Spy Camp and Midnight

Spy Slumber Party" and wondered why nobody had mentioned anything about them yet.

"We've got kids coming here to learn everything we can teach them about being a spy, so getting ready for camp is our top priority."

"To be fair, April, acquiring new objects for the museum is also a top priority," Matthew countered.

"But it's not *Gilda's* top priority," April snapped.

"If I can just interject something here," Gilda said, raising her hand as if she were a student in a classroom. "I'm a really good multitasker. Like at home, my mom never understands how I can do my homework while I'm also reading a bunch of novels and keeping up with my favorite TV shows, plus my own writing projects, but somehow I get it all done."

April's brow furrowed. *I bet that's how she looks at her two-year-old when she's telling him to poop on the potty,* Gilda thought.

"There's a lot to do for Spy Camp," said April, "and Janet has been busy all day cutting out cipher wheels. Do you think you could give her a hand?"

"I'm actually almost done," said Janet, sounding pleased with herself.

"And when that's done, the two of you can make sure all the disguises are in order."

"I'll get right on it," said Gilda.

OFFICE MEMO
To: April Shepherd
From: Gilda Joyce

TASKS COMPLETED:

1. Cutting out and assembling cipher wheels
   (decoder rings) in record time.
2. Disguises sorted, fluffed, spot-cleaned, and
   checked for bugs. Items checked: multicolored
   wigs, facial hair, makeup kits, sunglasses, and
   clothes.
3. Professional development highlight: resisted
   overwhelming urge to dress up in purple wig.
4. Suggestion for Spy Museum improvement: find
   more 1960s-inspired wigs and hairpieces like
   long ponytails and beehive hairstyles to add to
   the disguise collection!

Gilda found herself walking past the White House, past rows of sleek black cars, past somber-looking security guards. She thought she saw a shadowy face watching her through a front window. Gilda wanted to look more closely, so she made her way toward the White House, looking down and hoping the guards wouldn't stop her. As she reached the front entrance, she was surprised to find that the door opened easily, and the guards and police surrounding the White House made no move to stop her. *I suppose I've been invited,* she thought.

As Gilda opened the front door and entered the house, she sensed time slowing, the surrounding cars and trees receding, the afternoon light changing and becoming more subtle and beautiful. But once inside, she realized she had actually entered the

Spy Museum. She found herself in a model of an old-fashioned library—an exhibit about writers who were also spies. *I guess I'm here to do my work,* she thought.

Gilda took a seat behind an antique writer's desk stacked with leather-bound books, wax stamps for letters, a quill pen, and a bottle of ink. She was vaguely aware of tourists who moved around her like phantoms, blind to her presence.

Then Gilda heard a voice—a deep sigh filled with pain. It seemed as if the very walls in the room groaned. She slowly turned her head to look behind, and she saw the silhouette of a tall, lean man who wore a long overcoat and a top hat. He exuded melancholy, weariness, and something dusty and still that made her think of an old coffin. He moved closer and in the dim light of a candle she saw a somber, familiar face. *How strange*, Gilda thought. *It's Abraham Lincoln. What is he doing in the Spy Museum?*

"It hurts," he said.

"What hurts?" she asked.

Lincoln pointed to a gun sitting on the writer's desk—the lipstick gun the museum had acquired. The gun, in turn, seemed to point toward an object hanging on the wall. The shadowy man in the top hat extended a long arm, pointing in the same direction.

There, displayed on the wall next to the antique desk was the Jefferson cipher wheel—a wooden cylinder covered with small, carved letters.

Gilda watched as the letters rearranged themselves into a single word:

OAKHILL

"What does it mean?" Gilda turned back to Lincoln's ghost, thinking he might be able to explain the significance of the word. But when she turned around, she found herself staring into the barrel of a gun—the lipstick gun. The face behind the gun was featureless—a dark shadow.

10

The Message in the Cipher

Gilda awoke with a feeling of panic and sorrow, as if she had just learned that a friend had been fatally wounded. Her skin felt clammy. She grabbed the notebook she kept next to her bed so she could record her dream before it slipped back into her unconscious mind. She wrote the first word that popped into her mind—a word with a cryptic meaning:

OAKHILL

Why is that important? What does it mean?

```
TO: Gilda Joyce
FROM: Gilda Joyce
RE: PSYCHIC DREAM REPORT--POSSIBLE GHOST CONTACT


3:00 A.M.: I just woke from a dream that may contain
a psychic message! I was in the Spy Museum, and I
spoke to the ghost of Abraham Lincoln! He didn't
say much, but he told me that something "hurts."
    What does the ghost of President Lincoln have
to do with the Spy Museum and a lipstick gun?
```

Gilda sat back in her chair and rested her chin on her knee. Had the dream merely been her brain processing little pieces of information—a collage of images and thoughts from the past few days? Or did the dream contain a genuine message?

Gilda pulled her *Master Psychic's Handbook* from a side pocket in her suitcase. The book, written by Gilda's idol—famed psychic Balthazar Frobenius—was battered from years of being carried in Gilda's backpack, stuffed in the back of her school locker, wedged into suitcases, and basically accompanying Gilda just about everywhere. Even though she had read the book more times than she could count, she always found a new nugget of wisdom when she searched the book for insight into a problem. She turned to a chapter on dreams and read:

ON PSYCHIC DREAMS

Some people receive psychic messages best through dreams—when the mind is completely relaxed. Even people who do not aspire to psychic skills often perceive information during sleep that is normally concealed during their waking hours. This may be because relaxing the mind clears away the sensory clutter that ordinarily blocks one's deepest mental abilities—abilities including psychic perception of messages from spirits, information about the future, and the ability to read the thoughts of others.

With ongoing practice, aspiring psychics can learn the technique of "wakeful dreaming," which allows part of the mind to remain conscious during the dream state, thereby controlling this access to unconscious and even psychic information. The truly advanced practitioner may gain the ability to utilize dream states to project the mind through time and space—potentially gaining access to distant places and possibly even distant times.

Gilda thought for a moment, then turned back to her psychic-dream report:

```
Whatever psychic abilities I have often seem to
come through dreams--and sometimes the combination
of dreams and writing. It's hard to explain
exactly what it is that makes the dreams with
messages different than ordinary dreams, but they
often have a heightened feeling of reality.
     I feel certain that my dream contained a
message since Abraham Lincoln actually pointed
toward the cipher wheel hanging on the wall.
```

Gilda suddenly had a sinking feeling as she recalled the final image of her dream.

```
I was staring into the barrel of a gun.
Am I in danger? What if THAT's the message??
```

Wanting to call Wendy, Gilda picked up her cell phone and hesitated. She knew Wendy would be grumpy if she were wakened in the middle of the night.

But I owe Wendy a phone call, Gilda reasoned. And isn't that what best friends are for—someone to call at 3:00 A.M. if you're scared and really need to talk? Gilda decided to go ahead and dial Wendy's number.

Far away, in a neat bedroom in Ferndale, Michigan, Wendy Choy cursed and lurched out of bed at the sound of her cell phone, which was at the bottom of her backpack. She found the phone just in time to pick up Gilda's call.

"Lo," she said in a hoarse voice, peering at the clock on her bedside table.

"What are you doing?"

"Oh, I was just sitting here hoping someone would call."

"I was afraid I'd wake you up."

"Seriously, Gilda. I have to get up in the morning for math camp."

"How's that going, by the way? My brother's in that same program this summer, you know."

"I know. And it's good. I don't know. Why don't you ever call me at a normal hour to have a conversation? I've been wondering how you're doing in D.C., and I don't hear anything, and then you wake me up in the middle of the night."

"I've written you a bunch of letters; I just haven't mailed them yet."

"I have e-mail and a cell phone, Gilda. Why not just send a text message like a normal person?"

"With text messages there's nothing for posterity. Years from now when we're old and the technology is outdated, all those letters I write you will still be sitting there in your attic. See, if I only send you text messages—"

"Gilda, what do you want?"

"Something weird just happened."

"Every time you go somewhere something weird happens."

"Wendy, I don't even have to go anywhere and weird things happen."

"So what happened this time?"

Gilda told Wendy about the dream and how it seemed to contain a message of some kind. "And at the end, there was a gun pointing at me."

"Oh." Wendy grew quiet for a moment. She was well acquainted with ominous nightmares; during a trip to England, she had experienced some very disturbing dreams that made her feel certain that her life was in danger. She suddenly felt more sympathetic toward Gilda. "It was probably just an anxiety dream. You know; you're on your own in the big city and everything."

"But everything else about the dream seemed so significant."

"Or maybe the gun was just there because you were dreaming about President Lincoln. You know, he got assassinated, so that's not far-fetched."

"But it felt like he had something to *tell* me. Why me?"

"You're a psychic investigator, aren't you? Maybe Lincoln's ghost just wants to get to know you."

"I guess. . . ." Gilda's voice trailed off. She caught her breath because a light suddenly flashed in her room. She put the telephone down and watched as it happened again—and then again—a repetitive series of flashes: *on, off, on, off.*

"Gilda? Are you there?"

"Something's going on here, Wendy," Gilda whispered.

"What's happening?"

"I need to check this out. I'll call you later."

"But—"

Gilda hung up the phone and realized that the light was coming from outside her window. She opened the blinds and

looked across the courtyard into rows of apartments that were
dark—except for one fifth-floor window where lights were
flashing: *on, off, on, off.* Gilda watched for a minute, transfixed.
What was going on in that apartment?

Gilda remembered how the mousy woman had stared
through that same apartment window. Her face had been plain.
Maybe she wore glasses. There was nothing striking about her
at all, but the simple fact of seeing her staring with such intensity through the window had filled Gilda with trepidation.

```
TO: GILDA JOYCE

FROM: GILDA JOYCE

RE: ADDENDUM TO PSYCHIC REPORT--MYSTERIOUS
ELECTRICAL ACTIVITY IN CATHEDRAL TOWERS APARTMENTS


Following recording of potentially psychic dream
and conversation with Wendy Choy, lights are
seen flashing in a 5th-floor apartment where a
suspicious-looking woman lives.

   Is this a coincidence, or is there a connection
between the dream about Lincoln and the lights?
Could the lights be a signal of some kind--or
possible evidence of a poltergeist?
```

Now feeling even more bewildered and intrigued than when
she had first awoken from the dream about Abraham Lincoln,
Gilda pulled a book entitled *Haunted Government: The Famous
Ghosts of Washington, D.C.* from her suitcase and turned to a
passage about Lincoln's ghost.

LINCOLN — OUR "GUARDIAN GHOST"?

Abraham Lincoln's ghost has appeared to many visitors at the White House. Some have claimed to see his somber silhouette standing at the window of the Oval Office, gazing out at the nation with an attitude of concern.

Lincoln experienced personal tragedy and profound grief during his term in office, and the weighty emotions associated with his life may be one reason his spirit continues to linger after death. Adding to Lincoln's deep concern over the plight of the nation during the bloody battles of the Civil War was the trauma of the death of his beloved son Willie, who passed away from an illness during Lincoln's presidency. Lincoln's wife held séances in the Green Room of the White House, some of which Lincoln was reported to have attended.

President Lincoln was also known to sit for hours by his young son's tomb, weeping openly and even asking that the crypt be opened so he could view the boy's lifeless body once more.

While the moments of anguish associated with Lincoln's family are sufficient explanation for his ghost's moody presence around the White House, a perhaps more intriguing theory put forth by some psychics is the notion that Lincoln remains a "guardian spirit" of the nation, appearing at times of danger. Whether his ghost's message is perceived depends on the emotional and psychic sensitivity of the officials in the White House at any given time.

If Lincoln's ghost is a "guardian spirit" of the nation, is it possible that he has a message for me, is it possible that this word "Oakhill" and those flashing lights are pointing to some type of spy activity I'm supposed to investigate?

11

The Museum Ghost

Surrounded by an assortment of antique toiletries including "Southern Rose" hair oil, "Dri-Dew" deodorant, perfume bottles, and a silver hairbrush and mirror, the Spy Museum's manager of exhibit production stared at the lipstick pistol and secret-camera brooch he had just installed in the Sisterhood of Spies room. His name was Roger Selak, and although he resembled a young college student dressed in a baseball cap and blue jeans, he was actually a new father who had been up for exactly half the night pacing through his apartment with a colicky newborn. The other half of the night had been spent dozing on the couch and having whispered arguments with his wife about the possible cause of their baby's sleeplessness and which of the two of them was more tired than the other. Roger assumed it was sleep deprivation that caused him to feel lightheaded and dizzy as he considered the lipstick gun and spy-camera brooch in their case—objects he had originally intended to place among secret weapons of the Cold War. On the other hand, maybe the problem was the sneaky, vintage femininity of the exhibit, which was designed to resemble a dressing room of a Southern belle who was also a spy. The display contained dolls with hollow china heads, tiny Bibles containing secret handwritten notes, and a fake beard and mustache—the various tools of female spies who smuggled communications behind enemy lines during the Civil War.

Behind Roger, a film about female spies was projected from an ornate three-way mirror. Black-and-white photographs of women's faces emerged from the mirror, growing larger, then fading as the soft-voiced narrator told of the lives and deaths of spies including Mata Hari, Harriet Tubman, Sarah Edmonds, and Edith Cavell, the last of whom was executed by a firing squad.

I need sleep, Roger told himself, allowing himself to close his eyes for just a moment.

His thoughts were interrupted by a crackling, static sound. The image of Edith Cavell's face dissolved into grainy pixels and the narrator's voice fell silent. *Great,* he thought. *All I need is for something to go wrong with the show software.* He checked all the connections and hidden cords in the exhibit but could find nothing wrong.

The normal exhibit film had completely stopped. Roger stared at the mirror, first seeing his own reflection, then watching something that resembled a plume of smoke moving inside the glass. The plume of smoke grew darker and larger until it resembled a human head. . . . Was it a woman's face? *Whatever that is, it isn't a film image,* Roger thought. It was something more real and present—something that seemed to *watch* him. There was also an aroma—a sweet floral perfume that also smelled old, reminding him of a box of dried flowers or aging bottles of vanilla extract and bags of stale marshmallows in the back of his kitchen cabinet at home.

Roger often worked alone in the museum, so it was unusual for him to have the feeling he suddenly had—the immediate, childish knowledge that above all, he didn't want to be alone. He actually felt scared.

Leaving a rolling cart of tools behind, he hurried toward the staff offices, wanting to forget what he had just seen.

12

The Promotion

Sitting at her desk in the Spy Museum, Gilda logged into her computer and typed the words "OAK HILL" into a search engine just to see what she might find.

To her delight, a site for Oak Hill Cemetery in Washington, D.C., appeared. She clicked on the site, then grew even more excited when she realized that Oak Hill Cemetery was in the same neighborhood as Boris's house in Georgetown.

Surrounded by a quiet Georgetown neighborhood on R Street, Oak Hill Cemetery is a historic and atmospheric destination in Washington, D.C. You will find many graves from the Civil War era, including a family mausoleum where President Lincoln's son Willie was buried during Lincoln's presidency—until the president himself was assassinated, after which time both bodies were laid to rest in Springfield, Illinois. During his term in office, the president was known to spend hours sitting by his son's tomb in Oak Hill Cemetery.

IMPORTANT DISCOVERY!

There's a link between the word "Oakhill" and President Lincoln! If Lincoln's young son used to be buried there, that explains why he was pointing to that word.

Still—why would the ghost of Lincoln want to tell me about the place where his son was buried?

Gilda heard the sounds of museum security guards, information-desk attendants, and retail clerks arriving for work, pouring coffee, and slamming the refrigerator door shut as they put away lunches.

"You have a good night? Feels like you just left, huh."

"There's Mr. History. Oooo! You look sweaty! You run all the way to work today?"

Matthew Morrow made some comment Gilda couldn't quite hear.

"Only ten miles? You slackin' off, boy!"

Gilda heard voices approaching and turned to see Matthew and Jasper Clarke standing in the doorway and speaking in hushed, concerned tones.

A moment later, Janet trudged past Jasper and Matthew into the office. "Oh." She regarded Gilda with thinly disguised disappointment. "You're here early."

I bet she was hoping I'd be late so I'd get in trouble with April again, Gilda thought. *I can tell she's the competitive type.* "I couldn't sleep thinking about these cipher wheels that need to be finished," Gilda fibbed.

"Now we've got a lot more than cipher wheels to give us insomnia," said Janet, moving closer to Gilda's desk and speaking in a low voice. "April's freaking out because one of her Spy Camp counselors canceled at the last minute with a family emergency. Roger's freaking out because his colicky baby is keeping him up all night. When I passed him in the hallway just now, he told me he was heading home 'either to rest my eyes or be killed by my wife,' which sounded kind of disturbing. He looked like he had just seen a ghost."

"What kind of ghost?"

"Um, I think that's just a figure of speech." Janet opened her large purse and unloaded a can of Slim-Fast and a paperback titled *Love's Fever* into her desk drawer.

"Whatever you do," Janet added, "don't have any problems today."

"I wasn't planning on it."

April abruptly burst into the room with a colorful flurry of silk scarves, tote bags, and morning stress, pushing between Matthew and Jasper and breaking up their conversation in the process.

"Excuse you," said Matthew.

"Sorry, but I have an emergency." April tossed a tote bag onto her chair impatiently.

"Is everything okay? Is Gabriel sick again?"

"Gabriel's fine; it's our Spy Camp that's in trouble."

"We already heard about it," said Janet, clearly enjoying being the first to know.

"Heard what?" Jasper and Matthew looked perplexed.

"April is short one counselor," Janet announced. "I heard you talking on your cell phone in the hallway," she explained, noticing April's slightly annoyed stare.

"I already knew about it, too," Gilda added.

Janet rolled her eyes. "Gilda only knows because I told her."

"The first session of Spy Camp starts tomorrow, doesn't it?" Jasper leaned in the doorway casually, but he looked concerned.

"That's right; it starts tomorrow."

"So who are you going to call for a substitute counselor?"

"I've been calling everyone I can think of, and so far, everyone is working, out of town, or just avoiding my phone calls."

"I'm sure nobody in this city would avoid your phone calls, April."

April fixed Matthew with a broad, false-looking grin. "That sounded like the helpful comment of a volunteer. Yes! You, Matthew, are going to be my new camp counselor."

"Um—I don't think so."

"He can't," said Jasper. "We just accelerated his deadline on a couple of publishing projects, and he needs to be available to answer calls from the press."

"Thank you, sir," said Matthew, turning to Jasper. "You're a gentleman and a scholar."

"I'm not sure I'm doing you a favor; it would probably be more fun to do Spy Camp."

"What do you mean, 'probably'?" April slumped in her chair. "It would *definitely* be more fun."

Gilda cleared her throat loudly. *Why wasn't April jumping at the chance to make her a camp counselor? She was sitting right there!*

"I think you might have one volunteer." Matthew tilted his head in Gilda's direction.

"I'd love to," said Gilda, standing up. "I'm great with kids." 93

"You *are* a kid," said Janet.

I definitely do not like Janet, Gilda thought.

"Yeah, she's a little young," said April. "I mean, I appreciate that you're offering to help, Gilda, but you'd only be a few years older than some of the kids."

"So give me some of the younger ones and I'll whip 'em into shape. By the time they leave this place they'll be running circles around the CIA."

Jasper Clarke made a move to leave. "Well, it looks like you have this under control, April."

"Very funny."

"I have a meeting with our advisory board to discuss some museum development plans. I'm afraid I'll have to leave the four of you to figure this out." Jasper paused. "For what it's worth, I think you should give Gilda the job. She's a natural spy, so they'll never guess that she's only fifteen."

Make that fourteen going on fifteen, Gilda thought, a little guiltily.

The room fell quiet for a moment after Jasper left.

"I guess I *could* give her a smaller group," April suggested, "maybe some of the younger kids."

Janet looked skeptical. "Won't the younger kids be more difficult for her to control?"

"They might be more likely to respect her," said Matthew.

"I think we're forgetting the art of disguise," said Gilda wondering why nobody in the room was addressing her directly.

Everyone stared at her with surprise, as if she had just belched loudly.

"Aren't we in the Spy Museum? It shouldn't be hard to look a few years older than my real age with makeup and wigs."

"While we're at it, we could make you look like a little old man."

Janet and April wrinkled their noses as if trying to imagine Gilda disguised as an old man.

"Well!" April stood up and brushed invisible lint from her pants. "The bottom line is that there are a few busloads of kids showing up to attend this camp, so we'd better hustle. Gilda, I hope you're done cutting out those cipher wheels because you have some camp-counselor training to accomplish today."

"Awesome! And don't worry; I won't disappoint you."

13

The Dead-Drop Message

Instead of going directly into her apartment building after work, Gilda decided to investigate Oak Hill Cemetery to see if she could find any more clues to explain the strange dream about President Lincoln. She made her way down Wisconsin Avenue, past the rumbling of idling delivery trucks parked outside businesses, past the high wall of the Russian Embassy with its security gates and wary guards, and past Guy Mason Park, where toddlers played in the sand as bored nannies watched. As she neared Georgetown, the air filled with the smoky aroma of Rockland's Barbeque and an assortment of Thai and Italian restaurants where people sat at little tables along the sidewalks, fanning themselves in the heat.

Gilda turned onto R Street where the atmosphere was sullen with humidity and a heavy silence. Again, the street gave her the ominous feeling of being watched by quiet, empty houses—houses that *knew* things. Sweat trickled into her eyes and between her shoulder blades, staining the back of her yellow sundress.

Gilda froze: she suddenly spied Boris Volkov heading up

the walkway toward his house, his black jacket slung over one shoulder, his arm gently resting on the back of a well-dressed, middle-aged woman whose hair was dyed a very unnatural shade of red and styled in a stiff, hair-sprayed do. *That must be Boris's wife,* Gilda thought. She had an impulse to run up to the couple and say hello—to ask Boris's wife why she had wanted those KGB artifacts out of the house. Instead, Gilda hid behind a tree just as Boris turned to glance behind him.

Boris, you're breaking the "Moscow Rules" of spy tradecraft, Gilda thought. *Never look behind; it makes you look paranoid.*

More than anything, Gilda wanted to spy on Boris. She wished she had had the foresight and technical skills to set up some kind of surveillance bug inside Boris's house when she and Matthew had visited him.

Realizing it would be too dangerous to actually peek into the windows of Boris's house, Gilda decided she had better continue to Oak Hill Cemetery.

Gilda passed through the walled entrance to the cemetery and found herself gazing down over a terraced hillside and what looked like a little village of graves: cherubs, marble angels perched upon pedestals, tall obelisks. Under the trees, the play of light and shadow upon gray and white stones was eerily beautiful.

Gilda had printed a cemetery map from the Internet—a maze of swirling lines demarcating intertwined walkways dotted with numbers indicating the graves of notable people from the Civil War era including Lincoln's war secretary, a bunch of Union generals, and several women who had been "hanged as confederate spies." Then Gilda found what she was looking for on the map: at a distant edge of the cemetery was the grave where Lincoln's son had been buried.

> Willie (William Wallace) Lincoln—President's son
> who died in 1862; removed from Oak Hill after
> President Lincoln was assassinated.

Gilda followed a rocky path that wound down the steep hillside among the tombstones. The air was still and hot, but here and there were sudden cool gusts rising up from the earth like little sighs of cold breath.

Gilda was suddenly very aware of being *alone* in this graveyard among people who had been dead for more than a hundred years. She had the strange feeling she was entering a new territory where she was outnumbered.

What if something more sinister than the ghost of Lincoln was beckoning to me in my dreams—luring me toward this cemetery? Gilda's mind drifted to a memory of a zombie movie she and her brother Stephen had watched on late-night television after the last day of the school year.

Get a grip! Gilda warned herself. She reminded herself of a passage from *The Master Psychic's Handbook* she had memorized:

> The psychic must create a personal boundary. YOU control what spirits
> talk to you. YOU decide if they are welcome or not. If they are not welcome,
> tell them GO AWAY.

Gilda navigated cracked and broken stone steps down a very steep hillside descent without a railing. *Clearly people don't take leisurely walks around this part of the cemetery very often,* she thought.

A cloud passed over the sun and Gilda heard the whir of cicadas in the trees and the sad cooing of mourning doves. As she neared the tomb where Lincoln's son had been buried, she felt suddenly cold. She walked alongside tombstones that had been toppled over, as if someone had risen from the ground and knocked them down.

Finally Gilda reached a family mausoleum built into the hillside: it was a tomb enclosed behind a heavy stone façade and an iron gate—the place where Lincoln's son had been laid to rest.

I'm standing exactly where president Lincoln stood when he came to visit his dead son, Gilda thought. She pictured Lincoln sitting next to the tomb while his guards looked on. He rested his head in his hands, tears streaming down his long, bony fingers.

"I had a dream about you, President Lincoln," she whispered. "What did you want me to know?"

Gilda caught her breath at the sound of rustling behind her. She turned to gaze into a pair of wet, black eyes. For what seemed a long time, she looked directly into the hypnotizing eyes. *This is what writers mean when they say, 'time froze,'* Gilda thought. The face had a black nose and soft ears: it was a small fawn who stared at her without moving, almost as if it wanted to say something to her.

Gilda recalled a passage from her *Master Psychic's Handbook*:

> Sometimes an animal will appear with a message from a spirit: Animals are more receptive to spirits than many humans: the old horror movie scene where the dog perceives an unfriendly ghost before the rest of the family actually has some basis in reality. The spirits of children have a special affinity for animals. . . .

Without warning, the spell was broken: the young deer turned and bolted, bounding down the steep hillside, stumbling and knocking over loose stones lining the path.

Gilda was about to take out her notebook to record the encounter when something on the ground captured her attention. *One of the large, brick-sized stones the fawn had knocked loose was not a stone at all!* It had broken open to reveal a secret compartment and a folded piece of paper.

I have a feeling it's the message I'm supposed to find, Gilda thought.

Gilda glanced around just to make sure nobody was watching, then picked up the stone container. Upon closer investigation, she saw that the stone was not natural at all, but made of some kind of painted plastic that had opened very neatly in half to reveal its contents.

Gilda unfolded the piece of paper and read:

dear dear friend speed when I it expect comes
to to have this a I delivery should for prefer
you emigrating soon to some look country for
where my they usual make signal no blue
pretense gum of marking loving Anna liberty to
you Russia will for respond instance with where

pink despotism gum can on be Anna taken to
pure Jet and me without know the you base
alloy of received hypocrisy package the poet

I can't make heads or tails of it, Gilda thought. She sat down with
her back resting against the side of the mausoleum to study the
cryptic note more carefully.

*If I found this anywhere else, I'd probably assume that it's just the
ramblings of some demented person. But this was concealed in a large
fake rock—something a lot like some of the dead-drop concealment
devices I saw in the Spy Museum.*

Gilda remembered how almost any object ranging from a
fake tree stump to fake dog poop could be used to conceal
secret information intended for pickup by a spy. She recalled
how, instead of face-to-face meetings that could lead to arrest
if anyone witnessed a direct exchange of information, spies
used dead drops to hide secret messages and classified government documents. Gilda felt a surge of adrenaline as she contemplated the potential implications of her chance discovery.
She whipped out the reporter's notebook she always carried
to scribble a note:

What if this is an encoded message, and I've just intercepted a real dead drop? It might be a message from someone inside the CIA, the FBI, or the military who's selling
secret information to some foreign government or organization! (The words "Russia" and "signal," for example, look
a little suspicious, considering the fact that the note was in
a fake rock!)

Gilda remembered reading about moles—traitors within the U.S. government like Aldrich Ames, who worked for the CIA and sold classified information to the Soviet Union for many years. Whenever Ames was ready to make a drop of secret documents to sell to his Russian spy contacts, he would make a simple chalk mark on a mailbox to alert his foreign handlers. He would print secret information from his office computer in the Central Intelligence Agency, then hide the documents somewhere in a suburban park. *A remote place like this,* Gilda thought. Ames's Soviet contacts would pick up the information and replace it with a cash payment. Finally, the Russians would leave another signal mark to let Ames know they received the package. Ames's activities led directly to the deaths of at least ten U.S. spies.

Gilda was about to stuff the piece of paper in her bag, thinking she would take it back to the Spy Museum to show Matthew or Jasper Clarke when she had another sobering thought. *If this is a real dead drop,* she thought, *then I could be in the middle of something dangerous. What if the mole discovers that I removed it? At the very least, I'll never get to the bottom of the case because the spy would just change the dead-drop location.*

Then Gilda remembered one of the things she learned at the Spy Museum: a spy wouldn't remove a secret document; she would instead take pictures of the information so that nobody would discover anything missing. Grateful that she hadn't yet removed her old Polaroid camera from her shoulder bag following her arrival in D.C., Gilda took several images of the message at various angles, then put the prints in her bag and the original message back inside the fake-stone concealment device.

The evening was dusky and humid as Gilda trudged up the long incline of Wisconsin Avenue. She felt uneasy as the guards in front of the Russian Embassy seemed to watch her with more interest than usual. Was it her imagination, or did they move a little closer to the gate as she passed by?

Gilda walked faster, eager to get back to her apartment and to get started decoding the message.

14

The Secret Code

```
TO: Gilda Joyce
FROM: Gilda Joyce
RE: POSSIBLE DEAD-DROP MESSAGE--ANALYSIS AND
DECODING

This is clearly not a numerical code. It's also
not the kind of code where each letter represents
a different letter of the alphabet--the kind of
code you can use a cipher wheel to solve. There
are some potentially significant words here: "coun-
try," "emigrating," "signal," "Russia," "des-
potism," and "liberty." These words point to a
foreign contact (maybe Russian?) and something
having to do with governments.
```

Wearing her "Motor City" nightshirt, Gilda sat at her typewriter and studied the photos she had taken of the message.

She heard Caitlin enter the apartment, talking on her cell phone as she threw her keys on the table and tossed her backpack on the couch. Gilda knew that Caitlin was now sitting on the couch with her feet up on the coffee table as she continued her phone conversation. As far as Gilda could tell, Caitlin was virtually always on the phone—catching up with college friends who were establishing themselves in other cities, making plans to meet up with people for brunch or drinks in the city, planning dates with guys she met at work, at parties, and even through an online dating website. One of the things Gilda loved about the apartment she shared with Caitlin was that the walls were thin enough to allow for nearly effortless eavesdropping; she didn't even need to lean against a door or a wall to overhear Caitlin's conversations with remarkable clarity. On the other hand, Caitlin was proving to be one of the few people who could talk on the phone longer than Gilda could maintain interest in listening.

"So anyway," Caitlin was saying, "my boss doesn't like me. . . . I know, I said that before, but now he *totally* doesn't like me. Remember that chick I told you about—the one I call 'the princess'? She got actually got *promoted* today. I know! Here I've been copyediting about twice as many stories per week as her. . . . Yeah, she kind of flirts with him, but I think it's more that she never ever disagrees with anything he says. Even when he's totally wrong. He also loves her because she went to the same college as him. . . ."

Caitlin fell silent; it seemed that her friend had a story of her own to tell.

"Wow, so they promoted you to associate editor? That's really great," said Caitlin after a long silence. "And a huge raise too? Great." This was clearly news that Caitlin would have preferred not to hear at that moment.

"Oh, but I forgot to tell the other part of the story," Caitlin interjected, turning the conversation back to herself. "My boss's boss *really* likes me. And I don't think he likes Frank—that's my boss. So I'm thinking I might complain to him."

Gilda heard Caitlin turn on the television and flip to a news channel. "Yeah, I'm thinking of taking the LSATs, too—going to law school. But then I don't know. Everyone goes to law school. . . ."

The combination of Caitlin's anxious, competitive banter on the telephone, and the cryptic photographs sitting in front of her on her typewriter keyboard suddenly made Gilda feel weary and a little homesick. Spy Camp would begin the next morning—a week of day camp culminating in the Midnight Spy Slumber Party. Gilda realized she had better organize her wardrobe and supplies to get ready for her counseling job before going to bed.

SPY CAMP COUNSELOR ("SPY RECRUIT TRAINER")
CHECKLIST

- Walkie-talkie to stay in touch with "Spy Headquarters" (and for April Shepherd to reach me when she wants to tell me to do something)
- CD player (to play spy instructions from Headquarters)
- Spy Camp counselor attire--something authoritative and sophisticated, yet mysterious
- Spy gadgets ("tradecraft" materials borrowed from the Spy Museum including sunglasses with hidden video camera)

- Flashlight
- Tissues and wet wipes (for messy spy recruits)
- Hand sanitizer (for germy recruits)
- Cell phone
- First aid kit
- Rope, tape, and handcuffs (emergency restraints for hyperactive young spies)
- Tranquilizer dart gun (kidding)
- Equipment for slumber party: spy pajamas and sleeping bag

Dear Dad:

Can you believe it? I'm going to be a Spy Camp counselor--a training officer for young spies!

I admit I'm a tiny bit scared. What if the kids don't listen to me? What if some of them can tell I'm only a couple years older than they are?

What would you tell me if you were here, Dad?

"Listen, Gilda," you'd say, "you aren't just a kid. You've already solved three mysteries even though you haven't gotten the public recognition you deserve. Do you think those CIA agents really know what they're doing when they go into a foreign country and start attending cocktail parties and getting people in trouble? Of course not! They learn as they go. Your instincts are as good as anyone else's, so just suck it up and act like you know what you're doing. That's what

107

most of those clowns in Washington do."

Thanks, Dad--that makes me feel better!

Love,

Gilda

Before going to bed, Gilda placed the dead-drop photographs under her pillow, hoping some clues might seep into her brain during the night.

Just as she fell into a deep sleep, the light from the apartment across the courtyard flashed—*on, off, on, off, on, off*—and the pattern continued for what seemed a very long time.

15

Team Crypt

Hi, Wendy!

First, a lot has happened since I woke you up in the middle of the night. Let's just say that the dream I had about Abraham Lincoln and a lipstick gun pointing at me was about more than Lincoln's assassination or being in a new city. I can't say more due to national security concerns, but I'm investigating something that may have far-reaching implications.

I also got promoted to the job of Spy Camp counselor!

I'm sure you're just dying to know how my first day of work as a Spy Camp counselor went, so I'm sending you a highly detailed report.

MY <u>SPY</u> <u>CAMP</u> <u>WARDROBE</u>:

I got lucky; a heat wave broke with a heavy summer rainstorm in the morning, so I took the opportunity to wear my light blue spy trench coat over a sleeveless black dress and vinyl stretch boots. I styled my hair with hot rollers, teased the crown for extra "spy body," stuck a partial ponytail on top of my head, and froze the whole thing with hairspray. I call it "1960s spy hair."

MY COLLEAGUES:

Before the campers showed up, the camp counselors all met early in the morning in the Ultra Room—which is this large space in the Spy Museum with high ceilings, tables and chairs, and a big movie screen that comes down from the ceiling when the museum hosts lectures and movie nights.

I felt a little awkward when I walked in and realized that the other counselors were dressed in casual black jeans and T-shirts, and that they all seemed to be college students who knew each other from classes or other jobs or just meeting up at the bar. "Live your cover," I reminded myself. "Act as if you aren't afraid."

COVERS & LEGENDS ROOM—SPY CAMP ORIENTATION:

When we went to meet our young spy recruits, we were greeted with a motley assortment of kids in all sizes, shapes, and colors who stood in little groups, giggling and whispering. A few wore quirky T-shirts with phrases like "Beware of female spies" and "Think! It's not illegal yet!" A few of them had even turned up in attempts at disguises: I saw a handful of wigs and dark glasses.

It's funny when you see a bunch of younger kids
who remind you of yourself. They think everything
they're doing is so serious, but you can see how
it's really silly and cute, and of course, you
also see how much you've grown up since those
days. (No snide comments, please.)

AN OMINOUS EXCHANGE:

As I surveyed the group and tried to guess which
kids had been assigned to my spy team, I noticed
a weird exchange between a boy and his mom as
they said good-bye. The boy had a narrow, pale
face and long, greasy bangs that hung in his eyes.
His mother was freckle-faced with a broad, cheesy
smile.

"Have a good time!" said the mom.

The boy looked annoyed.

"Come on--SMILE!!" The mom pointed at her own
smile with an index finger.

The boy glared.

Believe me, I know how embarrassing and annoying parents can be when you're surrounded by kids
who are sizing you up and possibly judging you,
but something about what this boy did next gave
me chills. He suddenly held up his finger like a
handgun and pointed it at his mother, striking the
air several times as if to say, GET OUT NOW IF
YOU KNOW WHAT'S GOOD FOR YOU. His mom just giggled
nervously and left.

A SPOOKY MOMENT:

We led the kids into the Briefing Room, a small
auditorium with a huge map of the world that glows
on the walls, surrounding the audience in eerie
black light. A few of the kids looked uneasy by
the end of the film we watched: "The cost of spying
could be torture, imprisonment, deportation, or
DEATH," the movie warned.

Then, without explanation, the movie screen
went black for a minute and then started again,
repeating the word "DEATH." The kids giggled, but
I saw Roger Selak (our manager of exhibit production) and Jasper Clarke (the executive director of
the Spy Museum) whispering in the corner. Jasper
looked concerned and Roger just looked ill. (I've
heard through the museum grapevine that there have
been a few unexplained glitches in the audio and
video exhibits during the past couple days and
that Roger is baffled about the cause.)

Next, April Shepherd (my boss) got up to speak.

APRIL: So do you all think you have what it
takes to be spies?

KIDS (screaming, and totally forgetting their
fear during the orientation movie): YES!

APRIL: Good! Now I'm going to introduce you to
a real spy.

Jasper Clarke stood at the front of the room.
"First, I have to apologize to the young man I
was sitting next to who assumed I was someone's

dad. He told me that he thinks the CIA is—and I quote—'retarded'. He must now be rather surprised to discover that I'm actually the executive director of the Spy Museum and a former CIA intelligence officer."

Jasper proceeded to explain to the kids that their basic job as spies is "to get information that someone else doesn't want you to have."

"How do you get that information?" he asked. "Mostly by FORMING RELATIONSHIPS—getting to know the insiders who have that information. Sometimes you can use surveillance technology, too, but it's the relationships that are often most important.

"Now, what kinds of information will you be trying to learn as spies?"

The kids stared at him.

"Capabilities and intent, that's what. In other words, as a spy I want to know what you're able to do to me, and also what you're PLANNING—or even hoping to do. Spying only exists because governments never trust the information they tell each other directly."

"What's the biggest gun you've ever carried?" the kids wanted to know.

"Listen, most of spying isn't really about guns," said Jasper. "It's more about people and using your mind. You have to convince people to give you information."

I could tell a handful of the kids who had

watched lots of spy movies were still wondering
when we were ever going to get around to shooting
some guns.

TEAM CRYPT MEETING PLACE:

I decided to meet with my spy team in one of my
favorite spots in the museum: a model of a 1940s
movie theater with velvet curtains and rows of
velvet chairs. The theater is decorated with colorful vintage posters of spy movies with titles
like "International Woman--SHE'S DANGEROUS!" I
thought this would be the perfect spot for me to
try on my new role as a seasoned Spy Camp counselor and an expert in spy tradecraft.

A MOMENT OF DREAD & REMORSE:

THE BOY I SAW GLARING AT HIS MOTHER IS ON MY SPY
TEAM! For some reason, I immediately thought of
old Mrs. Weinstock in 8th grade. Remember how
she'd get really annoyed when I'd read my Master
Psychic's Handbook while she was trying to teach
us a lesson on something like semicolons or
gerunds? It's true that her classes were mind-
numbingly boring, but I suddenly had some sympa-
thy for her after all this time. Wherever you are,
Mrs. Weinstock (probably tuning in to All My
Children and already dreading the next school
year) I just wanted to say I'm sorry if I seemed

rude back in 8th grade!

The kids stared at me, expecting me to say something brilliant. Live your cover, I reminded myself.

"Welcome to Spy Camp," I said, "and welcome to your spy team—Team Crypt.

"Our time together will be brief, but you're going to learn things that will change your life forever. You're going to learn to disguise your identity so completely that your own parents won't recognize you. You're going to learn that for a spy, things aren't always what they seem: dog poop lying on the White House lawn or a dead rat carcass in the basement of a government building might be something merely disgusting, but it also might be an ingenious secret container for a very valuable classified message. It's up to you to find out which is which. You're going to learn about gadgets and spy tradecraft. You're going to learn how to make witty conversation at cocktail parties. And you're going to learn how to tell when someone is lying.

"Someday I'll share the true details of my life and the spy missions I've been involved in, but for now, all you need to know is that my code name is ZELDA. You can call me 'Case Officer Zelda.' My legend: I'm a fashion designer and stylist visiting D.C. to promote my latest clothing line and beauty products. My hobbies include karaoke singing and fine dining.

"You should know that most of what I just told
you is a lie--the 'legend,' or made-up life story
I use when I'm working undercover in D.C.

"Now it's your turn to choose a cover identity
and share something about yourselves with the rest
of your team."

SPY RECRUITS IN TEAM CRYPT:

Eddie Rizzoli
CODE NAME: THE COMEDIAN
Eddie is a cute, plump boy with big eyes and an
overbite that makes him look as if he has chipmunk
teeth. He sneezes a lot but never seems to have
a tissue. (Good thing I came prepared, or the
whole museum would be covered with boogers.) He's
also prone to falling down. When he introduced
himself, he spoke in a very convincing British
accent and only revealed a few minutes later that
he had never even been to England; he was just
pretending.

Hansen Stubbing
CODE NAME: THE MISANTHROPE
Hansen ("The Misanthrope") is that pale boy who
seemed weirdly angry at his mom when she dropped
him off.

Hobbies: picking locks and making homemade alarms

so he knows when his parents are coming into his room. (Good old traditional American pastimes!)

Likes: books and movies about spies

Dislikes: talking and people ("especially people at my school")

Camp counselor note for recruit's file:
Keep an eye on this kid. My guess is that he's used to being the "bad kid" and that he's been picked on in the past. To save time and maybe to protect himself from getting hurt, he decides he's not going to like anybody he meets from the out-set. I'm just a little worried that he wants to be a spy as a way of getting revenge on people he doesn't like.

Willow Merman
CODE NAME: STARGIRL
Willow ("Stargirl") wears a hat she knitted her-self with green yarn, long pigtails in corkscrew curls, horn-rim glasses, and an oversize T-shirt that says GREEN in sparkly letters. She's home-schooled and she keeps talking about how every-thing at her house is powered by solar energy.

She seems very smart, but she also has some zany, giggly tendencies. (No, I don't know anyone else who has those tendencies.)

<u>Sonya Vitchenko</u>

<u>CODE NAME: AGENT MOSCOW</u>

Sonya ("Agent Moscow") has butter-yellow hair that
has the stiff, sticky texture of cotton candy.
(The black roots are growing out and it looks like
she dyed it herself.) Unlike the other kids, she
actually dressed up for Spy Camp--but not in a
disguise: she wore high-heeled sandals with jeans,
a sparkly top and painstakingly applied makeup
(including liquid eyeliner, which you and I both
know is VERY difficult to apply correctly).

Interesting: Agent Moscow attends an elite boarding school in Virginia. Her parents (who are
apparently very wealthy and whom she calls "oli-
garchs," whatever that means) live in Moscow! She
had the choice of getting an education here or in
Europe and she chose the U.S.

　　She's in 8th grade now (although she acts like
she's about 20) and she's been on her own here in
the U.S. for the past three years. She's bilingual
and speaks English with a Russian accent.

NOTE FOR AGENT FILE:
Agent Moscow has a great background for a young
spy recruit if I've ever heard one! (<u>Unless, of
course, Agent Moscow is already a spy.</u> Keep an eye
on this one just in case.)

Demetrius Young

CODE NAME: JAMES BOND

Demetrius ("James Bond") is African American and
a social butterfly who knows how to act cute and
flatter grown-ups. (That's right; I'm considered a
grown-up at Spy Camp.)

"I like your jacket," he tells me. "You're the
only counselor here who looks like a real spy." I
explain to him that it's not such a great thing to
"look like a spy" since spies often get more information when they blend in with the crowd.

"Still," he said, "it's _cooler_ to look like a
spy."

He received a gold star for the day in his
agent file.

Dewey Decker

CODE NAME: SPIDERMAN

DOUBLE-SECRET CODE NAME: "BABY BOY"

Dewey ("Baby Boy") is six years old--by far the
youngest kid on my team. He's obviously in awe of
the other kids, but they tend to ignore him completely.

He's very cute, but sometimes I wonder if he
really understands what we're doing here.

Note for recruit's file from camp counselor:
Make sure Baby Boy doesn't get lost in the city
during activities. Scheduled bathroom breaks are a
good idea.

ME (addressing my spy recruits): Imagine this:
You're in a hostile environment and your cover has
been blown. You need to get out of this situation quickly, without being detected. You'll need
a fake passport, and you'll also need to disguise
your appearance. Get ready, because your first
lesson is the art of disguise.

KIDS: COOL!

THE COMEDIAN: I want to be a ninja!

BABY BOY: I want to be Darth Vader!

ME: Hold on, there! What's the difference between
a costume and a disguise? You wear a costume, but
you BECOME your disguise. The way you walk, the
way you talk, the story of your life--everything
changes with a disguise.

The kids grab wigs, hats, and sunglasses from a
big trunk. The Comedian disguises himself as a
character he called "the Russian belly dancer." He
uses three fake mustaches: one for a unibrow, one
for his upper lip, and one to create a strange,
two-tailed beard. He pulls on black boots, a fur
hat, and a scarf and dances around the room. A few
minutes later he complains that "the mustaches are
making me dizzy and disoriented." Then he sneezes
and wipes his nose on a wig.

James Bond disguises himself as a character

called "Body Hair Man." He uses spirit gum to incorporate nose, ear, and chest hair into his disguise along with a little mustache.

The Misanthrope disguises himself as a woman
and Agent Moscow disguises herself as a man. The
Misanthrope looks almost pretty as a woman with
long auburn hair. Agent Moscow, on the other hand,
just looks like a bearded lady from some old-
fashioned sideshow.

Stargirl disguises herself as a "goth girl"
with tattoos, black lipstick and nail polish, and
a jet-black wig.

Baby Boy is scared of the wigs and the fake
facial and body hair, so his disguise is limited
to sunglasses, a cowboy hat, and a scarf.

Interesting Observation: The entire group seemed
happier and friendlier once they're in disguise,
no matter what they wear. They feel free and
also safe: suddenly they're becoming friends and
laughing. Even The Misanthrope starts talking and
helping people try on fake noses. (See? I'm not
the only person who likes to pretend I'm someone
else!)

AN UNFORTUNATE MISHAP: Now liberated by their
disguised identities, the kids (particularly
the boys) become giddy. They start a game they
called "wigball" using water bottles for bats and
an assortment of wigs and fake noses for base-

balls. While running to catch a wig that's sailing through the air, The Comedian crashes into a disguise makeup table, knocking everything to the ground including several open containers of spirit gum. Now spirit gum and fake hair are everywhere. Our team spends the next 30 minutes applying baby oil to hair-covered objects. Agent file folders are now permanently coated in various shades of hair, which delights my recruits.

April Shepherd pulls me aside and asks if I need help "keeping my recruits under control." I tell her the whole thing was just an "icebreaker exercise."

"I'm all for breaking the ice," she said. "I just don't think it's a good idea when we have body hair and glue all over the place."

"I couldn't agree more," I tell her. "Body hair and glue detract from the learning environment."

"It looked like they were having fun, though," April added. "They seem to like you."

ASSESSMENT OF MY FIRST DAY AS SPY CAMP COUNSELOR—— Covered in fake hair and glue, but an overall success!

16

The Profiler

Gilda stuffed several letters to Wendy into three fat envelopes, addressed and stamped them, then dialed her mother's cell phone number, thinking she should probably check in on developments in Ferndale. Between Spy Camp and her discovery of the dead-drop site in the cemetery, she hadn't thought much about calling home, and it suddenly occurred to her that she hadn't heard from her mother.

"Gilda! Hello!"

Her mother's voice sounded more jolly than usual, which made Gilda suspicious.

"What are you doing?"

"I'm actually at work right now; I've been taking on a couple extra shifts, trying to save up some money for Stephen's college applications."

"Can't he just go to community college and keep mowing lawns part time?"

"He may have to if I don't get more money saved up here. But the good news is that his instructors at math camp think he could qualify for a scholarship to University of Michigan."

"That's great." Gilda knew that her older brother would go

to some great university and that he would find some way to pay for it. It practically went without saying because Stephen had been working hard all through school with a single-minded determination. Gilda was proud of him, but sometimes she envied his sense of clear, practical purpose—the way he knew exactly what he wanted to study and how to make that happen. Next to Stephen, her own aspirations sometimes seemed outlandish, unlikely, and hard to explain.

Gilda heard someone giggling in the background. Her mother covered the mouthpiece of the phone. "Are you sure?" she whispered. "Oh—I don't know. Oh, you're too much!"

"Aren't you supposed to be taking care of patients? It sounds like you're having a cocktail party over there."

"It's surprisingly slow on our shift right now, so my friend Lucy here is helping me with something." Gilda's mother covered the mouthpiece of the phone again and giggled. "That looks good."

"What are you *doing*?"

Gilda wished, as she often did, that she had surveillance equipment hooked up so she could simply push a button and see exactly what was going on. Why was her mother distracted and giggling like a teenager? Why wasn't she asking what Gilda was doing in Washington, D.C.?

"Your mother is a hottie," she heard a man in the background say.

"I beg your pardon!" Gilda practically shouted into the phone. "I demand to know what is going on over there!"

"Calm down, Gilda."

This only made Gilda feel more annoyed. Whenever her

mother said "Calm down, Gilda," it only made her more certain there was good reason to feel agitated.

"I'm sorry; you caught me at an awkward time. My friends here—" Mrs. Joyce broke into another fit of nervous laughter. "If you can believe it, my friends here have taken it upon themselves to write an online dating profile for me."

"An online dating profile? Like those classified ads that say 'Women seeking men'?" Gilda's Grandma Joyce sometimes read classified personal ads from the newspaper over her coffee and chortled at them with obvious contempt. Did people like her mother do that sort of thing? Wasn't her mother too old? Gilda didn't like the sound of this. Although she had managed to tolerate her mother's last ill-fated boyfriend, Brad, she had far preferred the past few months when her mother had had no dates at all and had spent her evenings taking up knitting and occasionally going bowling with some friends from work. Who knew what kind of loonies an "online dating profile" might bring into the house?

"Well—it's just a way to meet people, that's all. My friends think it might be a way to find someone I have something in common with."

"Grandma Joyce always says there are crazies out there on the dating scene."

"Yes—we've all heard Grandma Joyce say that many times. But just because she's too scared to try dating doesn't mean the rest of us have to spend the rest of our lives without finding someone."

What in the world was her mother talking about? The idea of Grandma Joyce "trying dating" was preposterous. And was that applause she was hearing among her mother's coworkers in the background? Did someone actually say, "You go, girl"?

"Mom, is this conversation taking place in front of a live studio audience or what?!"

"Sorry—sometimes people around here get a little carried away. Lucy—excuse me, hon, I just need to talk to my daughter for a second." Mrs. Joyce moved into the hallway, away from her friends.

"I'm sorry, Gilda. I shouldn't have told you about that; you don't have to worry, okay?"

"Who says I'm worried?"

"You sound upset."

"I'm fine. Just on my own here in a big city—all by myself in a huge apartment building surrounded by strangers. I was thinking of doing an online dating profile for myself, actually. Great way to meet people here in the nation's capital, don't you think?"

"Don't you dare."

"See how you are?"

"Gilda, I am in my forties. You don't need to worry about me."

"Well, why don't you worry about *me*?" The question popped out, surprising Gilda. As soon as she blurted it, she realized that it was true: it did bother her that her mother hadn't been calling since she arrived in D.C. She didn't want her mother to hover over her or thwart her adventures. On the other hand, how could her mother think about online dating profiles when her daughter was in a big city all by herself for the first time?

"Gilda, I do worry about you. I've been thinking about you all the time since you left."

"Could have fooled me. I call, and you're giggling about dating elderly men."

"Now that isn't fair. You know you don't like it when I nag you or check up on you too much. In fact, when I didn't hear from you right away, I called the Spy Museum to make sure you got to work okay. I spoke with a lovely woman, April Shepherd."

Gilda felt a little embarrassed to think her mother called her boss at work. "Did she say anything about me?"

"She asked if I shared your fashion sense."

"Definitely not."

"I told her, 'Gilda has her own style.'" Mrs. Joyce sighed. "The truth is, Gilda, it hit me hard when you left on this trip and Stephen drove down to Ann Arbor to start going to his math day camp. The house was so empty. . . . It made me think about how it's going to be when Stephen's away at college the year after next."

"What about me? I'll still be at home."

"I know, honey, but you're so independent. It made me start thinking that I need to find someone. At least, I need to make sure I have my own life."

"What's wrong with knitting and bowling?"

"Is that what you'd prefer? Your old mother, sitting in the corner knitting doilies?"

"Scarves would be more practical. And you wouldn't sit in the corner all the time. We'd take you out in your wheelchair for some fresh air now and then."

Mrs. Joyce laughed ruefully. "Sounds like I have a lot to look forward to."

"See? You have a very full life."

"So how is D.C.?"

"It's fine. Nothing too special." Ironically, now that her mother was finally questioning her, Gilda no longer wanted to talk about her own experiences.

"How is your internship?"

"It's cool. I'm a Spy Camp counselor now."

"You are? Do you play games with the kids?"

"Mom, it's a *spy* museum. I'm teaching spy tradecraft."

"Oh. That sounds interesting."

Mom knows absolutely zilch about spying, Gilda thought. *In fact, she would make a really good spy because nobody would ever expect that she knows anything.*

"Gilda, is it okay if I call you a little later? I'm getting paged to go see a patient, honey."

"That's okay. I was going to bed anyway; I have to get up early tomorrow."

"Gilda—I'm thinking of you all the time, honey. I'll start calling you more often."

"Well, don't go overboard. Oh, I almost forgot—can I read your online dating profile?"

"Why do you want to see that?"

"Just curious. And I'm a writer, so I could probably help you edit it and liven it up a little." Gilda couldn't help feeling curious to see what her mother had written even though the idea of her own mother having a dating profile made her recoil. "You can send it to my e-mail address at the Spy Museum."

Mrs. Joyce laughed. "If you read it, you have to be nice—no mean jokes."

"I've never made a mean joke in my life."

As Gilda stared into the refrigerator feeling ravenous, she had a sudden appreciation for her mother. The contents of the Joyces' refrigerator often left much to be desired, but at least there was food. What Gilda really wanted was a peanut butter, banana, and chocolate sandwich, and she realized that if she wanted to eat, she would have to walk all the way to a grocery store.

The front door of the apartment swung open, startling Gilda.

"Hey there!" Caitlin's dishwater blond hair was clipped in a messy updo, her face shiny with sweat. "You would think rain would have made it cooler, but it is *nasty* out there today. I need a shower." Caitlin tossed her black blazer over a chair and her briefcase on the couch. "Omigod! I have been such a bad roommate! You must be starving."

"No, I'm fine," said Gilda, not wanting Caitlin to view her in the same category as an abandoned housecat. "I was just about to walk over to the convenience store."

"Oh, I'll drive you down to Safeway. I need to pick up some things anyway, and it's way too hot out there to walk carrying bags of groceries right now."

Gilda and Caitlin meandered through the aisles of the grocery store, picking up ingredients for Gilda's peanut butter, banana, and chocolate sandwiches and other items Caitlin thought would "liven up the refrigerator": a jar of marshmallow cream, mint chocolate chip ice cream, raisin bagels, cream cheese, frozen veggie burgers, microwave popcorn, instant mocha mint coffee, and sugarless gum. At Gilda's suggestion, she also tossed in a couple fashion magazines.

This is way more fun than going shopping with my mom, Gilda thought. With Mom, the cart is full of things like broccoli, ground beef, onions, and no-brand macaroni.

"I suppose we should get some fruit and veggies for you, too," said Caitlin, staring at the items in the shopping cart. "I mean, you're still growing, aren't you? Aren't kids your age supposed to have vitamins and cod liver oil and stuff?"

"I don't need as many vitamins as most kids," said Gilda. "I've been eating Detroit school lunches for years, so I've kind of evolved to get along with less roughage."

"Really?"

"Anyway, I think I'm done growing," Gilda added. "Good thing I like high heels."

"I'm sure we can get a couple more inches out of you. Here, let's get some grapes and blueberries. Maybe some yogurt, too."

As Gilda and Caitlin purchased their groceries at the checkout, they joked about the celebrity tabloid magazines and discovered that they both loved Junior Mints. On the way home, Caitlin became chattier than ever. In between bites of Junior Mints, she revealed how she's a "daddy's girl" who grew up in Virginia Beach; she explained how her father really wants her to go to law school even though she isn't excited about it; she described how she dates all the time but just can't find the right person. "The truth is, Gilda, I've never really had a serious boyfriend. If I like him, he doesn't like me. If he likes me, I don't like him."

"We are so similar," said Gilda, who had only once come close to having a real boyfriend. *This is kind of like having an older sister for the summer,* she thought.

"Anyway," said Caitlin, "it's been nice having you here instead of my roommate Lauren."

"Why's that?"

"Oh, she's always nagging me about the dishes I left in the sink or a phone bill that's past due or something. You're more laid-back."

"Oh, thanks." Secretly, Gilda knew that she wasn't the least bit laid-back; she simply wasn't focused on Caitlin's dishes.

"I think she's at The Farm, you know."

"You're kidding. Your roommate's in the CIA?!" Gilda knew that "the farm" meant the CIA training facility for new recruits. This was interesting. Why hadn't Caitlin ever mentioned it before?

"Oh, I don't know *for sure* that she's there, but she says she's training to work as a 'foreign diplomat' and if you ask me, that's code for 'spy.' She'd be just the type, too. She *loves* keeping secrets, which drives me crazy."

As she followed Caitlin down the sidewalk and into the elegant apartment lobby carrying bags of groceries, Gilda reflected that she herself had quite a few secrets she hadn't yet shared with Caitlin. *Should I tell her about the message I found in the cemetery?* Gilda wondered.

The elevator doors opened to reveal a tiny, mousy woman

who glared angrily at the two girls. Her iron-gray hair was pulled back in a messy knot and she wore a shapeless dress with old sneakers. She looked nothing like the other residents of Cathedral Towers, most of whom were either young professionals dressed in suits or elderly ladies wearing pearls, coral lipstick, and Sunday hats.

Gilda felt her psychic radar blast into high-alert mode: *it's the woman who stared at me from across the courtyard,* she thought—*the woman who lives in the apartment where the lights flash in the middle of the night.* Moving to the back of the elevator where she could stare at the woman's messy granny bun, Gilda wondered what, exactly, made this tiny woman so scary.

As Gilda exited the elevator, she glanced back for a moment. Her stomach clenched as her eyes met the woman's hostile gaze.

"Do you know that lady?" Gilda whispered to Caitlin as they walked down the hallway toward their apartment.

"Not really," said Caitlin. "She seems kind of weird, though. She never says hello."

"This may sound odd, but did your roommate ever say anything about flashing lights coming from that woman's apartment?"

"Flashing lights?" Caitlin paused to dig through her purse, searching for her apartment key.

"They've been waking me up in the middle of the night since I got here."

"You're kidding." Caitlin opened the apartment door and abruptly dropped her grocery bags on the floor. "Let me tell you something about my roommate. Lauren could practically sleep through an earthquake; I'm not kidding." Caitlin began hurriedly stuffing items in the cabinets and refrigerator. "Once we had this huge party, and Lauren just left right in the middle of it and went to bed. It didn't even bother her that everyone was shouting at the top of their voices and dancing. About five people came knocking on our door, telling us to keep it down, but Lauren was out cold. She never drinks, either, so that wasn't the problem. Anyway, I don't think flashing lights would wake her up since she usually sets about five alarm clocks in the morning."

Gilda couldn't help wondering whether comatose sleeping habits might be a bad quality for an intelligence officer in training—if that was indeed what Lauren was.

On the other hand, Caitlin said that her roommate keeps secrets. If she is training for the CIA, it's possible she knows something about the flashing lights but just never said anything.

After Gilda and Caitlin unloaded groceries, Gilda assembled the peanut butter, banana, and chocolate sandwiches, then heated some butter in a pan to fry them. Caitlin added a dollop of marshmallow cream to her sandwich and turned the heat dial on the stove to high. "These are either going to be really great or really gross."

"Trust me; they'll be great." Now that she felt closer to Caitlin, Gilda was toying with the idea of letting her in on her discovery of the dead drop. She knew that a true spy would keep everything under wraps, but she found herself wanting to share the note she had found in Oak Hill Cemetery. What if Caitlin could offer some insights into the kind of person who had left the note?

"So," said Gilda, "I have a question for you."

"Shoot."

"Can you really analyze handwriting?"

"How did you know about that?"

"I saw your book when I moved in."

"I'm not bragging or anything," said Caitlin, licking a serving spoon coated with marshmallow cream, "but it's scary how well I can analyze handwriting. My friends practically think I'm psychic." Caitlin paused to flip the sandwiches that were sizzling on the stove. "The thing is, it's kind of a problem because as soon as I see a handwriting sample from someone I'm dating, I also see all their problems. It's like their whole personality is on paper in front of me."

Gilda nodded. "That's exactly the kind of skill I need. I wondered if you could take a look at something I found."

"Is it something for the Spy Museum?"

"I'll show you." Gilda went to her room to retrieve the photographs she had taken of the dead-drop message. She handed them to Caitlin. "Can you just look at the handwriting here and tell me what you think?"

"Testing me, huh? Okay—fine." Caitlin went to a drawer, took out a magnifying glass, and sat down at the dining room table. "I'm pretty serious about this stuff," she explained. As she examined the handwriting in the note, her demeanor changed. Suddenly she seemed far more studious and scientific than she had just moments ago.

"Well, I'm sure I don't have to tell you that there's no sentence structure here; in fact, the whole thing makes no sense. However, it doesn't appear to be the writing of an insane person; it's written this way very purposefully and with great care. I'd also say that it's written by someone who has something to hide."

Gilda nodded eagerly. "What else?"

"I'd say there's evidence of some criminal tendencies here. You see how every letter is so meticulously formed? It's almost kind of childish, like a kid who's just learning to write and who doesn't want to make a mistake. This is someone who's afraid of slipping up in some way—afraid of revealing his or her true self. This person doesn't want to be known. You can also see an antisocial tendency in the way the letters lean to the left instead of the right. I'd say this is also someone who's angry. You see these jabs in the paper here and there where the pen is practically stabbing the paper even though the writing is so neat? You see these places where the tail ends of letters curl down sharply like little claws? Some people call those 'felon's claws.' In short—I wouldn't advise anyone to date this person."

"Do you think it's a man or a woman?"

Caitlin wrinkled her nose. "Usually I can tell immediately, but the only thing I can say for sure is that this person wants to disguise his or her identity."

The shrill, metallic scream of the smoke detector combined with an acrid, smoky odor interrupted their conversation.

"Omigod!" Caitlin jumped onto a chair and struggled to deactivate the smoke alarm on the ceiling. "Shut up! Shut up!"

Gilda ran into the kitchen and seized the frying pan, from which smoke curled and billowed over two charred squares. She turned off the stove and tossed the entire pan into the sink, feeling almost grief-stricken at the loss of two perfectly yummy sandwiches. *But I guess Caitlin's handwriting analysis was well worth the sacrifice,* she thought.

Finally, Caitlin managed to turn off the smoke alarm. "Sorry—I forgot to tell you that I burn food a lot. It drove Lauren crazy all year; we had to buy a new pan about every other week." Caitlin poked the pan in the sink. "Yeah, this pan is toast." She ran cold water over the pan and a cloud of steam exploded into the air.

"I can make more sandwiches," Gilda offered.

"I think I lost my appetite."

Maybe that's how she stays so thin, Gilda thought. *She makes dinner, burns it, then throws away the pan.*

Caitlin retreated to take a shower while Gilda made another sandwich. Unable to find another pan, she decided to eat it cold while typing her investigation progress report.

CASE FILE: DEAD DROP IN OAK HILL CEMETERY
INVESTIGATION UPDATE--HANDWRITING ANALYSIS REPORT:

Handwriting analysis indicates "potential criminal intent" and someone "with something to hide." This supports my theory that I have indeed intercepted a real dead drop.

POSSIBLE "PERSONS OF INTEREST":
1. Boris Volkov (former KGB officer): I would
   classify Boris as a "person of interest"

because of his history with the KGB and because
he lives very close to Oak Hill Cemetery.
A dead drop in this location would be very
convenient for him. Besides, Matthew Morrow
seemed confident that he had "switched sides"
for good, but you never know, right? What if
he's pretending to advise the U.S. government
about the Russians, but secretly double-
dealing--giving the Russians--or someone else--
information about us?

2. Freaky old lady on the 5th floor (code name
   "Ms. Flash"): no evidence links her specifically
   with Oak Hill Cemetery, but I don't like the
   way she looks at me--as if she knows I'm up to
   something. Why do lights flash rhythmically from
   her apartment every night? Is it some kind of
   signal? Why was she looking into my apartment?
   Why does she look at me as if she hates me?

17

Lincoln's Ghost

Gilda found herself in the Spy Museum again—in the Literary Spies Room. *He's here again,* she thought.

There was the ghost of President Lincoln surrounded by high stacks of old leather-bound books: he leaned over his desk, dipping his quill pen into an inkwell and etching letters onto the page. Gilda tried to get closer to see what he was writing, but she couldn't make out the words.

Strangely, she also saw Mrs. Larson, her school librarian, who perched on a stool, opening the covers of books and stamping them with due dates. *What is she doing here?* Gilda wondered.

She had an unusual awareness that she was dreaming. *If this is a dream,* Gilda thought, *I should be able to wake up*. But she didn't wake up.

Instead, she decided to ask Lincoln a question. "What does it mean?" she heard herself ask. It was hard to talk. She sounded breathless, as if she had lost her voice.

Look at my letters, Lincoln replied without turning to look at her. He continued writing with great urgency and speed.

Gilda tried to get closer to see the letters Lincoln was writing, but the words were dense and tangled—a web of ornate lines. She sensed someone else standing very close to her—someone who watched her from behind. Mrs. Larson stopped stamping books. She grew pale, staring at something just over Gilda's shoulder.

Someone is standing behind me, Gilda thought. She wanted to see who it was, but at the same time, she didn't want to know.

Something that felt like a sharp fingernail—*or was it a gun?*—pressed into her spine.

Gilda whirled around, and stared into a stranger's masklike face—a woman's face with skin the color of frozen snow. Her smooth forehead was marked with a bright red stain in the shape of a five-pointed star.

Gilda sat up in bed and closed her eyes, trying to preserve her memory of the dream. She knew she had to record the dream right away, because dreams had a way of evaporating quickly if she didn't get them down on paper fast.

```
TO: GILDA JOYCE
FROM: GILDA JOYCE
RE: DREAM INTERPRETATION--REPORT ON POSSIBLE
PSYCHIC MESSAGE


The ghost of President Lincoln appears for the
second time in my dream. This time, he was writing
something with intense speed, but I couldn't make
out the words.
   LINCOLN'S MESSAGE: "LOOK AT MY LETTERS."
   What letters? Does he mean the letter he
appeared to be writing in the dream? I tried to
```

read it, but I couldn't understand what it said.

IMPORTANT: Who is that eerie-looking woman who appeared at the end of the dream?

Gilda picked up one of her photographs of the dead-drop message and scrutinized the letters. She remembered Caitlin's analysis: "This shows evidence of criminal intent."

Then Gilda remembered another important clue from her dream:

Mrs. Larson, the librarian from school, was in my dream and there were lots of old books stacked all around Lincoln while he was writing. Maybe there's something important about a librarian--or the library.

Gilda remembered her American history teacher commenting that "Lincoln was not only a great American president; he was a great American writer. Sometimes on a Saturday night, I open a volume of his letters just for light reading."

Maybe that's it; maybe I need to look at the letters Lincoln wrote!

TO DO: Visit the Library of Congress A.S.A.P. and look at volumes of Lincoln's letters. Maybe one of his letters contains a clue!

18

"The Man of Our Dreams"

Gilda got into her office at the Spy Museum early, planning to look up some information about President Lincoln and his letters on the Internet before her campers arrived. But when she turned on her computer, she was distracted by a message from her mother entitled "THINKING OF YOU RIGHT NOW!"

Uh-oh, Gilda thought. I bet she's sending me her dating profile.

Hi, honey!

I miss you, and just want you to know that I'm thinking of you EVERY MINUTE! Please be careful in the city, okay? Don't go anywhere after dark, and make sure you watch your purse when you're riding on the subway. Grandma Joyce said someone stole her purse when she was riding the train from Detroit to Chicago, so she wants you to be careful, and make sure you keep an eye on your belongings.

Stephen has been very busy at his math camp in Ann Arbor, but he thinks the Spy Museum sounds "very cool."

Pretty high praise coming from your brother!

That's impressive that they're letting you help with Spy Camp! Your father used to like spy movies. It sounds like you're having fun.

Last night, your brother was kind enough to help me "load off" my Match.com profile (or whatever it is you do to get stuff up there on the computer). Your mother isn't very good with computers, so I'm lucky I have my kids to help me, right?

Anyway, I just wanted you to see that this is all in fun and that you have nothing to worry about, but if you see any misspellings or sentences that sound silly, just tell me. I'm always telling my friends what a good writer you are.

Take care, be VERY CAREFUL—and call me soon.

Love,

Your mom

Gilda felt annoyed that Stephen had actually helped her mother post an online dating profile. Didn't the two of them have any sense?

Part of her didn't want to read it, but curiosity won out.

Gilda opened the attachment to her mother's message and found a picture of her mother that she had never seen before. Her mother looked younger and prettier than usual, and she sat in a restaurant Gilda didn't recognize, laughing happily.

One of her friends must have taken it, Gilda thought. *From that picture, you'd think Mom was just a barrel of laughs. You'd never know that she gets really upset when socks disappear in the dryer or when she finds crumbs under the couch cushions, or that she loves spending*

Saturday mornings cleaning the garage.

PATTY JOYCE

Single mom is young at heart!

Hobbies: bowling, dancing, love the nightlife.

Me: Fit, energetic, and cute. I'd love to meet up for
conversation or a night out. I'm a great companion and
a good listener. Seeking friendship and maybe more.

Gilda stared at the profile, feeling like she didn't quite
recognize her own mother. Who knew that her mother loved
"dancing" and "the nightlife"? She remembered her parents
going to a handful of parties where her father had apparently
danced in a very silly way, but that was about it.

It's weird, Gilda thought, *how you think you know everything
about your mom and then all of a sudden, you see something that
makes you realize you've only known a small part of her—that she
has these secret parts you discover later. I mean, here I'm supposed to
be a spy, and I had absolutely no idea that my own mother even knew
the phrase "the nightlife"!*

Gilda decided to take her mother up on the request to
look for silly-sounding sentences in her dating profile. She
composed a new e-mail, typing very quickly:

Hi, Mom,

Attached, please find my rewrite of your dating profile. I
think you need a little more info and "truth in advertising" here. (Also, just a heads-up that your line "friendship and maybe more" has a good chance of bringing in
the lecherous crowd.)

I've made a few changes that should help you find the man of our dreams.

Love,

Gilda

EAGER BUT NOT DESPERATE!
PATTY JOYCE (born Patty McDoogle)
Middle-aged widow and mother of difficult teenagers
still wants to believe in love!

Several years ago, the light of my life was extinguished
when my dear husband Nick Joyce left this earth for
heaven. After a long and semi-chaste mourning period,
I am ready to seize the day—ready to take a chance
on love again.
Are you ready, too?

Me: A "bottle redhead" who's easy on the eyes.
Just focus on the sun-kissed freckles on my nose,
and you won't notice the frown lines.
I'm a nurse so it takes a lot to make me squeamish.
If anyone pukes during our date, I'm on it, pronto!
Good thing at our age, huh?

Recent accomplishments: scarves knit for the whole
family while watching *Dancing with the Stars*.
Aspirations: shakin' my own booty on the dance floor.
Special distinction: daughter is psychic investigator,
spy-in-training, and novelist.

<u>YOU</u>: good-looking but not vain, filthy rich but not arrogant. You own your own home, and you prefer to stay there. You like to keep a low profile. You're self-sufficient and you need lots of space and time to yourself.

When you want to give a gift, you think in terms of ballroom dancing costumes, New York theater tickets, or European travel for the whole family, kids included.

In a nutshell: We hardly know you're around, yet our lives have vastly improved since we met you.

If you match the above qualifications, we're ready to give you a chance.

Gilda hit Send and glanced at the clock. She would have to do her research on Abraham Lincoln after work; it was time to go meet her recruits.

19

The Ghost in the Machine

Attention, Team Crypt!" April Shepherd stood facing Gilda's team of spy recruits. "This morning you're going to learn what it's like to find yourselves in a foreign, hostile environment. You'll have to use your surveillance skills to track down information about possible terrorist activity and a missing nuclear triggering device."

Gilda and her team were in a part of the Spy Museum that simulated the experience of spying in an imaginary foreign country where streets were lined with markets selling odd foods like "mutton puffs," secretive government offices containing incriminating documents, and hidden locations for spy surveillance stakeouts.

April Shepherd led the kids into a briefing room covered with maps, photographs of "people of interest," and diagrams illustrating complex relationships among agents. "Yesterday, Case Officer Zelda taught you the art of disguise—how to create a new identity for yourself and how to 'live your cover.' Some of you got a little carried away with the concept of fake body hair, but you saw that in order to be believable, a true disguise is something that becomes part of a whole life story.

"Now, you're going to expand your spying knowledge; you're going to learn how to use technology to gather information."

April led Gilda's team into an audio surveillance room filled with large machines covered with complex dials and knobs. Gilda noticed Roger Selak in a corner of the room examining the connections between the machines and various cables and wires.

"Everyone, I want to introduce you to Agent Shockwave, our technical operations specialist." April turned to Roger, whose eyes looked bloodshot and almost bruised with dark circles. "Agent Shockwave, are our surveillance machines up and running today?"

"I sure hope so." Roger had spent the morning trying to fix a baffling technical glitch: he heard strange sounds coming from the equipment but couldn't pinpoint the cause of the problem. He had spent hours checking the rack-mounted panel of electronic show software with no luck. Making matters worse was the fact that he had been up most of the night with a baby who screamed for no good reason that any adult could determine. The two problems had put Roger in a very glum mood: in the past, he had delighted in seeing the Spy Camp kids, but today, he just didn't have the energy to play the role of a spy in a foreign country.

"You look a little haggard today, Agent Shockwave," April observed.

She's right, Gilda thought, remembering Janet's comment. *He looks like he's just seen a ghost.*

Roger was not amused. "You would too if you spent the night with someone screaming in your ear."

"Kids, Agent Shockwave has been conducting audio surveillance with some pretty dangerous characters recently."

"That's one way to put it."

"Okay, we've gotten some information about a meeting taking place between one of our undercover agents and some suspected terrorists who may be plotting an attack on the government," April announced. "We've got our surveillance equipment set up to listen in on that meeting. It's going to be hard to hear what they're saying, so you're going to have to figure out how to get your equipment tuned in to the correct frequency pretty fast." April checked her watch. "Okay—it's time. Use those listening skills!"

Gilda helped her team get set up with headphones, positioning spy recruits in front of the audio surveillance machines.

"Hey!" shouted James Bond. "I hear someone talking!"

"Shhhhh!" Gilda whispered. "You have to listen so you don't miss anything."

"It sounds really fuzzy," The Comedian complained.

"I can't understand what they're saying!" Baby Boy cried.

"Team Crypt!" Gilda clapped her hands. "Stop talking and start listening!" The kids fell silent and Gilda had the galling realization that she had sounded exactly like one of the grumpy teachers at school. *I guess it really is true that you don't know why people say or do things until you have to spend a day in their shoes,* she thought.

Gilda's recruits leaned close to their machines, frantically turning dials one direction, then another, in an attempt to get information from the secret meeting.

"Wait a minute," said Stargirl, "someone's speaking in another language, but I can't understand it."

"Hey, yeah!" said James Bond. "Some foreign lady is talking now!"

Noticing that all the color had drained from Roger's face, Gilda grabbed a pair of headphones to listen for herself. She heard a man's heavily accented voice coming through heavy static. "We need to act quickly . . ." he said. "She's going to visit [something muffled] tonight . . ." Gilda knew that these voices were part of a prerecorded conversation—actors playing the role of suspected terrorists plotting their next moves. Then, in the background, Gilda perceived a soft female voice speaking in a foreign language. It was odd: the woman didn't seem to be having a conversation with the two men who were on tape. It reminded Gilda of times when she and her family had listened to the radio while driving on a long trip. Sometimes, as you moved farther from home, fragments of stations from other cities broke through, interrupting songs and other programs. *Is it possible that these audio surveillance machines are picking up some "spirit" frequency?* Gilda wondered.

Agent Moscow listened with a prim expression. She pressed her earphones closer to her head with a childlike hand painted with chipped red fingernail polish. "Eet's Russian," she said.

"Really?" This was intriguing, since they were supposed to be in the Spy Museum's imaginary country of Khandar. "What is she saying?"

"She speaks very soft, but I hear something about a meeting—'the last meeting.'" Agent Moscow frowned; a furrow appeared between her dark, thinly plucked eyebrows. "She says, *'Poét znáet'*—which means 'the poet knows'; *'Poslédnaya fstrécha'*—that means 'the last meeting'; *'Právda vsegda'*—'the truth lives forever'; *'Poét znáet'*—'the poet knows'. . ." Agent Moscow paused. "She's repeating the same phrases again."

Roger stared at Agent Moscow. "So—those words actually mean something?" His face looked pale and drawn, as if he were just recovering from a bout of the flu.

"Roger—I mean, Agent Shockwave—are you saying there *isn't s*upposed to be a Russian woman's voice on these audio surveillance machines?" Gilda demanded.

She felt a distinct tickle in her ear. There was something eerily significant about those phrases, "The poet knows . . . The last meeting . . . The truth lives forever . . ." and something about the pleading tone of the woman's voice made Gilda believe that this might be a significant message—something worth further investigation.

Something's definitely up at this museum, she thought. She remembered how, in a case she had investigated a few months before, she had learned that ghosts can use the capabilities of machines as a kind of "voice box" to help them speak to the living. *Roger seems baffled by this voice,* she thought. *My guess is that we've got a genuine haunting here.*

"If you're hearing a voice on the machine, I'm sure there's supposed to be a voice," April snapped.

Ignoring April's comment, Roger grabbed a pair of headphones and put them on. "I worked to get rid of that voice all day yesterday, and I thought it was finally gone. And now it's back again." He shook his head ruefully. "Gilda is right," he said. "That voice *isn't* supposed to be there. I even called the company who created the show software, and they couldn't figure out why it's happening, either. I have no idea where that voice came from."

The members of Team Crypt whispered among themselves:

"What did he say?"

"He said something's wrong with the surveillance equipment."

"It's broken?"

"No, it's probably sabotage from a rat agent on one of the other teams."

April looked annoyed. "Roger—our recruits are supposed to be honing their audio surveillance skills right now. Maybe you can investigate these little technical glitches later." April didn't like wasting time, and she hated any suggestion that the fantasy situations created at Spy Camp were not the *real* thing.

"Actually," said Roger, completely ignoring April's criticism, "this is good because you all heard that voice, too, which means that I'm not crazy."

"Excellent news, Roger," said April, sardonically.

"I was beginning to wonder." He stood with his hands on his hips, shaking his head at the equipment as if it had just attempted a malicious practical joke. "But if you're hearing it, too, it's not just me."

"Recruits!" April clapped her hands. "Everyone listen up! Time to move on to video surveillance!"

As she dutifully followed April and her recruits from the audio room, Gilda noticed Roger leaning against a wall, still holding one headphone to his ear and listening to the voice. He had the concerned, disappointed look of someone who had just completed a complex jigsaw puzzle only to discover that a single piece was missing.

20

The Frightening Face

The video surveillance room featured an enormous video screen on one wall and stations resembling pinball machines or video games equipped with smaller screens along with various buttons and levers to control the movement of cameras. Gilda's recruits immediately began pushing levers and trying to make the screens work.

"Okay, recruits, since it looks like some enemy agents have sabotaged our audio surveillance equipment, we're going to work on your video monitoring skills instead."

"Cool!"

April held up a photograph of an attractive, olive-skinned woman wearing a business suit. "Your job is to follow this woman. Her code name is *Agent Topaz*. Watch her closely and see where she goes and who she talks to."

"Agent Zelda," said April, looking at Gilda, "can you tell your recruits to stop playing with the equipment until they understand how to use it?" April eyed James Bond and The Misanthrope, who were all but taking out wrenches and screwdrivers to disassemble the video monitors.

"Stop touching stuff," said Gilda, walking over to the boys. This was a phrase Gilda's brother had used with Gilda through-out her life—usually in reference to the interior of his car, his computer, or any other object he owned. It usually deterred her for about half a minute.

"But we already know how to use this equipment," said The Misanthrope. "When you push this button, you see the view from camera one. This one is camera two—"

"Alert!" April shouted and waved at the front of the room. "Agent Topaz has entered the hotel. Everyone in positions; we need to get a clear picture of what she's up to and who she's meeting with. Start working those surveillance cameras, and don't lose sight of her, whatever you do!"

The large video screen at the front of the room showed the empty lobby of a hotel. A thin, elegant woman entered the lobby, deep in conversation with a man.

"There she is!" yelled The Comedian. "Get her!"

The kids frantically pushed buttons and pulled levers at their stations, zooming the view on their video monitoring screens in and out, doing their best to switch camera controls to follow the constant motion of the woman through hallways and into stairwells where she paused to have whispered conversations with suspicious-looking contacts.

Gilda had to give her team credit; they really did know how to work the surveillance equipment.

"They're actually doing pretty well," April whispered in Gilda's ear. "They're tracking her better than the other teams did. I'm going to run to the ladies' room; looks like you have everything under control here."

Gilda's spy recruits had just managed to close in on Agent Topaz and were turning up their dials in an attempt to get an audio reading when every screen in the room went black.

"Hey!" James Bond shouted. "Who turned out the lights?"

"Probably just a power outage," Gilda suggested. "Real spies have to deal with unexpected technical problems all the time."

"I don't think it's a power outage," said The Misanthrope. "The overhead lights are still working."

Gilda was just about to fetch Roger for help when every video screen filled with grainy gray and black dots. Gilda's left ear tickled. She felt a prickly sensation all over her skin as a staticky electrical roar filled the room.

"Hey! The video is coming back!"

Everyone waited for the image of a hotel interior to re-emerge on their screens, but instead, the screens only blurred with more black dots that moved faster and faster, clustering together in what seemed an attempt to form an image.

"I bet this never happens when you have a solar-powered system," said Stargirl.

"Cool!"

"Weird! What's going on, Case Officer Zelda?"

The temperature in the room plummeted. Gilda shivered, sensing a presence that was gathering energy—struggling to gain enough strength to reveal itself. Then, with the unexpected immediacy of a flash of lightning, a face peered from every screen.

Baby Boy screamed.

"Omigod!" squealed Stargirl.

The other kids fell silent, transfixed by the face's sightless,

155

open eyes. Dark makeup smudged the eyes and black-red blood trickled from a wound on the woman's head.

It was the face of a dead woman. Upon the woman's throat was a brooch in the shape of a star. Gilda had the disturbing feeling that she *recognized* the face. The recognition was particularly upsetting because there was only one place she had ever seen this woman.

It's her, she thought. *It's the face from my dream.*

After recovering from their shock, Gilda's spy recruits seemed to decide that the face on their video screens must be part of the surveillance test—something intentionally created by the Spy Museum to scare them.

"Like I said before, I bet a rat agent from another spy team is sabotaging our surveillance equipment," The Misanthrope suggested.

"That's a good theory," said Gilda. "We'd better all keep our eyes open for double agents." *The truth is that he just saw a ghost,* she thought.

Deciding that everyone needed to recover from the surveillance activity and hoping to learn more about the events of the morning, Gilda sent her team on a bathroom break and told them to meet her back in the Ultra Room for lunch.

It's very weird that at the moment, I'm acting as an adult who's concealing true information from kids. It's ironic because I HATE it when adults do that. On the other hand, I now understand something: I think so-called grown-ups hide or even lie about the truth when they don't have a

clue what to say about it to kids. They're scared and confused and don't know how to explain what's going on, so
they don't say anything. For example, if the grown-up in
charge (me) doesn't know exactly who or what that face
on the video screens was that we all saw, how are the kids
supposed to feel safe? Hence, not talking about it at all and
hoping they'll forget they ever saw it.

Deciding that everyone needed to recover from the surveillance activity and hoping to learn more about the events of the
morning, Gilda sent her team on a bathroom break and told
them to meet her back in the Ultra Room for lunch.

With a couple minutes to spare before lunchtime, Gilda
decided to take the opportunity to look for Roger in his office.

Roger worked on a laptop computer, but most of his work-
space resembled a utility closet.

Gilda opened the door to find Roger sitting in a chair with
his eyes closed as if he had dozed off without realizing it. "Oh!
Sorry."

Roger rubbed his eyes. "Was I asleep?"

"Maybe just for a minute."

"Don't tell April. She's loves that I'm experiencing this
whole colicky baby thing on top of everything else going on
here. She thinks it's hilarious. 'See, Roger? Now you know
how I felt a couple years ago.'" Roger took off his baseball
cap, rubbed the top of his head as if this might help wake
him up, and reapplied the baseball cap. "To be honest," he
said, "I'm still kind of spooked out by that stuff in the audio
room."

"Good thing you weren't in the video room a few minutes ago."

"What happened?"

Gilda explained what she and her spy recruits had just seen—the woman's face that had suddenly peered at them through the video screens.

"I've seen a lot of technical problems, but this is definitely the weirdest. I even started to wonder whether someone might be tampering with the equipment or the software in the control room. I asked the security staff to check out the museum's surveillance cameras but we couldn't find anything that looked suspicious."

"Roger, I think we're dealing with a haunting." Gilda watched Roger carefully to gauge his reaction.

He looked doubtful. "I know there are supposed to be a lot of ghosts around D.C., but that seems far-fetched. Why the Spy Museum?"

"Why *not* the Spy Museum? Ghosts gravitate to places or objects they used during their lives, and this place is full of old objects with tons of history. Plus, ghosts often turn up more often when people die amid intense emotions or unfinished business."

"There's plenty of unfinished business around here; that's for sure."

"Exactly. This place is just filled with stories of intrigue and betrayal, not to mention all the spies who got killed before they finished whatever they had set out to do. Maybe one of them wants us to know something about her."

"Maybe." Roger's face clouded as if he were angry with the ghost for interfering with the exhibits he had so carefully designed.

"Has anything like this happened before?"

"No." Roger thought for a moment. "Well—there was one thing. When I placed that new gold lipstick pistol and the star brooch in the Sisterhood of Spies exhibit, I saw something strange in the mirror where that film about female spies plays."

At the mention of the lipstick pistol and star brooch, Gilda's ears perked up. She pulled out her reporter's notebook to take notes. "Tell me more," she said. "Tell me exactly what you saw."

"It was like the regular film stopped, and this weird smoky thing appeared. . . . It kind of looked like a person, but I wasn't sure what it was. All I knew was that it was looking at me—and I wanted to get away." He picked up a screwdriver and began flipping and catching it in one hand nervously. "I made myself forget about it because I couldn't find any way to explain it. When I checked the equipment, I couldn't find a single thing to explain what happened."

"Was that the *first* time you experienced this kind of strange event in the museum?"

"I think so."

Gilda nodded. "That backs up my theory."

"What theory?"

"I think this is all connected with the new artifacts we acquired from Boris Volkov; I just have to figure out exactly how."

TO: Gilda Joyce

FROM: Gilda Joyce

RE: SPY MUSEUM HAUNTING INVESTIGATION--UPDATE

HYPOTHESIS: The Spy Museum may be haunted by the
ghost of a female spy who has some connection
with the artifacts acquired from Boris Volkov.
The camera-concealing star-shaped brooch seems
particularly significant. Images of blood and death
are linked with this ghost; maybe she was a KGB
officer who was murdered?

QUESTIONS TO INVESTIGATE:

1. WHAT DOES THE SPY MUSEUM GHOST WANT TO TELL ME?
   I need to find out more about the ghost's identity and how (if at all) she's linked with the
   lipstick gun and camera-concealing brooch. Find
   a way to interrogate Boris Volkov. (This might
   prove difficult.)

2. WHAT DO THE FOLLOWING PHRASES MEAN, AND WHAT IS
   THEIR SIGNIFICANCE TO THE SPY MUSEUM GHOST?
   "The Last Meeting"
   "The poet knows"
   "The truth lives forever"

3. In my dreams, the Spy Museum ghost, Lincoln's
   ghost, and clues pointing to Oak Hill Cemetery
   are linked together. ARE THESE CLUES ALL RE-
   LATED, OR AM I REALLY PURSUING TWO SEPARATE
   INVESTIGATIONS? HOW ARE ALL THESE EERIE IMAGES
   AND MESSAGES CONNECTED?

21

Two Truths and a Lie

Dear Wendy,

BIG development: there's a ghost in the Spy Museum who's turning up in audio and video exhibits. Meanwhile, I've got a situation that potentially involves a national security issue and the ghost of President Lincoln. I can't go into the details yet, but I'm planning to go to the Library of Congress after work today to do some research that should help me decipher a code.

If all of that isn't enough: at this very moment, I'm sitting here watching my spy recruits play yet another lively game of "wigball." (That's right—wigball. The kids use the museum's spy wigs and false noses as balls and water bottles as bats.)

ME: (watching a wig sail through the air, nearly colliding with my boss's head) Hey, you guys! That's enough.

KIDS: But we're just playing wigball. Can't we just finish this game?

It's weird when you find yourself on the receiving end of the same excuses you've used all your life. How many times

has my mom said to me, "Gilda, turn off _Saved by the Bell_; it's time for dinner now." My response: "But I just want to see what happens next" (even though I've seen the rerun about twelve times already). Well, now I'm in the position of being the authority figure, and at the moment, the kids aren't listening to me. Maybe I need to get one of those annoying whistles that our playground supervisors wore around their necks when we were in elementary school.
Now wigs are sailing through the room, whizzing past the other teams' tables. Uh-oh—I think I just saw one of them land on April Shepherd's head. She's giving me a warning look. Okay—I've got to do something about this. I'll write more later!

"Come over here, guys!" Gilda did her best to entice her recruits away from their rowdy game of wigball. "I have a really cool spy game to teach you!"

"What is it?" asked James Bond as he tossed a blond wig in the air and used a soda bottle to whack it across the room.

"It can't be more fun than this game of wigball," said Stargirl, deftly catching the wig.

Gilda did her best to think fast. "You're going to practice telling lies."

This got her recruits' attention: for a moment they looked both intrigued and stunned.

"But lying is wrong," said Baby Boy.

"That's right, Baby Boy," said Gilda. "Lying is wrong."

"My code name isn't Baby Boy; it's Spider-Man."

"Lying is wrong," Gilda continued, "but spies have to do it

all the time. What do you think you're doing when you put on a disguise and use a fake passport and let someone believe that your cover story is your authentic identity? You're essentially telling a lie in order to do your job as a spy. If you're a good spy, you're lying as a means to an end: in order to get important information that will help protect others from danger. But of course, you will be trying to get information from people who might be lying to you as well. For example, you have to watch out for double agents. If you want to be a spy, you have to get good at sensing when other people are lying to you."

"I can tell when people are lying," said Stargirl. "They get really twitchy and nervous."

"Lots of people do," said Gilda. "But some people don't. In fact, I once knew a girl who kept herself incredibly still while she was lying. She was pretty, popular, liked by everyone. And she made perfect eye contact and practically stopped blinking while she was lying through her teeth to the teachers and the school principal denying her involvement in a criminal activity. The only way you can catch people like her lying is when they slip up at some point in telling their story. That's why, if you're interrogating someone, you have to keep asking the same question lots of different ways."

"And if you're the one making up a cover story and a legend, you'd better know your own story really well," said James Bond.

"Exactly. Which leads us to a little game we're going to play: it's called Two Truths and a Lie."

"Oh, I think I've played that before at a slumber party," said Stargirl. "It's like we all say three things about ourselves: two things that are true and one thing that's a lie. Then we all see if we can guess which is which."

"That actually sums it up pretty well, Stargirl."

"Oh! Can I go first?" The Comedian asked.

"Go ahead."

"Okay—here goes. Number one: I've won seventeen karate tournaments."

The Comedian ignored the giggles and broad grins that followed this statement. He was well aware his plump physique made it hard to imagine him pursuing any sport quite so seriously.

"Number two: once I was standing in a bakery, and a car crashed through a wall. I was saved by a display of chocolate croissants that stopped the car before it could crash into me."

"What are croissants?" Baby Boy asked.

"Pastries," said The Misanthrope. "Kind of like flaky bread. And not something you usually see blocking a car crash."

"A car crashed into bread?"

"In other words, that was a lie," said James Bond.

"Are you *sure*?" said The Comedian. "Number three: I'm twelve years old."

"If you subtract six years of mental age," said James Bond.

"Hey, I think he told two lies instead of two truths," said The Misanthrope. "No offense, but I don't believe he's a karate champion, and I definitely don't believe he was saved from a car crash by croissants."

"Doughnuts, maybe," quipped James Bond, "but not croissants. Too fancy."

"Yeah, eet sounded like a movie," said Agent Moscow. "Kind of hard to believe."

Gilda smiled, feeling certain she knew which statement was the lie. "Do you want to tell everyone the lie?"

"I'm actually eleven years old," said the Comedian, clearly pleased with himself. "*That* was the lie."

"I knew it!" Gilda blurted.

"You knew his age because you've seen our records," said The Misanthrope.

"No, I suspected he was lying because 'I'm twelve years old' was the most boring thing he's said since he got here. It wasn't in character."

"It's like that saying," said Stargirl, "truth is stranger than fiction."

"Exactly. Have any of you ever told the truth to someone who assumed you were lying simply because your story sounded too odd or unexpected?"

Gilda's recruits all nodded.

"A lot of people *prefer* hearing lies," said The Misanthrope.

"What are you talking about?" Stargirl frowned. "I don't know anyone who prefers lies."

"I sure do," said The Misanthrope.

"Like who?" James Bond asked.

"A lot of people." The Misanthrope shrugged. "People at my school who shoplift even though they're rich but would never admit it. People who are considered smart and popular but who cheat on every test. Their parents know they do it but they pretend not to know because they want them to get into college someday. My mom, who tells everyone she has 'the perfect family' and does her best to fit in with that whole group of phonies." His voice rose at the end, and Gilda got the feeling he might have burst into tears if he had been alone.

The group fell silent, momentarily unnerved by the harsh honesty of his words. Sitting on the floor, The Misanthrope played with one of the shoelaces on his sneakers. "I guess, with a lot of people I know, when you tell them something they don't want to hear, it's like they become deaf."

Okay—now's the time I need some mature words of wisdom to put this all in perspective as their camp counselor, Gilda thought, wondering how they had veered from the topic of spy tradecraft into something that suddenly felt more like a group-therapy session. *Maybe this is what happens in the intelligence community when spies have to work under pressure and nobody in the "outside world" can know what's really going on with them. Do they confide in one another, or do they just become distrustful of everyone?*

"Eet can feel lonely when you can tell nobody what ees really going on," said Agent Moscow quietly.

The Misanthrope glanced up at Agent Moscow with appreciation but quickly went back to staring at his shoelaces as if hoping they would come to his protection in some way.

"What do you mean, Agent Moscow?" Gilda asked, feeling very curious about Agent Moscow and also relieved that one of the kids had at least attempted to offer a helpful response to The Misanthrope's confession.

"My parents—I don't tiell dem much because dey are so far away in Russia. Dey can do nothing to hielp when something goes wrong, and I don't want to worry dem. Sometimes I lie.

Or I just don't tiell everyting—and dat is lonely sometimes."

Gilda had to admit she could relate to some of the feelings her team members described: she had felt vaguely lonely ever since she arrived in the nation's capital. While she was too busy with work and her investigation to dwell on the feeling, the truth was that trying to solve a complicated mystery while living far from anyone who knew her well was harder than she had expected.

"Feeling lonely or even kind of alienated is common for spies," said Gilda, thinking that she should try to direct the discussion back to the subject of espionage. "Think about it: imagine you're an intelligence officer based in a foreign country, and you've assumed a false identity. If you're able to make some friends in the local community, they won't know who you *really* are: they'll only know invented facts about you—your made-up 'legend.' When you're having a hard time getting secret information, you won't be able to call your best friend from high school and complain because your work will be secret from everyone except a very small circle of spies—maybe one or two family members. Hopefully, you'll know that you're doing important work, but most of the time, you'll be the only person who will know what's going on in your life." *Now that I think of it,* Gilda thought, *simply being lonely is one of the risks of being a spy that the Spy Museum movie didn't mention.*

"That's partly *why* I want to be a spy," said The Misanthrope. "I usually don't like being around people anyway."

"How are you going to get secret information from anyone if you hate being around people?" Stargirl demanded.

The Misanthrope shrugged. "I didn't mean that I can't be

around people *at all.* I just don't think I would mind too much if I was just living undercover, wearing disguises, with nobody in the neighborhood who knew much about me."

"I think that would be hard," said Stargirl.

"That's why we spies have to stick together," said James Bond. "Right, Case Officer Zelda?"

"Absolutely. Spies working on the same team have to trust and rely on one another."

"But if spies are always lying to other people," said Stargirl, "how do they know that they aren't also lying to each other?"

"Lie detector machine," commented The Misanthrope.

"He's partly right," said Gilda. "Ever since they found moles in the CIA and FBI, they've had to double-check everyone from time to time."

"So what about you, Case Officer Zelda?" James Bond grinned at Gilda.

"What about me?"

"Aren't you going to take a turn playing Two Truths and a Lie?"

"Yeah!" the other kids chimed in. "It's Zelda's turn!"

Gilda felt flattered by their curiosity—their sudden desire to make her a closer part of the group. And while she usually delighted in her own independence and complete autonomy, she suddenly felt an overwhelming urge to forge a stronger connection with her campers—to let them in on one of the secrets she had been keeping.

"Okay," she said, leaning forward and lowering her voice so that none of the other counselors would overhear her, "see if you can tell whether I'm lying or telling the truth."

Team Crypt leaned toward Gilda eagerly.

"One: I love peanut butter, banana, and chocolate sandwiches."

"Gross!" said Baby Boy.

"Two: I'm a psychic investigator."

The Misanthrope snorted with derision.

"Three: I hate wearing wigs."

"She can't be a psychic investigator," said James Bond.

"Why not?" said Stargirl.

"Eet's possible," countered Agent Moscow.

"Because—if she was like a psychic investigator, she wouldn't be here doing Spy Camp; she'd be on television or something."

"She *might* be a psychic investigator outside of her camp-counselor work," said Stargirl.

"What's a psychic investigator?" Baby Boy asked.

"I think it's someone who investigates hauntings and stuff like that."

"Oh, I believe in ghosts."

"I don't."

Gilda listened as her team members argued among themselves, half wishing she could take back the information she had told them. *I really let the cat out of the bag now,* she thought.

"The lie she told is about eating the peanut butter, banana, and chocolate sandwiches, because that sounds way too yucky!" Baby Boy announced.

"Listen, team," said Gilda, glancing at the time on her cell phone, "we're running out of time and we need to begin our next project, so I'll go ahead and tell you. The first two statements are true, and the last statement is a lie. I actually *love* wearing wigs, and I own several."

"See?" Stargirl poked James Bond. "I was right!"

The Comedian stared at Gilda, bug-eyed. "That means you're a *real* psychic investigator."

"Yup," said Gilda, "and I've solved several cases."

"You mean, you talk to ghosts and stuff?"

"Not only do I make contact with ghosts," Gilda whispered, now enjoying her team's rapt attention, "I have reason to believe there's a ghost right here in the Spy Museum." *A true professional would have kept that a secret,* Gilda thought. But it was too late to take back the truth now: for better or worse, she was letting her team in on a big part of her investigation. "You know that face that appeared on the video monitors when you were practicing your surveillance?"

Gilda's recruits nodded silently. She had their complete attention.

"I'm pretty sure we were actually seeing a ghost."

Team Crypt stared, wide-eyed, as if they were sitting around a campfire listening to a spooky story.

"Yes," said Agent Moscow, quietly and with great certainty. "Eet *was* a ghost."

22

Dream of the Psychic Spy

The psychic spy reclined in his chair in the secret office where he worked. There, across the room, was Loomis Trench, his supervisor. As always, Loomis wore his yellow bow tie and neatly pressed dark suit. As always, Loomis frowned and took detailed notes, recording everything the psychic spy said during his trance.

The spy's current target was a remote industrial facility in an unfriendly foreign country. Entering a trance state, he projected his mind to a distant location and began to search for evidence of covert weapons development.

The psychic spy felt his body moving through a misty realm where there was no sky and no earth. Then, as he approached the industrial building—his target—he looked for his spirit guide. Once again, the girl failed to appear. Why had she abandoned him? Without her, his readings had become unpredictable, unreliable.

Loomis had brought the psychic spy to the CIA to prove that a professional psychic could contribute something of genuine value to intelligence gathering, but recently, the psychic spy's readings had become inexplicably faulty. Increasingly, his remote viewing sessions were disregarded by skeptical higher-ups in the agency. Nevertheless, Loomis showed no signs of giving up the project. He continued his dogged persuit of one target after another.

I'm in the wrong place, the psychic spy realized. Instead of viewing the industrial site Loomis had told him to target, he found himself in a spare, dingy apartment where damp laundry hung to dry across the living room. He felt his stomach drop with surprise when, tacked to the wall, he saw a calendar displaying the date: 1988. *I'm viewing the past,* he thought. *And I seem to be in a foreign country. Is it Russia? Why am I seeing this?*

It was a woman's apartment—a woman who looked very familiar. She stared into a mirror, first applying bright violet eyeshadow, then carefully affixing a star-shaped brooch to the colorful scarf around her neck. The psychic spy knew that there was something very special about the brooch: it allowed the woman to take secret photographs. He knew something else: *she's going to die.* Suddenly he made the connection: *It's her,* he thought, now recognizing the face. Several of his remote viewing sessions had been interrupted by this same woman's dead, bloodstained face! But why? He had no idea who she was.

"Who are you?" the psychic spy asked the woman.

As usual, she would not answer him. She picked up a slim red book: he saw that it was a book of poems by the Russian poet Anna Akhmatova.

From a distance, the psychic spy heard his supervisor speaking to him. "Here," said Loomis, his voice sounding hollow and muffled, as if he were speaking underwater. "Wear this." Loomis roughly put a blindfold over the psychic spy's eyes.

Panicked, the spy awoke to find himself in his bedroom. He was in a small Washington, D.C., hotel in a building that used to be a Victorian mansion. Moonlight streamed into the window, illuminating the purple and dark green hues of the painted walls and carpeting. His bed was surrounded by an antique birdcage and an assortment of paintings and small sculptures. Amid the clutter of shapes in his room, it took a few minutes for the psychic spy to perceive the girl's shadowy silhouette: *his spirit guide sat in a chair in the corner.*

Seeing the girl, he felt a surge of happiness and relief. "You came back," he whispered.

The psychic spy had aged, but his spirit guide was eternally eleven years old. She called herself "Lavender"; she was freckle-nosed and petite with long, chestnut braids that hung past her delicate shoulders. But something about her had changed: perhaps she looked more serious than usual.

"Where have you been?" he asked. "Why haven't you been helping me?"

"I've been helping you," she snapped. She was very real, yet he could see through her body to the pattern of a purple velvet cushion propped behind her. "*You* haven't been listening and paying attention."

"Look, the work I'm doing right now is more important than anything I've done before. I'm trying to view foreign targets for the Central Intelligence Agency. It's important for the country, for the whole field of psychic research, and yes—for my career. I need your help: I keep seeing a woman I don't even recognize. If that isn't bad enough, a couple times when I was getting close to reading the access code for some top-secret files, the image of a teenage girl wearing cat's-eye sunglasses turned up for absolutely no reason!"

"The people you're seeing are trying to help you, but you aren't really paying attention," the girl retorted.

"Is that all you can tell me?" It was unusual for the psychic to feel frustrated with his spirit guide. Ever since her death when they were both children, he had trusted their connection—kept faith in the knowledge she gave him through dreams and visions. Now, for the first time, he felt impatient with the limitations of his knowledge—annoyed with these cryptic appearances from unwelcome phantoms.

"The government is entrusting me with highly classified information," he insisted. "Think how many foreign governments would love to know about the weapons systems, access codes, and undercover agents I've targeted in various countries. I want to do a good job, and I need your help."

"I guess you won't be able to see the truth until you're ready," said the girl. She vanished, leaving only a glimmer of moonlight on the velvet chair.

23

Cracking the Code

The atmosphere in the city was languid and sleepy as Gilda exited the Union Station Metro stop and headed toward the Library of Congress, where she planned to meet Caitlin. The warm, musky scent of black-eyed Susans and marigolds permeated the air, and idling tour buses parked along the streets filled the air with a low, rumbling sound. Gilda walked through a quiet park where trees were labeled with little plaques to identify their species. Here and there, office workers wearing high-heeled pumps sat on benches talking on cell phones or munching on sandwiches.

She turned down First Street and walked past the Supreme Court, pausing for a moment to read the façade proclaiming EQUAL JUSTICE UNDER THE LAW, absorb the solemn aura that surrounded the building's gleaming white marble.

Gilda felt immediately happy when she entered the cathedral-like Great Hall of the Library of Congress. Gilda loved libraries of all kinds, and this was quite simply the most spectacular library she had ever visited. She was surrounded by high ceilings, marble arches, pillars, marble mosaics, and murals. Everywhere she looked, sculptures and paintings portrayed

175

f freedom and knowledge. Gilda had paused to view a
of paintings depicting the long journey of progress from
men scribbling on cave walls through the development of
he written word and printed books when she heard Caitlin's
breathless voice calling her name.

"Gilda! Oh, good, you're here!" Caitlin rushed toward her,
the casual flip-flops she wore with her black pantsuit slapping
against the floor. "My friend Joe is a reference librarian in the
reading room here, and he says you can come in and do your
research today as a special favor to me. Like I told you, you'd
normally have to be at least eighteen years old to do research
here, so you're getting special access."

"That's great!" Now that she was in the Library of Congress,
Gilda was itching to begin her research.

"Follow me," said Caitlin. "I'm in a rush because my lovely
employer has given me some extra stories to proofread plus
a story to write for the newsletter before the end of the day,
so I have to get over to a Judiciary Committee meeting and
then back to the office to write it. Come on, I'll introduce you
to Joe."

Caitlin led Gilda into the main reading room of the library.
Gilda looked up at the domed ceiling soaring overhead. Statues
representing religion, history, art, philosophy, law, and science
gazed down at her like the faces of angels.

"What are you researching?" Joe was a young man with
glasses and a goatee.

"Um—do you have any books about President Lincoln—
like collections of letters he wrote to people and things like
that?"

"Not only do we have books on Lincoln, we have books on Lincoln in hundreds of languages. We have tunnels between the Capitol Building and the library with conveyor belts that shoot books back and forth all day long. So yes—I think I can dredge up at least a couple books on Abraham Lincoln for you."

"You came here to research Abraham Lincoln?" Caitlin asked. "I thought you needed to come here to do some research on an espionage case or something."

"It's actually related to espionage research; it's just kind of complicated."

"Whatever it is, Joe can help you. Right, Joe?"

"That's what I'm here for—to help the public."

"Joe's not like me; he never complains about his job."

"That's right. I only complain about people who never return favors."

"Good thing we don't know anyone like that."

"So when are you going to make me that gourmet meal you promised me *last* time I did you a favor?"

"Omigod, Joe. This month has been so totally crazed with work."

"Plus all those dates."

"A girl has to have a life, Joe. Oh, and Gilda, honey, I'm sorry I won't be able to make you dinner tonight, either. I'm going to be at the office late to finish this story."

"That's okay." Gilda couldn't help feeling that this was an absurd statement; with the exception of the scorched sandwiches, Caitlin hadn't made a single meal since Gilda had moved in.

"She means she won't be there to help you open the jar of

marshmallow cream." Joe winked at Gilda and Gilda laughed.

"As you can tell, Joe's known me since college."

"That's right; I know your ways."

Caitlin glanced at her cell phone. "I'm going to be late for my meeting if I don't get going."

"Okay—thanks, Caitlin." Gilda admired Caitlin's ability to sweep in, get a quick favor done and then run off to an important-sounding Judiciary Committee meeting.

Gilda found a quiet spot at a desk with a reading lamp, and a few minutes later, a tall stack of President Lincoln's writings popped up from the underground tunnel. Joe placed them in front of Gilda. "Enjoy," he said.

Gilda stared at the towering stack of leather-bound books. Lincoln had written *a lot*—speeches, letters, even poems. As she flipped through the volumes, she realized that she had no idea what to look for or where to begin.

Gilda took out the photographs of the dead-drop message and arranged them on her desk. *Maybe the words in the message will give me some clue about where to look first,* she thought.

dear dear friend speed when I it expect comes
to to have this a I delivery should for prefer
you emigrating soon to some look country for
where my they usual make signal no blue
pretense gum of marking loving Anna liberty to
you Russia will for respond instance with where
pink despotism gum can on be Anna taken to
pure let and me without know the you base
alloy of received hypocrisy package the poet

Gilda leaned back in her chair and closed her eyes. She recalled her last dream about Abraham Lincoln. *Look at my letters,* the ghost had said.

But which letters? There were so many volumes.

Flipping through her reporter's notebook in search of more clues, Gilda noticed a phrase:

Lincoln was writing with great speed. . . .

Gilda looked back at the first line of the message:

dear dear friend speed. . . .

Following her instincts, Gilda looked up the word *speed* in the index of a volume of Lincoln's letters. She felt a little tickle growing in her left ear as she flipped through the pages and a surge of excitement when she found an entry entitled "Letter to Joshua Speed." Was it just chance that the corner of that particular page was folded, as if someone had marked it for her?

Gilda quickly flipped to the letter. Dated August 24, 1855, it was a letter from Abraham Lincoln to a friend from the South. The letter seemed to be about Lincoln's rejection of slavery, but what really caught Gilda's attention was a passage containing several significant words that also appeared in the dead-drop message:

Dear Speed,
. . . When it comes to this I should prefer emigrating to some
country where they make no pretense of loving liberty—to

Russia, for instance, where despotism can be taken pure, and without the base alloy of hypocrisy [sic].

She placed the coded message next to the passage from Lincoln's letter, examining both closely.

It's so obvious now, she thought. *Why didn't I see it before?*

Now she understood that the sentence from Lincoln's letter was just a disguise—a "cover" to distract her from the *real* message.

Gilda rewrote the dead-drop message, this time removing every word that also appeared in Lincoln's letter.

> Dear Friend,
> I expect to have a delivery for you soon. Look for my usual signal—blue gum marking Anna. You will respond with pink gum on Anna to let me know you have received the package. —The Poet

I did it, Gilda thought. *I cracked the code. It really is a dead-drop message!*

Clearly, the message announced a signal and the transfer of a secret package of some kind.

But who is Anna? Gilda wondered. *And is "The Poet" a code name, or is it something else entirely?*

DEAD-DROP INVESTIGATION PROBLEMS:

1. Timing: My Spy Savvy book says that spies usually agree to check for dead-drop "signals" at regular intervals--maybe once a day or once

a week. I've been too busy with Spy Camp to
monitor the dead-drop location every day, and
I have no way of knowing when, exactly, the
package will be dropped off and picked up. I
need to find the "signal site" so I'll have some
advance notice of when he or she is going to
make the next move.

2. In order to find the signal site, I need
to know the significance of "Anna." It could
be a name on one of the tombstones in Oak
Hill Cemetery--maybe the signal is a piece
of chewing gum stuck to the grave marker?
On the other hand, the cemetery wouldn't
be a convenient place for a spy to check
for a signal every day. A signal site is
usually a more ordinary place--a mailbox,
a signpost--something so innocuous and
obvious that passersby never really look at
it carefully.
IMPORTANT: FIND THE SIGNIFICANCE OF "ANNA."

24

A Dangerous Encounter

Gilda heard the rumbling of thunder as she left the Library of Congress and made her way back through the park. She passed people who walked home from work with brisk, hurried steps and a homeless man who mumbled about "exposing the government" as he shuffled slowly along the sidewalk. The trees trembled as a warm breeze rose and dark clouds gathered overhead.

Inside Union Station, a parade of people streamed from the trains, dragging suitcases and talking on cell phones as they converged on shops selling ice cream and coffee.

Gilda followed a crowd of people down the escalator to the underground train. She waited on the platform, sensing the fuming impatience of weary people staring silently at each other across the tracks. Deciding she might as well contemplate the next steps in her investigation while she waited for the train, Gilda pulled one of her photographs of the dead-drop message from her purse to examine it for more clues.

A moment later, the skin on the back of her neck felt warm: she could literally *feel* someone staring at her—looking over her shoulder.

Gilda turned to see a man staring at the photograph in her

hand with great interest. He had a round, sunburned face with a high forehead above which sparse, spiky hair sprouted. A close-cropped, reddish mustache and beard framed his face. He wasn't much taller than Gilda: in fact, there was something almost elfin or gnomish about the man, but the piercing intensity in his gaze unnerved her. *He knows something about me,* Gilda thought. *How long has he been watching me?*

For a moment their eyes locked, but before he could speak, Gilda instinctively stuffed the photograph back into her handbag. She abruptly opened her cell phone and pretended to check messages as she walked down the train platform, attempting to create some distance between herself and the man. She glanced up and felt another surge of anxiety when she found him still staring in her direction, slowly making his way toward her. The lights lining the train tracks flashed, announcing the arrival of a train. *Hurry up, hurry up!* The train simply couldn't arrive fast enough. Gilda had no idea who she was running from—only a gut feeling that this stranger seemed to have a very special interest in her.

The train rushed into the station and Gilda joined a group of people clustering together at the doorway. She scooted inside the train and watched with relief as the doors closed behind her before the man was able to follow her into her car of the train.

Gilda opened her notebook:

Was it just my imagination, or was that man VERY interested in the dead-drop message I was reading?

If he has something to do with that message—and if he knows who I am—I could be in danger.

I HAVE A FEELING I'M BEING WATCHED.

25

An Unpleasant Discovery

Following her decoding of the dead-drop message, Gilda wanted to go down to Oak Hill Cemetery to look for more clues and conduct surveillance, but the steady rain pounding on the windows of her apartment made the idea of navigating the crumbling walkways in the cemetery very unappealing. Besides, the idea of venturing into a cemetery alone after her scare in the Metro station suddenly felt too risky.

Gilda pulled some blueberries out of the refrigerator, mixed them with a dollop of yogurt, and sat down in front of the television. Unable to find anything worth watching, she stood up and paced around the apartment, thinking about the tangled maze of clues that seemed to grow ever more complicated and dangerous. *What if that man knows where I live?* she wondered. *What if he's been conducting surveillance and already knows all about my investigation?*

She examined the walls of the living room, wondering if there was any possibility her apartment was bugged. *We are always being watched,* Boris Volkov had complained.

"Okay, Gilda—just stop it," Gilda told herself. "You're getting too paranoid."

Feeling the need to get her mind off her investigation for at least a few minutes, Gilda decided to do something she usually avoided: she called her mother. "Hi, Mom."

"Gilda! How are you?"

"Pretty good. I guess."

"Anything wrong?"

"No." Gilda wasn't about to tell her mother that a suspicious-looking man had been staring at her with great interest in the Metro station.

"What have you been up to?"

"Nothing, really. You know—just working hard. Same old, same old." It was a banal expression she often heard her mother use with coworkers.

"I'm sure *something* interesting must be going on in the nation's capital."

"Not really." *Maybe this is how spies live with their families,* Gilda thought. *There are so many details they have to keep secret, they end up saying nothing at all.*

"What about you?" Gilda asked. "Any luck with your dating profile?"

"Well, as a matter of fact, today was my day off from work, and I met a nice gentleman for coffee."

"What kind of 'nice gentleman'? Did he meet the qualifications I outlined in your posting?"

"I don't think anyone could meet those qualifications."

"That would be the ideal, though."

"Maybe for one of us."

"Well?"

"Well, what?"

"Tell me about your date!"

"Please do not yell into the phone, Gilda."

"Sorry. I just need to know what kinds of 'gentlemen callers' to expect when I get back home." Gilda walked into her bedroom and pulled open the blinds. "I need to prepare my interview questions for when they come to the house to pick you up."

"I don't think this man will be coming to the house."

"One of the crazies, huh?"

"He was a little older than I expected."

Maybe you were a little older than he expected, too, Gilda thought.

"He's a widower, so we had that aspect in common. It was just odd; he kept talking about his deceased wife."

"That's very loyal of him."

"But it's not the kind of thing you do on a date. It was a little off-putting, to be honest. I almost began to feel that she was sitting at the table right there with us."

"Maybe she was." Gilda pictured her mother and an elderly man sitting at a small table at Starbucks. Next to them were two ghosts—the ghost of her father and the ghost of the man's wife. "Maybe she was there."

"Oh—but there was one funny surprise."

"He likes knitting and bowling, too?"

"I looked over, and who do I see at a nearby table but your brother and your friend Wendy just sitting there drinking Frappuccinos."

"You saw *what*??!!" What on earth was Wendy doing drinking Frappuccinos with Stephen? Even more appalling: why was she hearing this news from her mother?

"They were pretty surprised to see me, too."

"What were they *doing*? Why doesn't anyone ever tell me *anything*??"

"Gilda, they were just working on a problem from their math camp together. Seems they got paired up on an advanced project of some kind, and on their way home they decided to stop for coffee and try to do some work. I can't make heads or tails of that stuff; I really don't know how your brother knows how to—"

"I can't *believe* Wendy didn't call to tell me that. She owes me several letters and phone calls."

"Gilda, I'm sure she's just as busy as you are."

"Believe me, she's much *less* busy than I am. Nobody is as busy as I am right now."

"Honey, maybe you need some sleep. You sound a little grouchy."

You'd be grouchy, too, if you were being haunted by Abraham Lincoln and stalked by a short man with a red beard while also trying to train a group of children to become spies within a week, Gilda thought.

"Sorry, Mom," said Gilda, "I just realized I left something on the stove."

"Are you eating any vegetables? I hope you're taking a vitamin, because—"

"I'll call you back later, Mom. Bye!" Gilda hung up and immediately dialed Wendy's number.

"Hey!" Wendy answered. "I was just about to call you."

"Is there something you want to share with me?"

"I don't know. I don't think so."

"Frappuccinos with Stephen? My mother on a date? No phone calls to report on any of the above?"

"Oh—that."

"Yes—that."

"It wasn't a big deal, Gilda. Your mom didn't look too into that guy; he kind of looked like someone's grandpa or something. I doubt you'll be seeing him again."

"The point is, you should have *told* me about it."

"But you always have a stress fit about that stuff."

"I'm not having a 'stress fit.' Although I'm not sure exactly what a 'stress fit' even means. Is that some kind of Chinese term?"

"You know what I mean."

"And?"

"And what?"

"What about your math date with Stephen?!"

"This problem we were working on was super-difficult, and Stephen's been giving me a ride to camp during the past few days—"

"Stephen's been giving you a ride to camp?"

"I mean, we're both going to the same place."

"But you didn't tell me that."

"I'm telling you now."

Now isn't soon enough, Gilda thought. *That's the problem with being a spy based in another city; all the regular people you want to keep tabs on keep going about their business and you lose track of them.*

"Anyway," Wendy continued, "we stopped at the coffee shop to sit down and work on this assignment."

"Does Stephen get on your nerves when you're riding in his car?"

"No. He's actually really nice."

"Because when I ride with him in his car he always tells me, 'Stop touching stuff.'"

"Well, I didn't change the radio station every two minutes or grab the rearview mirror to check my lipstick, so I guess he didn't have to."

"I bet he's acting dweeby at math camp. Is he making jokes about numbers and stuff like that?"

"He's actually one of the cool ones at math camp."

"No way."

"Gilda, your brother is really smart."

"He gets that from me."

"He's funny, too."

"Again—from me."

"And he's kind of cute."

Gilda felt a seismic shift taking place in her friendship with Wendy, as if everything she had always counted on was getting ready to change. "Omigod. Are you actually telling me you're in love with a doofus?"

"I'm not in *love* with him. Maybe just a little crush."

"That is so sick."

"Why is it sick?"

"You're practically like my sister. It's illegal, Wendy."

"I'm *not* your sister."

"How long has this little infatuation been going on?"

"Not very long. I mean, I always thought he was kind of cute—"

"You always thought my brother was 'kind of cute,' and you never *told* me?"

"Because I knew you would act this way. And I don't necessarily tell you every single thought that passes through my head."

"Why not? I'd be interested."

"Yeah, right."

"Wendy, I just think you should know that my brother can be really gross. My mom told me that once, when he was a baby, he ate his own poop."

"I assume he doesn't do that anymore."

"When he goes in the bathroom, he stays in there a really long time. That's all I'm going to say."

"I'm sure he would appreciate you talking this way about him."

Gilda looked out the window and felt her spirits lift ever so slightly when she found she could peer directly into the bathroom window of the suit-wearing man whom she thought of as "the politician." He was gazing into a mirror and shaving his chin very carefully. "Is this a mutual thing between you and Stephen?"

"I don't know. I mean, it was his idea to go get a coffee together and work on this project. And we had a really great conversation. I guess we're friends."

Why does that bother me? Gilda wondered. "Hey, I know! I'll call my brother and find out if he's going to ask you on a date, and then I'll give you the scoop."

"Don't you dare."

"Don't you want to know if he thinks you're cute?"

"You won't be able to find out."

"I'm a spy, Wendy; it's my job."

"He wouldn't tell you. And besides, if you say anything about it, he'll think of me as your little friend instead of a potential girlfriend."

"But you are my little friend."

"You know what I mean. Like, ever since math camp, Stephen sees me differently. Before, he never knew that I was smart or cute or a real person or anything; he just thought we were little kids doing dumb stuff around the house."

That's why it bugs me that she likes Stephen, Gilda thought. "Wendy, Stephen wouldn't know a psychic investigation if it came up and bit him on his skinny butt." Gilda resented Stephen's skeptical and often condescending attitude toward her interest in paranormal phenomena. It sometimes seemed that no matter what she did, he always thought of her as a mere "little sister."

"Just don't say anything to him, Gilda. Promise?"

"Okay." Gilda sighed. "I promise I won't say anything."

```
Dear Dad:

I just learned that Wendy and Stephen are
"friends," and that Wendy goes for the dweeby
type. I should be happy, shouldn't I? Wendy's my
best friend and Stephen's my brother.

   But what if they become boyfriend and
girlfriend and then, every time Wendy comes over
to our house, she only wants to see Stephen and
not me? Worse: what if the two of them become
```

boyfriend and girlfriend and then they break up
after Wendy realizes that Stephen really can be
a doofus? Wendy would probably <u>never</u> want to come
over to our house anymore.

What do you think, Dad?

I remember what you used to tell me when I'd
worry about something one of my friends did. You'd
say, "Keep your eye on your own game, Gilda."
Like--stop trying to control what happens with
other people so much.

I'll try, Dad, but it's hard. I guess that's
one thing I have in common with the spies in the
CIA; I have this need to get entangled in other
people's business.

Gilda watched with fascination as the man in the window secured his hair with a cap and began carefully applying makeup: thick foundation, then blush, powder, eye shadow, eyeliner, and mascara.

When he was nearly finished, he seemed to realize that he had left the blinds up and pulled them shut abruptly, blocking Gilda's view.

It's amazing what you can learn about people just by peeking in their windows, Gilda thought.

She crawled into bed but she couldn't sleep. She felt strangely uneasy being in the apartment by herself. Every sound seemed magnified: footsteps pacing overhead in the room above hers, the hum of the refrigerator, the rush of the air conditioner, the sounds of murmuring voices and keys turning in hallway locks.

I wish Caitlin would get home, Gilda thought. I'd tell her about decoding the message and the man on the Metro.

But Caitlin didn't get home; she had gone to meet some coworkers at an after-work "happy hour" gathering that was showing signs of morphing into a club-hopping late night.

When the flashing lights began their rhythmic blinking, illuminating her blinds like a bright neon sign (*on, off, on, off*), Gilda squeezed her eyes shut and buried her head under a pillow. She finally fell asleep that way, never seeing the pale face watching her from the vanity table mirror—a ghostly face with dark eyes, a bloodstained forehead, and a perfect red star around her neck.

26

The Graffiti Ghost

April pointed accusingly at a graffiti-covered wall. She had called an emergency meeting with her Spy Camp counselors because something had been discovered earlier that morning in the "Cold War in East Berlin" exhibit—a portion of the museum designed to re-create the experience of being a spy in the Communist-controlled sector of Berlin.

At first, Gilda couldn't tell what April was so upset about, because the graffiti-spattered city wall spray-painted with the phrase "THE COLDEST PLACE ON EARTH" looked just the same as it always had. Near the wall there was a model of a Berlin café, a black sedan parked next to an old-fashioned telephone booth, and a government office that contained sinister-looking jars of scented rags—bits of clothing used to set attack dogs on the trail of any individual regarded as "suspicious" by the secret police.

Roger stood a few feet away with his hands on his hips and a dirty rag hanging from his back pocket. A sullen female security guard leaned against a wall next to him.

Finally, Gilda saw what April was pointing at: further down on the wall, in spooky-looking black letters, was a single word:

ANNA

Gilda felt a tickle in her left ear. She remembered the cryptic phrase in the dead-drop message: *Look for my usual signal: blue gum marking* Anna.

Gilda scooted in front of the other counselors to take a closer look at the wall. She rubbed the wall and examined her fingers, but saw no residue of ink or paint. There was definitely no sign of gum. The other counselors regarded Gilda with interest: she wore her *Avengers*-style spy catsuit (actually black leggings, high-heeled ankle boots, and a sleeveless black tunic) and her hair in a high ponytail in honor of a special event taking place at the museum later that afternoon.

"Gilda, what are you doing?" April demanded. "Roger has already been trying to get rid of this graffiti all morning. In fact, I only found out about it because I saw the poor guy trying to wipe it off with a rag."

"So what are you saying, April?" one of the counselors demanded. "You're saying one of us did this?"

"Of course not. I'm saying that one of the campers did it. We want the kids to have a great time—even get a little silly and crazy." April glanced in Gilda's direction. "But we do *not* want them defacing museum property."

"I didn't let my campers out of my sight all day," said a tall, athletic counselor named Raymond.

"Me, either," said another counselor standing next to him. "None of my campers would have done this."

"Mine, either."

"Well, didn't any of the security guards see who did it?"

Shauna, the security guard standing nearby, piped up. "I was standin' right here the whole time. I turned my back for maybe half a minute to check the other room. Half a minute, okay? I didn't see any campers or counselors do this."

More evidence of a supernatural cause, Gilda thought.

"What about your team, Gilda?"

Gilda wasn't entirely certain that one of her campers *wouldn't* have done this if given the opportunity. After all, there was The Misanthrope with his history of picking locks; and Agent Moscow, who was something of a mystery; and Baby Boy, who might have regressed into toddlerhood for a moment. On the other hand, why would any of her recruits write a single word—*Anna*? And what about the fact that this exact name also appeared in the dead-drop message?

As Gilda contemplated these questions, she pulled her Polaroid from her bag and snapped a photograph of the word on the wall, thinking she should record the evidence just in case it was relevant to her psychic research.

"Gilda, may I ask why you're taking a picture of the wall?"

"Oh—I just thought I'd show my team the evidence and ask them who's responsible. If nobody comes clean, I'll hook them up to those lie detector machines we made yesterday." As an activity, Gilda's team had made small "lie detectors" using batteries, wires, and tiny lightbulbs; the machine functioned by detecting tiny amounts of sweat causing a bulb to light up when the subject became nervous. Gilda's recruits had tested the gadgets during yet another game of Two Truths and a Lie, with decidedly unreliable results.

April and the counselors laughed at Gilda's suggestion.

"That's a good idea, but I'm not sure how accurate those lie detectors are."

As Gilda held the print from her Polaroid, waiting for the image to dry, she noticed another clue—an unusual aroma that was both floral and spicy, like a very sweet perfume.

"My point," April continued, "is that you need to know where your kids are at all times. 'Have fun while avoiding costly damages' will be our motto from this stage forward, okay? Okay! Well, the campers are arriving, so we need to get going with our day."

As April and the camp counselors headed up to the Venona Room to meet their campers, Gilda approached Roger, who remained behind, examining the wall.

"It wasn't the kids who did this," he blurted.

"Then why didn't you say something to April?"

"I don't know." Roger pulled the rag from his back pocket, sprayed some WD-40 on it, and rubbed the wall without success. "I'm not so sure of myself right now. I'm functioning on about two hours of very bad sleep and I haven't showered in two days because the hot water in our condo isn't working, and I also have a baby spit-up stain on my shirt."

"It doesn't really show." Gilda noticed a dried white patch that resembled a residue of bird poop on Roger's blue T-shirt.

Roger sighed. "When I found this graffiti on the wall, I had security check out a surveillance camera that's focused on this exhibit because I wanted to know exactly what happened before I got everyone else involved."

"Did it show anything?"

197

"It was so weird. Like, at one moment, everything in the exhibit looks normal. Then, in the next microsecond, there's that word *Anna* on the wall, like it just appeared on its own, out of nowhere."

Gilda felt a surge of excitement. "More evidence of our ghost," she said, remembering a passage in her *Master Psychic's Handbook* about rare ghosts who leave messages in the form of "ghost graffiti"—words or images that appear on the walls of houses and then mysteriously vanish without a trace. "Roger, I feel like there's something she wants us to understand. I mean, assuming the ghost is a she."

"She can't just write us a note with paper and a pencil?"

"That wouldn't really get our attention, would it?"

"I guess not. Just between you and me, I'm no fan of this ghost, if that's what it really is. I'm ready to call in a ghost exterminator."

Gilda realized she was going to be late to meet her campers if she didn't hurry up. "Tell me if you see anything else, okay?"

"It's a deal. Tell me if you find me collapsed and unconscious on the floor, okay?"

"You got it."

As Gilda climbed the stairs, walking past the Nuclear Age exhibit posters displaying posters from the 1950s with such headlines as "How to Survive a Nuclear Attack: *Don't Be There!*", Gilda examined the photograph she had taken. She immediately stopped and stood motionless, staring at the photograph with awe and near-disbelief. A message had appeared in the photograph—*a message that hadn't been on the wall*:

ANNA
THE LAST MEETING

Those words definitely weren't visible when I took the picture, and now here they are. This is the first time I've ever captured evidence of a ghost in a photograph!

Gilda's *Master Psychic's Handbook* recounted many stories of ghosts who communicated through photographs: some of them appeared as shadowy figures in the background of family portraits. "Often you will not see the ghosts and apparitions around you with the naked eye," Balthazar Frobenius wrote. "You will only discover them after you develop your pictures."

However, note that light sources, natural mist, and water droplets can all create "false positives" if they are not avoided while shooting pictures. How often the amateur ghost hunter rushes excitedly to announce that he has captured a ghost, only to be told that a television screen in the living room or the moon shining through a window was the true source of the phantom image in his photograph.

But this isn't some phantom image, Gilda thought. *This isn't some weird plume of smoke or little orb of light.* Gilda was also pretty sure she remembered this phrase from the incident in the audio surveillance room, and she was almost positive that Agent Moscow had said the words meant "the last meeting."

But what in the world did these clues—"Anna" and "the last meeting" actually *mean* to her investigation?

"Listen," said Gilda, lowering her voice as Team Crypt gathered around her. "Remember how I told you that the Spy Museum might be haunted?"

They all nodded.

"Well, something very interesting was discovered in the museum earlier today—an actual written message from the ghost."

Baby Boy's eyes grew large, and his mouth hung open with fascination and fear. The entire group fell very silent. "I have reason to believe it may be the ghost of a spy who got killed," Gilda added.

She showed her recruits the photograph she had taken and described the mysterious clues that had turned up on the wall and in her photograph.

The Misanthrope frowned. "How do we know you didn't doctor up this photograph?"

I guess we don't call him The Misanthrope for nothing, Gilda thought. "Listen, I have better things to do with my time than trick my spy recruits. We're a team, and if we're going to solve this, you have to trust what I tell you."

Agent Moscow picked up the photograph and held it gingerly between two chipped red nails. She studied it with great interest.

27

Spy Games

A buzz of conversation filled the Venona Room as people wearing business attire filed in to see a lecture by Boris Volkov. He had recently published a book entitled *Memoirs of a Russian Spy: My Life in the KGB*—a book that fascinated Gilda. During her lunch break, she had borrowed a copy from Matthew and read as much as she could in anticipation of the event:

> Book Notes Re: Boris Volkov's Memoir of the KGB
> By Gilda Joyce
>
> Boris's memoir tells the story of his years in the Russian Embassy in Washington, D.C. Throughout much of the Cold War, he posed undercover as a Soviet journalist. While he went to press events and wrote news stories, he was also working as a spy.
> But gradually, Boris perceived major problems with the Soviet system. "I warned my bosses in Moscow that economic collapse was imminent—that the whole thing was going to blow up in their faces," he writes. But when he tried to tell the truth to the senior Soviet officers, they not

only ignored him; they demoted him. "Talk about blaming the messenger!" Boris writes.

Shortly thereafter, Boris realized that he was better suited to the American way of life. "Irreverent late-night talk shows, weekend shopping trips at Target, and Mc-Donald's cheeseburgers had become part of my DNA," he writes. "As much a part of me as the vodka and sausages of my motherland."

So Boris defected, and after a lengthy process of interrogation, he switched sides for good and began to work for the CIA and FBI.

After her campers had left the museum for the day, Gilda, Janet, Matthew, Marla, and some of the museum's technical staff had busied themselves with preparing for Boris's presentation: they arranged rows of chairs and set up a projector and microphones. Standing next to Marla, Gilda observed people shaking hands and exchanging business cards as she took their tickets and crossed names off a list of guests with special invitations.

"A lot of these people are special agents in the FBI or former CIA intelligence officers," Marla whispered. "See that woman?" She pointed to a tall woman wearing a dark, conservative suit—the kind of person who looked as if she might be a banker or a lawyer. "She's a former chief of disguise for the CIA."

"She looks kind of ordinary to be a chief of disguise."

"Well, she doesn't go around wearing fake mustaches and noses all the time—at least not at these events. Besides, when you're a spy, the point is to blend in with the crowd. Now see that guy over there?" Marla pointed to a short man with curly dark hair who stood in a corner, interviewing Jasper Clarke and Boris Volkov. "He writes a lot about intelligence issues for the *Washington Post*."

I'd love to ask Boris a few questions myself, Gilda thought, watching as Boris answered the reporter's questions while shaking hands with friends who passed by. *I'd like to find out exactly why he got rid of those artifacts he donated to the museum. But Jasper wouldn't like it if I put him on the spot in front of all these people; I'm sure he doesn't want a story about a haunting at the Spy Museum turning up in the* Washington Post.

Gilda spotted a mushroom cloud of sunset-red hair moving through the audience. Beneath the hair there was a middle-aged woman in a well-tailored skirt and jacket who walked gracefully on sling-back pumps. She paused to kiss Boris, then made her way to her seat.

"Psst, Marla." Gilda pointed at the woman. "Do you know that lady?"

"That's Boris Volkov's wife, Jacqueline," said Marla as she took tickets from incoming guests. "She's French."

"I see." Gilda remembered how Boris had mocked his wife's attitude toward the artifacts: "My wife has the idea that they are bad luck," he had commented.

There was a momentary lull in the flow of guests into the room: *an opportunity for me to go talk to Boris's wife,* Gilda thought, feeling she had to seize the moment. "Excuse me, Marla," said Gilda, "I just need to ask someone a quick question."

"Okay, but hurry back."

Boris's wife had taken her seat in a corner of the room, away from the rest of the audience. *That's good,* Gilda thought; *maybe we can talk without being overheard.*

"Excuse me—Madame Volkov?"

"*Oui.*"

Gilda wished she had signed up for French class at school. At the moment, the only French words she could think of were *croissant* and *bonjour.*

"Um, do you speak English?"

"Of course." Jacqueline regarded Gilda with impatience. She struck Gilda as an elegant, haughty woman.

"I work for the Spy Museum, and I wanted to ask you something about the artifacts we acquired from your husband—the lipstick pistol and the camera brooch."

Jacqueline thrust up her hand as if she were a traffic cop at a stoplight. "We cannot take them back."

That was an odd thing for her to say, Gilda thought. "Oh, don't worry, Mrs. Volkov; nobody wants you to take them back." Gilda slipped into the empty seat next to Jacqueline. "Mrs. Volkov," she said, lowering her voice, "your husband said you wanted the objects out of the house because you thought that they were bad luck."

Jacqueline looked very directly into Gilda's eyes. "Have you seen her?"

She means the ghost, Gilda thought. "Seen who?" she asked, playing dumb just to see what Jacqueline would tell her.

Jacqueline drew in her breath. "That face: I don't ever want to think of it again. The headaches I had—the nightmares—the television and radio turning on and off all through the night . . . Do you know that for years, I thought it was my house that was haunted?" She shook her head, then placed a hand on her chest, peering at Gilda earnestly. "Because I am very sensitive. Boris—nothing." She waved her hand dismissively and blew raspberries. "He sleeps like a big, fat baby all night while I am lying there, hearing footsteps and voices.

"One night I hear a woman crying in the attic above our bedroom. I *know* something is up there. So I go up to the attic, and something tells me I must look through old boxes. And what do I find? Buried in a corner, an old box Boris brought from his very last trip to Moscow. And when I see what is in it, I wake him up, shaking him. 'I want these things out of the house,' I tell him. And he looks at me and says, 'Oh, I thought I had lost those! That gun is worth a lot of money. I'll find a collector and sell it!' And I say, 'No. I want these things out of our house *now*. Either you call the Spy Museum first thing in the morning and donate them, or I will put them in the Dumpster!' So!" Jacqueline made a swiping gesture, as if washing her hands of something dirty. "Once they are out of my house, everything is quiet. And now I sleep like a baby, too."

"Did your husband ever tell you anything else about the artifacts—who used them—or anything else about them?"

"I didn't want to know anything," said Jacqueline. "I only know my husband take them from a senior officer in Moscow—his boss. . . . It was a man he hated."

"Gilda!" Gilda realized Marla was waving her back to the ticket collection table because a line of people had entered the room. Janet scowled in Gilda's direction, having jumped in to help Marla.

"Excuse me, Mrs. Volkov," said Gilda. "I'd better get back to work. But thanks so much for your help."

"Of course. I hope that this ghost will leave you alone."

"I'm working on it." Gilda jumped up and hurried back toward the ticket table.

"Gilda," said Marla, swiftly gathering tickets from a group of guests, "can you please help this gentleman?"

"I can't imagine why I'm not on this list!" A man wearing a yellow bow tie, a dark suit, and square rimless glasses stood at the table, looking very displeased.

"Um, do you have a ticket for the event, sir?" Gilda asked.

"No, I do *not* have a ticket for the event. I am a longstanding member of the intelligence community, and my name should be on that list of special guests!"

He's one of those people who goes around getting annoyed about dumb things all the time, Gilda thought, half hoping that his name wouldn't be on the list. "And your name is?"

He pursed his lips at the question, irritated that Gilda even needed to ask.

"Loomis," he hissed. "Loomis Trench."

"Good cover identity." She realized her impulsive little joke was likely to annoy him further, but she couldn't resist.

"It's my real name."

"That's what they all say. Well, Mr. Wrench—"

"Trench!"

"Mr. Trench, I'm sorry, but I honestly don't see your name

here. If you'll just fork over a few dollars, we'll be happy to let you in on the secrets of a former Russian spy."

The man grew pale. He seemed to tremble, as if he were too angry for words.

Uh-oh, Gilda thought. She could tell he was gearing up to create a scene.

"What are you clowns *doing* in this organization?!" His voice rose and several people turned to look in his direction.

"Sir," said Gilda, "we are attempting to run a Spy Museum here."

Marla waved to Jasper and shot him a warning glance from across the room: *We've got a meltdown over here!*

"So, Mr. Treck, I suggest you take your daffodil-colored bow tie, and—"

"Loomis! Good to see you!" Jasper Clarke approached and clapped a friendly hand on Loomis's shoulder, interrupting the standoff between him and Gilda.

Loomis offered a wan smile that was more of a grimace. "We have a problem here, Jasper," he said.

"Oh? What's that?"

"Look, I know we never saw eye-to-eye at the agency, and I know you and a bunch of your cronies in this room did everything in your power to shut down the remote viewing program. But keeping my name off a list of invites is really beneath you."

Gilda felt her investigative radar blast into "high alert" mode: she had read about "remote viewing"—a technique used by psychics to perceive objects and people from great distances.

She had also read that the CIA and military had conducted experiments with the technique. How strange that this grumpy man—Loomis Trench—was actually involved with a remote viewing program for the CIA—and that Jasper Clarke had some connection to the program as well! It was all Gilda could do to resist grabbing both Jasper and Loomis and arm-wrestling them into telling her more details immediately.

At the moment, Jasper looked as if he wished he could find a container large enough to seal and store Loomis Trench until the lecture had ended.

"Gilda," said Jasper, "I think it will be okay if Mr. Trench takes his seat without a ticket today. After all, he is a member of the intelligence community."

"Yes, sir," said Gilda, giving Jasper a wink. "I'll put him on the 'special list.'"

"Miss, was that a sarcastic comment?" Loomis demanded.

"Loomis, here's a perfect seat for you," said Jasper, steering Loomis away before Gilda could respond.

With his meaty hands gripping the podium and high forehead beaded with perspiration, Boris Volkov stood at the front of the room, before a packed audience. He spoke in a booming voice, illustrating his tale of Cold War intrigue with photographs and film clips projected onto a large movie screen behind him. His talk was punctuated by bursts of laughter from the audience as he joked about his ill-fated meetings with "lovely ladies," his attempts to know the ways of the CIA by watching popular American spy movies and television shows, and the "vodka truth serum" he preferred using to ferret out potential double agents. "In many ways, we in the KGB were living in fantasy land—each doing our jobs the way we always had while the nation was going down the drain," he said. "There is a lesson in that for any country.

"But of course, the Americans had their own fantasies, too. I always found it funny how, in the movies, they viewed us in the KGB as ruthless and efficient. Most hilarious was their fear that we were psychics—that we had the ability to read and control minds. Because the Americans were certain we must be researching this. Believing the KGB had special 'mind tools,' the CIA started Project Stargate to study psychic espionage. Of course, as you know, that project unfortunately became a joke in the media and never had much success that could aid operations in any practical way."

"Excuse me!"

All eyes turned to the back of the room, where Loomis Trench stood up, his hand raised. "Pardon the interruption, but I must take issue with something you just said, Mr. Volkov."

"We'll take questions at the end of the presentation, please," said Jasper Clarke, eyeing Loomis warily and speaking from the sidelines of the room.

"It's just a quick comment," Loomis insisted.

People in the audience whispered. Gilda saw a couple of them roll their eyes in exasperation when they saw the speaker. *I bet some of them are his coworkers,* she thought.

"You have no basis for saying that the Americans achieved nothing worthwhile in psychic research," said Loomis. "I realize there are people here who have done everything in their power to shut down that research, and, of course, you're all so smugly contemptuous of something you know absolutely nothing about—something you couldn't begin to understand." Loomis trembled with barely controlled rage. "And Boris, I have to question what you really know of the Russian intelligence system anyway since you've had no ties with it for years—"

"Your comments remind me of an argument I had with my wife last night," Boris joked, cutting off Loomis's tirade and effectively diffusing the tension in the room. "She says to me, 'it is so hilarious that you ever worked in a field called "intelligence"'!" Having successfully redirected everyone's attention back to his presentation, Boris proceeded to show a segment from a KGB training film that generated many chuckles.

Gilda kept an eye on Loomis. He sulked and fidgeted for a minute, then quietly slipped from his chair and exited the room.

There's something fishy about that man, Loomis Trench, Gilda thought.

28

Shaking a Tail

After Boris's Spy Museum lecture, Gilda sat in a Starbucks near the Spy Museum and reflected on the strange events of the day. The café was across the street from the FBI building, and men wearing white shirts with ties and rumpled, pleated pants sat at little tables all around Gilda, their federal ID badges dangling from their necks. Some listened to headphones while studying stacks of papers and sipping lattes. Most of them looked perturbed and overworked, their careworn faces gray with exhaustion. With her high ponytail, catsuit, and high-heeled boots, Gilda was a striking contrast. She sat at a small table by the window, scribbling in her reporter's notebook:

BIZARRE OUTBURST DURING BORIS VOLKOV'S SPY MU-
SEUM PRESENTATION:

Something about that weird guy, Loomis Trench, just
isn't right. What kind of CIA employee makes a public scene
and draws that much attention to himself?

Even more interesting: clearly, the CIA was conducting
psychic research that was apparently shut down. I'm not too
impressed with Mr. Loomis Trench, but I am VERY curious

about his role in that CIA espionage research program—"Project Stargate"!

<u>SPY MUSEUM HAUNTING & DEAD-DROP INVESTIGA-TION UPDATE:</u>
ACTIVE CLUES:

1. "THE LAST MEETING": Those words have turned up twice now—first on the audio surveillance tapes and then on the photograph I took.

2. "ANNA": It appears twice in the dead-drop message I decoded. Suddenly, it also appears on the wall of the Spy Museum.

<u>ONGOING QUESTION: IS THERE A CONNECTION BE-TWEEN THE SPY MUSEUM GHOST AND THE DEAD DROP IN OAK HILL CEMETERY?</u>

Gilda paused and gazed out the window. She suddenly wished she had her binoculars with her because she spied Jasper Clarke and Boris Volkov crossing the street together, deep in conversation. Boris gestured exuberantly as he spoke. She wished she could hear what they were talking about.

Gilda's attention was distracted by a group of tourists walking into the café to order Frappuccinos. "Can we go to the Spy Museum now, Dad?" The girl wore a T-shirt that announced: I'D RATHER BE FISHING.

"Honey, we'll do that tomorrow. It's getting late and we need to get back to the hotel to meet your mom."

"But all we did around here was that Lincoln stuff!"

Gilda's ears perked up at this comment. *What "Lincoln stuff" is around here?* She pulled out her Washington, D.C., travel guide from her purse, looked up "Lincoln" in the index, and was amazed to discover that both Ford's Theatre, where Lincoln was shot, and Petersen House, the house across the street from the theatre, where Lincoln actually died, were just footsteps away from the Spy Museum.

I can't believe I never noticed this until now, Gilda thought.

Hoping to find some clue to explain her dreams about Abraham Lincoln's ghost, Gilda jumped up from her table and headed down 10th Street toward Ford's Theatre and Petersen House. The street simmered in the late afternoon sun: everyone walked slowly and silently, as if any speech or extra movement would make things hotter.

It's funny, Gilda thought, *that the place where Abraham Lincoln was shot is now surrounded by the Hard Rock Café and the Lincoln Bar & Grill*. She saw a crowd of tourists heading into Petersen House for a tour, so she followed them inside.

PETERSEN HOUSE

On the night of April 14, 1865, President Abraham Lincoln was shot while watching a play at Ford's Theatre—the theatre across the street from this house. Theatregoers carried the president into Petersen House, where he died the next day. This home has been preserved to look just as it was at the time of the president's death.

Gilda felt claustrophobic in the dimly lit house as she followed slow-moving tourists into a sitting room where black-and-white pictures hung on the walls, then back to a bedroom filled with antique toiletry bottles, books, and mirrors. The short, narrow bed seemed too small for Lincoln's tall stature. Gilda was ready for any signs of Lincoln's ghost, but she had to admit she felt nothing out of the ordinary. If anything, the room had a sense of peace—the somber sense of a place where something ended.

Maybe there are too many people around for me to make contact with a spirit, Gilda speculated.

She left Petersen House and crossed the street to Ford's Theatre. A tour guide pointed her toward the basement of the theatre, now a museum filled with an assortment of eerie objects: the clothes Lincoln wore on the evening he was assassinated, bottles of embalming fluid used to prepare Lincoln for burial, the drumsticks that played "Hail to the Chief" shortly before his death, and a dark hood worn by Mary Surratt—the only woman in the group of four people who were executed for conspiring to assassinate the president.

Gilda made her way upstairs into the auditorium of the theatre. *Now I'm close to the very spot where Lincoln was killed,* she thought, sitting in one of the chairs facing the stage.

Gilda looked up at the gold drapes, antique lace, and old American flags decorating the presidential box where Lincoln sat on the night he was killed. She closed her eyes and concentrated. *President Lincoln—are you here? Do you have a message for me?*

Gilda imagined the theatre packed with people watching a play: *A handsome man walks straight through the front door of the theatre, up the stairs. He hands a calling card to a presidential messenger, then enters the presidential box. He waits because he knows a very funny line in the play is coming. Now everyone is laughing. The president is laughing. The man's finger is on the trigger of his gun. . . .*

The sound of an explosion startled Gilda. She whirled around and realized it was just a toddler playing with an electronic battleship toy. His parents reprimanded him and struggled to wrench the ship from his grasp. Other tourists in the theatre shot reproachful glances in the family's direction.

Then Gilda felt as if her heart had stopped. Just a few feet away, in the back row of the theatre, was the man with the reddish beard—the very same man who had stared at her with such unnerving interest in the Metro station.

Gilda now felt sure of one thing: *he's following me.*

Don't panic, Gilda thought, wishing there was a trapdoor in the floor beneath her feet. *Trust your gut.*

She slowly donned her cat's-eye sunglasses, picked up her purse, stood up, and walked swiftly up the theatre aisle toward the door.

Out of the corner of her eye, Gilda saw the man get up from his seat as she passed by. Her heart pounded.

As she exited the theatre and walked into the furnace-blast of heat on the city sidewalk, she longed to glance back to see if the man was behind her.

Never look behind, the Moscow Rules advised.

Instead, she walked faster and faster, wanting to run. *I need to lose him,* she thought. *I can't let him follow me home. Who knows how long he's been trailing me? He may already know where I live. He clearly knows the neighborhood where I work; how else would he know to find me at Ford's Theatre of all places?*

Gilda ducked into an art gallery and pretended to look at colorful paintings of plump women holding equally plump cats while subtly monitoring the sidewalk. A moment later, the bearded man appeared on the sidewalk across the street. He wore a loose-fitting shirt with a Hawaiian print, shorts, and flip-flops. *He looks like a tourist, but I'm guessing that's just a disguise,* Gilda thought.

The man glanced up and down the street, clearly looking for someone. Finally he stuck his hands in his pockets and walked away.

Gilda whipped out her reporter's notebook and furiously scribbled some notes:

> Who is this man who's following me, and what, exactly, does he know about me?

The man was nowhere in sight, but Gilda was still scared to go back outside. What if he was waiting for her around the corner?

Get a grip! Gilda told herself.

> You wanted to be a spy, so stop loitering in this art shop filled with second-rate paintings of rotund women, and start using the tradecraft you've been teaching all week to your recruits! Stop feeling scared and sorry for yourself, and start acting like a real spy!

Gilda realized that this was exactly the sort of situation that called for something the CIA called a "quick-change" disguise, just in case the man actually *was* watching for her around the corner or in one of the galleries or restaurants that lined the street.

She opened her handbag and felt grateful to discover that she still had a wig and a couple of the fake noses she had confiscated following a game of wigball. Unfortunately, it happened to be a wig upon which The Comedian had sneezed, but she didn't have the luxury of feeling squeamish about a few boogers. Gilda stuffed her ponytail into the wig. The young, fashionable gallery owner who had been quietly watching Gilda from her desk in the corner now stood up from her chair and looked alarmed.

"I have a date," Gilda explained, stuffing wisps of her hair into the wig. She opened her compact mirror and did her best to quickly apply the false nose with bits of spirit gum, smoothing the edges with powder. It was a large, bulbous nose that would have been unattractive on a man's face in the best of circumstances. Gilda peered into her compact mirror and decided that the nose and wig made her virtually unrecognizable.

"That must be some date," said the woman in the corner.

"You know how it is," said Gilda. "It's so hard to just be yourself."

"You'll definitely make an impression."

Wishing she had an oversized jacket to cover her black catsuit, Gilda tied the scarf around her neck in hopes of disguising her outfit and made her way into the heat of the late afternoon. She walked slowly to the Metro station, watching for the man and surreptitiously adjusting her false nose when perspiration caused it to slip.

Sitting on the train, she pretended to read a copy of the *Washington Post* that someone had left on the seat. She peeked over the paper from time to time, half expecting to see a man with a suspicious-looking red beard boarding the train at every stop.

29

The Last Meeting

Gilda dreamed she walked through a maze of very small tombstones. The sun was bright and hot, and Gilda wished for a hat or some spot of shade—somewhere to hide. *He'll find me here,* she worried.

Gilda turned a corner and saw that at the end of the path, a woman waited for her: it was the same pale woman—the dead woman whose face had peered out of video screens. But this time the woman was alive.

"Who are you?" Gilda asked. "What do you want?"

"You're getting closer," the woman said. "But you must hurry."

"I still don't understand."

A pink bubble emerged from the woman's mouth. It grew larger, until it popped.

Gilda awoke suddenly, feeling uneasy.

PSYCHIC DREAM—NOTES:

   I just had a weird dream about that same spooky
woman. But this time there was something different on her

mouth—a bubble. GUM??? Is it a clue? Also odd: why were the tombstones surrounding me so small?

"I haf something to tiell you."

Gilda was surprised to see Agent Moscow at the Spy Museum so early in the morning, before the other campers and counselors had arrived. Gilda herself had left home much earlier than usual in an effort to throw the stalker she now thought of as "Redbeard" off-track, just in case he was planning to trail her to work.

"Is something wrong?" Gilda noticed that Agent Moscow looked tired. She wore no makeup and her blond hair wasn't styled as meticulously as usual.

Agent Moscow handed Gilda a book. She had marked a page with a poem by the poet Anna Akhmatova: "Song of the Last Meeting."

"I tink it may be a clue," she said. "Eet's strange. I was just seeting in my bed in de middle of de night, and I see dis book on my shelf. Eet's a book of Russian poems—a book I never looked at before. So I get out of bed, and open dees book—and what do you know: I open right to dis poem and the page is folded down even dough I never read it."

Agent Moscow handed Gilda the book, and Gilda saw that it featured both the original Russian poems and English translations by a man named Pete Biebow. As Gilda read "Song of the Last Meeting," she sensed something significant about the poem's lonely, ominous mood. *The link with the clues "Anna" and "The Last Meeting" seems important,* she thought.

My chest grew helplessly cold,
But my feet were light and deft,
I pulled a glove on my right hand—
The one that was meant for my left.

It seemed the steps were many,
But I knew—there were only three!
Amid maples, autumn's whisper
Pled softly: "Die with me!

My fate so fickle and evil—
Has coldly betrayed me anew."
I answered, "My dearest, my darling,
Mine too. I will die with you."

The song of the very last meeting.
I glanced at the darkened home.
In the bedroom the candles were burning
With an indifferent, yellowish glow.

Gilda's left ear tickled. The poem made her picture a woman walking into a wintry evening, feeling alone and betrayed. It seemed to tell a sad story about the end of a love affair. *This poem must mean something to the Spy Museum ghost,* Gilda thought. *It must be an attempt to communicate—maybe with Agent Moscow since she speaks Russian.*

"Agent Moscow, what do you know about this poet Anna Akhmatova?"

"Not much. I mean, I never heard she was spy or anyting like dat."

Gilda thought for a moment. "We have some time before the other kids show up. Why don't we go to my office to look up some information on the computer?"

As she and Agent Moscow walked down the hallway, Gilda heard Janet and Matthew Morrow talking; they were already in the office. She listened for a moment, curious to hear what they were talking about. "So—" said Janet, "got any plans for the weekend?"

Gilda hid just outside the office door and gestured to Agent Moscow to do the same.

"Huh?" Matthew grunted.

"The weekend. Any plans?"

"Not really. How about you?"

"I have an extra ticket for the Shakespeare Theater. I mean, if you'd like to go with me."

Omigod, Gilda thought. *Janet just asked Matthew Morrow to go out with her!*

"Oh!" Matthew seemed to realize that he was being asked out on a date. "Hmm. Let me see. I might be busy doing a really long run. . . . Can I get back to you on that?"

Gilda whipped out her notebook.

Clearly, Matthew has no interest in Janet, which isn't surprising since she reads romance novels on the Metro and has commented that she "hates exercise," which seems to be Matthew's main passion in life, aside from researching

222   and writing about the history of spying.

Plus, I have no idea how old Janet really is, but she kind of looks like she could be Matthew's mom. Maybe she goes for younger men and then makes lots of cipher wheels for their apartments.

"What are you doing?" Agent Moscow whispered.

"It's important to take notes when spying," Gilda replied. "Make sure you always have something to write with."

Janet's overture had apparently ended all communication between her and Matthew, so Gilda and Agent Moscow breezed into the office to look up information on Gilda's computer. As the two girls skimmed the contents of several historical websites, Gilda took notes:

Anna Akhmatova—NOTES:

Akhmatova was a Russian poet who was persecuted by the KGB throughout her life.

<u>Interesting fact:</u> a Russian astronomer later named a star after her.

<u>Any resemblance to the Spy Museum ghost?</u> No. We did find one painting of Anna Akhmatova: she had an interesting look, but it definitely wasn't the same face we saw on the video screens—the "ghost face." We found no evidence that Anna Akhmatova was a spy.

"It seems like this poem 'Song of the Last Meeting' is a clue of some kind," said Gilda, "but I don't think we're dealing with the ghost of Anna Akhmatova. It must mean something else."

"Excuse me." Matthew spun around in his swivel chair. "Did

I actually hear you say the words 'dealing with the ghost of Anna Akhmatova'?!"

"Agent Moscow," said Gilda, "this is Matthew Morrow, the Spy Museum historian. Matthew, I didn't realize you were eavesdropping on our conversation."

"In the Spy Museum, everyone eavesdrops," Janet interjected. "And by the way, Roger also thinks the museum is haunted." Janet declared this news headline with obvious pride at her insider knowledge, completely unaware that it was Gilda who had put that idea in Roger's head in the first place. "But April thinks that's silly," she continued. "She says Roger is just sleep-deprived and that it's a prank some of the kids are playing."

"Sounds like April might be right for once," said Matthew.

"Janet," said Gilda, "is there any history of a haunting in the Spy Museum?"

"Not that I know of." Janet reached into her desk drawer and retrieved a can of Slim-Fast. "But I do believe in ghosts. This city is full of them." She glanced in Matthew's direction, as if he might be a ghost himself.

"What do *you* think, Matthew?" Gilda asked.

"I think I have a lot of *real* work to do." His telephone rang. "If you'll excuse me, I'm getting a lot of calls from the press today. Since nobody inside the CIA will tell them anything, they call the Spy Museum historian with their questions."

"Well," said Janet, sticking a straw into her Slim-Fast, "I'll be seeing you both soon."

"You will?"

"You know. Spy Camp training this morning?" Janet raised

an eyebrow pointedly as if to say, *Don't you even know what's going on with your campers? How do you function in the world?*

"Oh—right." Gilda suddenly remembered that Janet was going to play the role of an enemy agent in a Spy Camp activity. *She'll probably do a good job in that role,* Gilda thought.

Gilda and Agent Moscow left the office to head back to the Venona Room.

On Gilda's desk, the computer screen displayed the poem "Song of the Last Meeting." Neither Matthew nor Janet noticed the face that appeared—the eerie eyes that gazed into the room through the words of the poem.

30

Secret Cameras
and a Drugstore Fiasco

This woman may look like someone's grandmother, but she's actually very dangerous." Gilda stood in front of her spy recruits displaying a photograph of Janet disguised with makeup and a brown wig. "Her code name is Ms. Frumpus and she's suspected of selling top-secret intelligence to terrorists and unfriendly foreign governments. Your assignment is to find her, trail her, and capture her on film. In other words, take her picture. But here's the catch: you need to take her picture before she even notices you looking at her. And I'm going to show you how to do that part in a minute.

"Now, if you find Ms. Frumpus having a meeting or exchanging information with an enemy agent, we definitely want that on film. She might be in disguise, so look *very* carefully. I should also warn you that she's known to have a rather surly disposition and she dislikes children, so watch out. Got it?"

Gilda's team stared at the photo. The recruits nodded silently and Gilda felt satisfied that she had scared them into momentary silence.

"So if we find this Frumpus lady," James Bond ventured, "what are we supposed to do with her?"

"Team Crypt, what did I just tell you to do?"

"I mean, shouldn't we try to catch her and put her in handcuffs?"

"Yeah," said The Misanthrope. "It sounds like we need to get her off the streets, not just take her picture."

Gilda chuckled, imagining how surprised Janet would be if a group of kids suddenly wrestled her to the ground and placed her in handcuffs.

"For this mission, your job is just to get accurate *information* by snapping a secret photograph. The actual arrest will be left to Special Operations after you do your job."

"Ooh, can I be in Special Operations?" Baby Boy pleaded.

"That's another lesson. This time it's photography."

Gilda showed her team the spy gadgets they would use to take their secret pictures: sunglasses with a hidden video recording device, a Cold War–era buttonhole camera, a writing pen that concealed a camera, a tiny Minox camera, and a video camera disguised as a pack of chewing gum. April had hastily showed Gilda how to use each of the gadgets, but while she wasn't completely confident in her own technical skills, her team didn't seem the least bit daunted by the devices.

"Now, who wants to try this secret buttonhole camera?"

"OH! OH! OH!!! ME! ME! ME!!!"

"Let me rephrase that question," said Gilda, holding the buttonhole camera over several sets of outstretched hands.

"Who feels sure that he or she can operate this correctly and successfully to capture a clear image of our target *and still stay undercover?*"

"ME! ME! ME!!!! I DO!!!"

Gilda distributed gadgets and watched her team examine them with a boisterous, clumsy curiosity that made her think of some young chimps she had once observed at the zoo. *I guess they'll learn on the job,* she told herself.

```
TO: TEAM CRYPT

FROM: GILDA JOYCE ("CASE OFFICER ZELDA")

CC: APRIL SHEPHERD

RE: REPORT ON SPY PHOTOGRAPHY MISSION


EVIDENCE OF SPY DEVELOPMENT: As you made your way
to the surveillance location, I was pleased to
see that you were always on the lookout for dead
drops. In fact, you photographed every empty soda
can and bit of dirty paper you came across just
in case it was something important. That's paying
attention to the details! (Remember, though: some-
times trash is just trash.)


AREA FOR IMPROVEMENT #1: Failure to keep a low
profile. Giggling and chasing each other like baby
squirrels as you walk down the street toward
the local drugstore draws too much attention. A
traveling circus would have been less noticeable.
```

AREA FOR IMPROVEMENT #2: Proper use of spy photography equipment.

The Comedian: you pulled the buttonhole camera from your pocket and openly examined it in full view of customers in the drugstore just to make sure you were pushing the right button.

James Bond: You took numerous pictures of the ground with your Minox camera.

Stargirl: When you wear spy-sunglasses-with-built-in-video-surveillance-camera on top of your head, you end up taking extensive footage of clouds and the sky. It's pleasant up there, but last time I checked, Ms. Frumpus is not a bird.

AREA FOR IMPROVEMENT #3: Acting normal in public. You had the right impulse to act as if you were shopping in the drugstore, but some of you played the role with a little too much enthusiasm.

The Comedian: Loud comments like "Are there any nasal inhalers in this store? Something for mucus removal? I need a mucus removal system!" draw too much unwanted attention.

AREA FOR IMPROVEMENT #4: Identifying the proper target. You spotted a matronly woman wearing a sunhat and shopping for laxatives, and you brazenly photographed her. THIS WAS NOT THE CORRECT ENEMY AGENT. Incidentally, the real enemy agent (Ms. Frumpus) was offended, because the woman you targeted was at least ten years older than her and about forty pounds heavier. Sure, there was a resemblance, but act carefully and subtly until you're sure.

MISSION FIASCO:

1. Matronly lady complains to store manager that youngsters are making fun of her purchases.
2. Store manager tells recruits to leave.
3. Agent Frumpus stands in the corner eating graham crackers out of a box. She giggles as she watches the entire mission implode.

OVERALL ASSESSMENT: You all would have been arrested or worse had this been a real mission.

31

The Interrogation

Wanting to lift her team's spirits following the failure of their most recent mission, Gilda took her recruits down to the Spy City Café for lunch. Once inside the kitschy, modern restaurant decorated with photographs of real dead-drop locations and other historic spy landmarks in the city, the team turned its attention to ordering hot dogs with spy names like "Havana Dog" and "Red Square Dog." Gilda noticed Boris Volkov and Jasper Clarke sitting together at a corner table, discussing something. Boris gestured broadly while taking large bites of a hamburger and scribbling notes on a napkin. Jasper Clarke appeared to be doing more listening than talking as he sipped a cup of coffee.

What were the two of them up to? Gilda suddenly wanted to approach their table: she had no idea what she was going to say, but this was a rare opportunity to try to get more information about Boris. *After all,* Gilda told herself, *he's still a person of interest in connection with the dead drop in Oak Hill Cemetery. I need to check him out more thoroughly.*

"Hi, there," said Gilda, breaking up their conversation with what she hoped looked like a casually friendly impulse.

She immediately felt awkward; Jasper and Boris looked surprised and not very pleased that she had interrupted their discussion.

"It's lovely Lady Gilda," said Boris, tactfully.

"You know our new intern?" Jasper was obviously surprised, and, Gilda sensed, impressed that Boris already knew Gilda.

"Of course. Gilda assisted Mr. Morrow in acquiring the new artifacts."

"Oh, I see," said Jasper. "Wonderful additions to our collection."

"There's actually something I've been meaning to ask you about the artifacts, Mr. Volkov," said Gilda, realizing she would have to get right to the point. "Your wife told me about the anomalies she experienced during the time you had the artifacts in your home."

"Did she tiell you about the vodka she drank each time she saw these 'anomalies'?" Boris winked at Jasper.

"Well, no—but I'm sure that by now you've both heard the rumors that the Spy Museum has been haunted ever since we acquired those two objects from Mr. Volkov."

Boris burst into nervous laughter.

"Actually, I have heard no such rumors, Gilda," said Jasper, frowning.

How can that be? Gilda thought. *Aren't intelligence officers supposed to know what's going on all around them? But then, his office is so separate from all the gossip and intrigue; he'd have to set up a surveillance bug to get the scoop on what's going on inside his own museum.*

"Gilda, do you think this can wait for a later meeting? Boris and I are discussing some important plans for a new lecture series."

Gilda knew she was pushing her luck, but she felt compelled to take a risk. She remembered the phrase from her cryptic dream: *You have to hurry.* "Just one more question, Mr. Volkov. Are you *sure* you can't tell me who those objects belonged to back in Moscow? I know you acquired them from someone in the KGB years ago, but do you know *anything* at all about the person who owned them—or someone who might have used them in her work as a spy?"

Boris opened his hands in a gesture of equivocation. "It is hard to say what the truth is. During those years, everyone is lying to one another. But—I tiell you what I do know. First, a confession: technically, I stole the artifacts from the office of my boss in the KGB—a horrible man who made everyone around him miserable." He raised a finger in the air as if to defend himself and emphasize his point. "But when I take these things I knew I was never going back to Moscow again; I thought I may need these things to prove who I am to the Americans— or maybe, who knows, to sell them if I need money. As far as who used them in spying activities? I don't know. The rumor was that my boss used his girlfriends and maybe even his wife to hielp him conduct missions, secret assassinations, you name it. So maybe it was one of these women he used."

Interesting, Gilda thought. *So are we dealing with the ghost of Boris's boss's girlfriend or wife?* At the same time, Gilda felt frustrated that nothing in Boris's story helped her answer her questions about the Anna Akhmatova poem or how any of this connected with the message she uncovered in the cemetery.

Boris glanced around the room nervously, as if worried that he had said too much—worried that some Russian spy in

Washington might be trailing him with secret orders to punish him for his defection to the United States—his betrayal of his motherland.

Jasper Clarke also glanced around the room as he leaned back in his chair and dabbed his mouth in an artificial gesture of contented boredom.

As both men were looking away, Gilda seized an opportunity to get a more revealing profile of Boris: she swiped a table napkin upon which Boris had scribbled some notes. She wanted to find out whether there was any possibility that Boris had left the message she found in Oak Hill Cemetery, and she knew his handwriting would help her get to the bottom of that question.

32

The Mind of a Spy

Well, he's quite a womanizer," said Caitlin, peering at the napkin upon which Boris had scribbled a list of book titles among what seemed to be a personal shopping list for a party: the words *cocktails, hors d'oeuvres,* and *cake* appeared next to little sketches of cartoon figures with pineapples for heads and large feet. "Or at least he would like to be—that's for sure."

"How can you tell?"

"See here? He has a lot of large loops in the lower region of his handwriting. I see that all the time from guys who have girlfriends, but who still try to pick me up at the bar when they write down their names and phone numbers."

"What else do you see?"

Pushing her cappuccino aside, Caitlin placed Boris's table-napkin doodles and handwriting next to the photographs Gilda had taken of the dead-drop message. She took a magnifying glass out of her backpack to examine the letters more closely.

"You carry a magnifying glass with you?"

"Gilda, I'm telling you; people come up to me all the time and ask me to look at handwriting samples. 'Should I hire this person?' 'Should I date this person?' I'm beginning to think I should start charging for my services."

"But this is free right now, right?"

"For you, it's on the house. Now," said Caitlin, "we can obviously see that these two handwriting samples are completely different. Anyone can tell that."

"But someone leaving a dead-drop message might disguise his handwriting, right?"

"Even when people attempt to disguise their handwriting, they usually give themselves away. Little bits of their own handwriting creep in—a letter here and there, a different stroke. It's like when an American tries to speak in a British accent: every now and then you're going to slip a little unless you're an exceptional actor. Same with handwriting."

Caitlin squinted at the handwriting. "What I *don't* see in Boris's handwriting is any evidence of tension—those little angry strokes where the pen presses into the paper too hard. Whereas I see *a lot* of that in the message you photographed.

"Now this guy Boris has an ego, for sure, but he's got a lot of openings at the tops of his letters, suggesting more openness in his personality. My sense is that he's really more interested in seeking connections with people than hiding things from them, whereas this other person in the photographed message doesn't ever want anyone to know what he's up to. He's probably one of those people who even keeps secrets from *himself.* My guess is that he started off as a petty grudge-holder who evolved into someone with criminal tendencies—mainly because he strikes me as the kind of person who blames others for all his problems."

"In that case, I guess I should remove Boris from my list of suspects." Gilda sighed and rested her chin in her hand.

"What's wrong? That isn't the answer you expected?"

"It's not that . . ." Gilda liked Boris, so she was glad he was no longer a suspect. On the other hand, she now had absolutely no idea who a more plausible suspect might be.

"Isn't this just a game for the Spy Museum? I mean, it seems like you're taking it so seriously."

"It isn't a game at all!" Gilda blurted. She suddenly realized that while she had shown Caitlin the photograph of the dead-drop message and mentioned the mysterious flashing lights in their building, she had never had a chance to explain all the facts of her investigation. Caitlin knew nothing about her discovery in the cemetery or the haunting in the museum.

"Do you want to tell me what's really going on with you?" Caitlin asked. "As your substitute mom for the summer, I demand to know."

"It's kind of complicated." Gilda took a deep breath and described everything—finding the fake rock that contained the cryptic message, the dreams in which a dead woman's face appeared, the spooky events in the Spy Museum.

"Gilda, I'm glad I know you well enough to know you aren't crazy, because if you had told me all that on the first day you moved in, I probably would have had to put you back on a plane bound for Michigan. But now that we're friends—aren't roommates supposed to tell each other what's going on? Why didn't you tell me about all of this before?"

"A real spy wouldn't need to tell anyone."

"Oh, poo on being a 'real spy.' Listen, Gilda, you're human, and you have to be able to trust somebody. People get weird when they keep too many secrets."

"I guess."

"Besides, maybe I could help."

"Well, the problem I have now is that I can't connect the clues in the museum with all the other pieces of the puzzle."

"Like what?"

"Like this." Gilda showed Caitlin the poem by Anna Akhmatova. She explained how the name Anna had appeared on a wall in the museum and how the phrase "the last meeting" had mysteriously appeared in a photograph.

Caitlin read the poem. "I like this poem," she said, thoughtfully. "It sounds like she had a love affair and this is about their last meeting." She chewed on a coffee stirrer and thought for a moment. "I know!"

"What?"

"The Alley of the Russian Poets!"

"What's that?"

Caitlin leaned forward and whispered, as if she and Gilda were plotting something. "If I were a mole in the D.C. intelligence community, I think the Alley of the Russian Poets would be the perfect signal site. It's a walkway lined with stones that look like little tombstones with the names of Russian poets—and there's a tree planted for each poet. I'm almost positive I've seen a stone engraved with this poet's name—Anna Akhmatova. It's perfect! It's walking distance from Oak Hill Cemetery; it's just down the street from the Russian Embassy, next to Guy Mason Park."

Hearing Caitlin's description, Gilda felt an electric charge of energy coursing through her veins. *It sounds a lot like the dream I had where I was walking through a maze of tiny tombstones,* she thought. She jumped up from the table, feeling as if she didn't have a second to lose. "Thanks soooo much, Caitlin. You've been the best substitute mom ever!"

"You're going there *now?*"

"I just have this feeling I have to act fast." Gilda again recalled the words from her dream: *"You're getting closer, but you must hurry."*

33

The Alley of the Russian Poets

Nobody would suspect that the Alley of the Russian Poets was also a spy's signal site. The peaceful, tree-lined path was marked with carved stones—each engraved with a Russian poet's name. Someone had left a red rose at the foot of each stone in tribute to the poets.

Nearby, parents led children to and from a small brick building used for recreational activities and a tiny garden where bees and butterflies hovered over wilting hydrangeas, lilies, and foxgloves.

Gilda felt giddy to discover the stone dedicated to Anna Akhmatova. *Look for my usual signal,* the spy had written, *blue gum marking Anna.*

There, stuck to the side of the stone was a wad of blue chewing gum! It looked so innocuous and ordinary, Gilda never would have noticed the gum if she hadn't been looking for it. *That must mean he or she has just made a drop of information.*

Gilda knew she had to act fast, before the mole's contact picked up the information. *I have to try to get a photograph of whatever secret information he or she leaves at the cemetery drop site.*

Maybe I'll even catch a glimpse of the person picking up the material and get a license plate number or something. . . .

Gilda resisted the urge to sprint down Wisconsin Avenue toward Oak Hill Cemetery. *Slow down,* she told herself. *You need to look as if you're merely out for a stroll in case anyone follows you.*

Gilda slowed her stride to a leisurely, casual pace, but her heart raced. The late afternoon sun sank lower in the sky, and her shadow lengthened as she made her way toward Oak Hill Cemetery.

Act confident, Gilda reminded herself, bolstering her resolve to get to the bottom of the mystery once and for all. *Never look behind.*

The cemetery was dappled with honey-colored light. As Gilda walked down the pathway, she heard the sound of mourning doves and rustling leaves. Here and there, shadows darted behind tombstones—fleeting signs of spirit activity.

Down the steep hill, past crumbling tombstones, Gilda navigated the cracked and broken stone steps leading to the dead-drop location. Was it just her imagination, or did she hear something stirring inside one of the graves?

Maybe it's a deer again, she thought. Or was it the sound of a person clearing his throat?

She approached the iron-gated mausoleum built into the hillside. Gilda froze for a moment, listening to the cooing of birds, the rustling of small animals in the leaves. When she reached the foot of the steps and turned to face the row of mausoleums, her entire body flooded with panic and nauseating disappointment at the realization that she had stepped directly into a trap.

She wasn't alone.

He was already there, leaning against the tomb and waiting for her. It was the man who had followed her twice before: Redbeard.

34

The Master Psychic

The psychic spy struggled to understand the vision that led him to Oak Hill Cemetery. He had clearly seen the ghost of Abraham Lincoln grieving at his dead son's tomb; he had seen phantoms of fallen generals and spies from years past.

Still, he knew there was some other reason he was supposed to come to the cemetery.

Then she appeared: a teenage girl wearing a yellow sundress and cat's-eye sunglasses at the foot of the stone steps. The psychic spy immediately recognized her pale, freckled face and dark hair from his visions. He had also seen her in the city—at the Metro station and at Ford's Theatre. The girl bore a striking resemblance to his spirit guide, but she was several years older. And this girl was most definitely alive.

The psychic spy realized that the girl was terrified—ready to bolt like a young fawn.

"I'm sorry I startled you," he said, hoping he could find some way to convince her that he meant no harm. "I know this sounds odd, but I'm supposed to meet you."

Gilda dug in her handbag, searching for her cell phone and something that might work as a weapon. She grabbed her apartment keys, thinking these would have to suffice as a means of defending herself against Redbeard if needed. *Go for vulnerable parts of the attacker's body,* a self-defense handbook she had read advised.

"I should introduce myself," said the psychic spy. "My name is Balthazar Frobenius."

Gilda stopped digging through her purse. Her mouth fell open. "Is this someone's idea of a joke?"

"I realize it's a pretty outlandish name."

"You mean—you're *the* Balthazar Frobenius—the great psychic?!"

"You know about me?"

Gilda dropped her apartment keys and pulled her tattered *Master Psychic's Handbook* from her purse instead. She waved the book in the air. "I carry this with me everywhere!"

Throughout his career, Balthazar had been surrounded by people craving answers, but he had never really had a true fan—someone who genuinely wanted to follow in his footsteps. The realization that this girl knew so much about him actually scared him a little.

Balthazar chuckled nervously as Gilda handed him her book, which bore the stains of quite a few peanut butter, banana, and chocolate sandwiches. "Ah, yes." He flipped through the pages and gazed at the book with nostalgia. "That book is probably still my best work."

"It changed my entire life! I know most of it by heart." Gilda took the dog-eared book from Balthazar and stuffed it back into her bag. "You know, if there had been an author portrait of you on your book, I would have recognized you. I mean, I assumed you were just a weird stalker or something."

"I doubt you would have recognized me even if there had been a picture in that book. It was published many years ago and most of my old friends would say that my looks have declined terribly." He patted his belly. "This is all muscle, though," he joked. "Anyway, these days I prefer to stay incognito."

"So what are you doing here?" Gilda whispered. "Are we both working on the same case?"

"I was hoping you could help me answer that question. During the past few weeks I've been completely unable to work because the most intense visions keep interrupting me. Some of them are people . . ." Balthazar thought of the pale woman and the images of Gilda herself that had interrupted his remote viewing sessions. "Some are very specific places in the city. What's unusual for me is that I have no idea what I'm really looking for."

Gilda nodded. "I know the feeling." She walked along the stones lining the path, searching for the one special stone that was actually a secret container. All the stones looked very similar, and for a moment she panicked, worried that she would never find it again. After all, she had first made the discovery accidentally.

Finally, Gilda spotted the large, fake stone positioned in the crumbling edging of the pathway: it was slightly smoother than the others around it and it also weighed much less than its appearance suggested.

"We're supposed to find this." Gilda lifted the stone and

pulled it apart to reveal the interior secret compartment. She stared in awe at the contents of the concealment device. "It really happened!" she whispered.

Balthazar stared in awe as Gilda unfolded a pile of classified documents.

- TOP SECRET -

Background: In 1994 the United States discontinued Project STARGATE—a program to gather foreign intelligence using remote viewing techniques. Intelligence officers in the U.S. military who were identified as having psychic potential were trained to perceive global targets using mental telepathy.

Project MINDSCAPE continues, however, in a highly classified setting, using select psychic professionals. These highly classified contents are top secret because they reveal targets and information of interest to the United States. The information that follows is relevant to secret U.S. military and foreign policy strategy.

Gilda flipped through the pages, reading a series of memos and notes that clearly documented recent, active attempts to spy on international targets by means of psychic readings. *Balthazar has been working for the CIA!* Gilda realized. *But someone's been passing along the information he discovers.*

TARGET #2: RUSSIAN DEFENSE MINISTRY (Balthazar Frobenius attempt to view secret documents) . . .

"Mr. Frobenius—"

"Call me Balthazar."

"Balthazar, do you realize your name is on each of these documents?" *If he's able to use psychic skills to perceive targets all over the world,* Gilda thought, *why didn't he know about the documents in this dead drop?*

Balthazar stared at the documents. His sunburned face now looked ashen. "May I?"

Gilda handed him the papers and he read them silently, his hand shaking with combined anger and excitement. "So that's why I've been so confused and blocked! I thought this whole Project MINDSCAPE was a failure, but the truth is, the Russians have been following every reading I do!" For a moment, Balthazar felt almost happy at the notion that his psychic abilities were being tracked by other spies—that the readings had in fact been significant enough to be a source of international intrigue.

Then he sighed wearily, realizing how blind he had been to the significance of the clues and warnings he had received. *All because I wanted to feel that my work was really important to the government,* he thought. He sat down on a small stone bench for mourners, rubbing his large, shiny forehead with his palms. "Now I understand. Now it all makes sense."

Realizing they didn't have much time, Gilda took the documents from Balthazar and did her best to take as many pictures as she could for evidence. She was eager to ask Balthazar about a million questions, but she was also worried that the foreign spy picking up the information drop would turn up while they were still loitering near the mausoleums.

"Gilda," said Balthazar, "I'll tell you something that isn't in that *Master Psychic's Handbook* I wrote. Maybe you can learn from my mistake."

"What's that?

"Even psychics can be totally blind to difficult truths that are very close to us personally. Here I was gathering intelligence information for the CIA—my mind soaring over the globe to remote locations where I could see everything quite clearly. I thought I was doing something to protect my country and others around the world. Meanwhile, right next to me was a source of destruction—that blasted Loomis Trench!"

"Loomis Trench?!" Gilda remembered the man with square glasses who had challenged Boris Volkov during the Spy Museum lecture. "Omigod—I think I met that guy at the Spy Museum! He was so weird. He was really uptight, and then he made a big scene."

Balthazar chuckled ruefully. "Yes, that sounds like him. Loomis is the man I've been reporting to at the CIA. He's heading up a secret arm of something the CIA used to call the remote viewing program. They used to train military servicemen to develop psychic skills, but Loomis—in his great wisdom—decided to hire me. But I guess I wasn't psychic enough to perceive the mole working right next to me—Loomis himself!"

"So Loomis Trench is definitely the CIA mole—the guy who's passing along this information?"

"I'm sure of it."

"But—how do you know he's the one who's doing it?"

"I just *know*. I've had too many visions that point in that direction. . . . Yes—on this one, I have to trust my gut. Not that my gut has been particularly trustworthy lately." He shook his head and looked dejected.

"Balthazar, don't be too hard on yourself for not knowing that guy Loomis was a mole. I mean, I've had the same best friend for years, and I never realized until a few days ago that she has a crush on my brother!"

"A very similar situation," said Balthazar, sarcastically.

"Oh, and I also never knew my mom likes dancing and 'the nightlife' until I read her online dating profile. You'd think I'd know my own mother better than that."

Balthazar suddenly tensed as if he were a rabbit sensing the approach of a predator. "We need to go," he whispered. "Someone is coming."

Gilda turned to head back up the steps, but Balthazar took her arm. "No," he whispered. "We have to go this way."

They walked down the path, taking a circuitous route through rows of tombs, then back up the hill.

When they approached the entrance to the cemetery, Balthazar quickly pulled Gilda aside just as a dark-haired woman pushing a stroller entered the cemetery and headed in the direction of the dead-drop location.

Gilda was sure she had seen this same woman leaving the Russian Embassy before. *The perfect cover,* Gilda thought. *You think you're seeing a mother taking her child for an evening stroll when in reality you're witnessing a Russian spy collecting U.S. intelligence. It's all happening right before our eyes, and if you only glance at the surface, you never know what's really going on.*

"What do we do now?" Gilda whispered.

"I don't know about you," said Balthazar, "but I'm hungry. How about discussing a plan over a plate of macaroni and cheese?"

"I guess I'm kind of hungry, too," said Gilda.

"Good. Come on; let's find a taxi. You'll be amazed when you see the place I have in mind."

35

The Mansion on O Street

You'll find this place interesting," said Balthazar, punching in a secret code that gave him access to the Mansion on O Street—a group of interlinked Victorian houses near Dupont Circle. "It's a very unique hotel because it's also an art gallery, a restaurant, and an antiques emporium all mixed up together. It's the perfect place to stay when you're working on something covert because the owner never reveals the names of her guests." Balthazar explained that lots of celebrities stayed at the Mansion when they visited D.C. "I'm no celebrity, but I like to pretend I'm one now and then." He winked at Gilda.

We have so much in common, Gilda thought. *I'm actually standing next to Balthazar Frobenius, the famous psychic. We're working together on a case involving national security!*

They entered a banquet room in which chandeliers dripping with crystal hung from gilded ceilings. Elegant little tables with white linen cloths and roses were set for dinner, but the room was virtually empty except for a couple seated in a corner who spoke in hushed tones. As Gilda took in the details of the large, dim room, she realized the atmosphere was overwhelming because it was at once elegant and so totally zany and cluttered, it was hard to know where to focus her attention.

Everywhere she looked, Gilda's eye rested on something unexpected: amid Victorian lamps and enormous bouquets of silk roses were sculptures and paintings of angels, ridiculous marionettes that hung from the ceiling and walls, and knick-knacks and figurines featuring everything from fat ladies to elves and fairies. Hundreds of paintings and books on every topic imaginable were stacked in precarious towers and stuffed into nooks and crannies.

"Good evening, Mr. Frobenius," said a hostess. "Will you be having dinner with us tonight?"

"Yes, and my colleague Ms. Gilda Joyce will be joining me."

I'm Balthazar's colleague, Gilda thought.

"Sit anywhere you like. As you know, dinner is buffet-style; you just help yourself."

"I have a feeling Gilda might like to take a look around first."

Gilda realized she must have been staring at the room with her mouth open.

"You can go anywhere except the rooms marked private. There are about one hundred rooms, thirty-two secret door-ways, and twenty thousand books. Enjoy your evening."

"Did she say 'thirty-two secret doorways'?" Gilda whis-pered.

"I thought this would be your kind of place," said Balthazar. "For some reason, I find that the whimsical noise from all the clutter in here keeps out some of the negativity and stress from the outside world—at least temporarily. I'm going to sit down and think about things for a minute; why don't you take a look around? Just don't get lost."

Feeling as if she had stepped into one of the magical worlds in a children's book where a secret doorway or magic mirror might lead into another universe, Gilda wandered from room to room, sometimes touching paintings or bookshelves that turned out to be secret doorways leading into yet another room.

"This hotel is disorienting," she scribbled in her reporter's notebook.

It's kind of like walking through a mystery. One clue leads to another, and just when you think you've found a solution, you realize you're really only seeing a small part of the whole picture—or that you're looking at something different than what you thought you were seeing.

There were bathrooms with games of chess set up on crystal tables, secret reading nooks, bedrooms with colorful skies painted on ceilings, a billiards table perched upon gilded dragons, and numerous stairways decorated with stacks of precariously teetering china dishes.

By the time Gilda found her way back down to the first floor, Balthazar was in the banquet room piling a plate with macaroni and cheese, meatballs, and biscuits.

"My appetite got the best of me," he said.

Gilda surveyed the sprawling buffet and was delighted that whimsical, silly foods like licorice sticks, lollipops, and even marshmallow cream were available next to more serious meals like pasta, meatballs, grilled chicken, mashed potatoes, and bean salad. She was also delighted to find books displayed alongside the foods.

She and Balthazar loaded up their plates and then found a secluded table.

"Now," said Balthazar, spreading a napkin on his lap. "I'm sure you have a lot of questions for me."

Gilda hardly knew what to ask first. How did Balthazar develop his psychic skills in the first place—or was he just born that way? How should the two of them catch this CIA mole Loomis Trench? And who, exactly, was the ghost in the Spy Museum?

While Gilda contemplated these questions, Balthazar stared at her with a strange intensity.

"What's the matter?"

"You remind me of someone. My sister, actually."

"Isn't she a lot older than me?"

"She would have been." Balthazar wiped his mouth and Gilda perceived the faintest quiver of emotion in his voice. "Sadly, she passed away when she was much younger than you; she was only eleven years old."

"What happened to her? I mean, if you don't mind my asking?"

"It's complicated. To make a long story short, we both became very ill one winter. I recovered and she didn't. She was truly psychic; she had far more natural talent than I do."

"No way."

"It's true. When we were young, she had remarkably vivid dreams with exact details of things that were going to happen to us the next day. 'You'd better study your spelling words tonight,' she'd say, 'because Mr. King is going to give us a pop quiz tomorrow.' And she was always right. She also had an uncanny ability to sense danger before it happened. She saved my life on at least one occasion."

Balthazar paused as if uncertain whether he wanted to open a floodgate of memories. "Anyway, after my sister died, I changed. I suppose that's when I started to become psychic; it was as if a new channel had opened in my brain."

Gilda listened intently; she literally perched on the edge of her seat, nibbling on a rope of red licorice.

"My sister spoke to me every night in dreams. But now, instead of telling me whether my teacher was going to give a pop quiz, she would tell me about other people. Sometimes I would read an article in the newspaper about a shooting in the neighborhood or a family who perished in an arson fire, and that night my sister would show me *how* it had happened. She would tell me who did it. Sometimes she even showed me where bodies were hidden. After I awoke the next morning, I would try to forget, but I couldn't. I *knew*.

"So I began sending anonymous tips to the police department. Sometimes they would act on them, and usually they would ignore them. It wasn't until many years later that I developed the courage to accept my role as a psychic—to develop my skills so I could use them to help people without being afraid of what I might learn. Of course, as I was reminded today, nobody's perfect. We're always students of the craft." He regarded Gilda pointedly. "But you already know that."

"Know what?" Gilda put down her licorice. "What do you mean?"

"I mean that you've clearly been studying your craft, and now you're actually becoming a psychic."

"I am? You really think so?" Gilda had always believed she had potential as a psychic even though her gifts were not completely natural; she had had to work hard to develop whatever psychic skills she possessed. Hearing this affirmation from Balthazar Frobenius himself was a dream come true.

"Gilda, if not for your work on this case, I might still be in the dark, oblivious to the fact that every reading I ever did for the CIA has been sabotaged. I think you have a unique talent, but more important, the focus, creativity, and spirit to really want to get to the truth. Not too many people have that."

Gilda smiled, wishing she could somehow put the moment in a container, freeze it, and then take it out to relive it the next time someone doubted her ability to solve a mystery. "Balthazar," she ventured, "I know you probably always get asked stuff like this—"

"Don't tell me; you want to know if I'm picking up anything from your father, right?"

Gilda froze. She met his eyes, hoping.

"His name was Nick?"

"Yes!" Gilda felt as if fire were racing through her veins. *He knows Dad's name.*

Balthazar closed his eyes and concentrated. "For some reason, I'm picking up something odd his spirit wants to say to you—something about . . . orange peanuts?"

Gilda felt ridiculous because without warning, she felt tears welling up—tears of surprise and nostalgia. These days, she often found it hard to picture her father's face, but she could vividly imagine the sweet, chalky smell and texture of those orange circus peanuts he used to share with her. For a moment, it was as if her dad were right there at the table. *You aren't alone,* he seemed to be saying. *I'm always here for you.*

Gilda giggled as she wiped her eyes on a napkin. "Of all the things he could say to me right now when I'm sitting here with Balthazar Frobenius—he picks 'orange peanuts'!"

"I admit I have no idea what that means."

"Oh, it was just something silly my father did when I was little. I'd go with him to the hardware store and he'd always buy me these bags of circus peanuts—you know, those really fake-looking orange candies—because I thought they were so funny-looking." The more she thought about those orange peanuts and the memory of her father, the happier she felt. She looked across the room where a vintage poster of President Lincoln was displayed next to a Beatles album cover. "I think Dad would like this place," she added.

"Sounds like he appreciated the silly side of life." Balthazar took the opportunity to steal a Twinkie from Gilda's plate of assorted junk foods.

"That's for sure."

"Now," Balthazar whispered, leaning closer. "While you were looking around the mansion, I came up with a plan—a way we can make sure Loomis Trench makes one more drop of information. Only this time he'll get caught in the act."

TO: GILDA JOYCE

FROM: GILDA JOYCE

RE: !!!!!!!!PSYCHIC INVESTIGATION
BREAKTHROUGH!!!!!!!!!!!!!!!

IDENTITY OF PERSON LEAVING DEAD-DROP NOTES
DISCOVERED--CIA MOLE LOOMIS TRENCH UNCOVERED!!

A man with the highly suspicious-sounding name
"Loomis Trench" has been selling classified information to the Russian government.

OUR PLAN: Balthazar and I need solid proof--some
kind of hard evidence to prove without a doubt
that Loomis is a CIA mole.

Tonight Balthazar will call Loomis Trench and
tell him he wants to meet for an emergency remote
viewing session. Balthazar will say he's picking
up some very interesting information that the
American government needs to know. (In truth,
he'll just be making up something about the
identity and location of some Russian or Middle
Eastern spy.) Then, we're hoping that once Loomis
Trench has this new, juicy "information," he'll
want to pass it along to the Russians right away.

But when Loomis turns up to leave the information, he'll get a big surprise. Ta-da! The CIA and
FBI will be there waiting to catch him!

Balthazar and I will be heroes! I can already imagine the headlines in all the papers:

"ANYONE WOULD HAVE DONE WHAT I DID TO SAVE THE U.S.A.," CLAIMS PSYCHIC SLEUTH GILDA JOYCE

NEW SPY MUSEUM EXHIBIT FEATURES TYPEWRITER, TRADECRAFT ITEMS USED BY RENOWNED PSYCHIC SPY GILDA JOYCE

Caption: typewriter (model), half-eaten peanut butter, banana, and chocolate sandwich (model), Jackie Kennedy-style office wear, and assorted spy gear used by Gilda Joyce in her heroic mission to track down and capture CIA mole Loomis Trench.

SPY MUSEUM HAUNTING:

Tomorrow night I have a rare opportunity to spend the whole night inside the Spy Museum. Chances of spirit activity are strong. Now that I know the identity of the mole who's been leaving notes in Oak Hill Cemetery, I'm hoping to figure out the specific identity of the Spy Museum ghost. Based on the clues that turned up in the museum, my guess is that she wants the truth about Loomis Trench to be known. She wants him to get caught once and for all.

36

Midnight Spy Slumber Party

We kind of want to see a ghost, but now we're kind of scared, too," said Stargirl.

She and Agent Moscow had decided to camp out in the East Berlin exhibit, thinking that they might see more ghost graffiti.

"I don't think this ghost would harm anyone," said Gilda, trying to sound more fearless and confident than she actually felt. "Just call me on my cell phone right away if you see anything unusual."

Throughout the evening, Gilda had kept an eye out for signs of spirit activity in the Spy Museum, but so far nothing had happened.

The boys on Team Crypt all opted to camp out in the exhibit featuring a classic spy car from a James Bond movie. Gilda was surprised and not a little suspicious when they all climbed into their sleeping bags at the very moment the museum lights dimmed.

"We're really tired," said James Bond.

"Yeah, we're totally exhausted," said Baby Boy, scooting into his Spider-Man sleeping bag and feigning loud snoring.

"Good night," said Gilda, making a mental note to check in on them frequently.

After saying good night to her recruits, Gilda crawled into the sleeping bag she had borrowed from April Shepherd. After sensing a strong tickle in her ear near the Spy Museum's model of a 1940s-era movie theater, Gilda had decided this spot had lots of psychic potential, and decided to camp out there on her own. During the day, the theater played a series of short films dating from World War II, including a cartoon that warned people not to blab military information that might be overheard by the spies lurking in ordinary places around town. "Loose lips sink ships!" the cartoons warned.

Now the theater was silent: the dramatic, colorful posters decorating the walls and the moody velvet curtains draping the movie screen looked spooky in the dim glow of Gilda's flashlight.

Gilda was just drifting into sleep when she heard scuttling and rustling sounds that made her think of a sinister little animal—an animal that made choking, gasping, snuffling sounds. She gasped, fumbling for her flashlight. A shadow slipped into the room, moving close to the ground.

Finally locating her flashlight, she pointed it in the direction of the creature. Illuminated in the beam of light was a row of garishly painted faces with dark smudges for eyes, mouths covered in red lipstick, and multicolored hair. One wore an incongruous mustache. "Oooooooo! I am the ghost who lives in the Spy Museum!"

"Nice try," said Gilda, doing her best not to appear as unnerved as she felt. "I knew you had something up your sleeves." She was now fully awake.

"How come you didn't scream?" Baby Boy asked.

"Because I knew it was you guys." The truth was that Gilda had been fooled for the first few seconds.

"Now we're going to sneak up on the girls in the East Berlin exhibit," said Baby Boy.

"No," said Gilda, "you're going to go back to your sleeping bags, or I'll have to call your parents."

"But we aren't tired."

"No buts. Just take off your makeup, wash your faces, and get your butts under the covers."

"I thought you said 'No butts,'" The Comedian joked.

"No puns, either," Gilda retorted.

"Is a pun like a 'bottom burp'?" Baby Boy asked.

"A 'bottom burp'?!" The boys broke into laughter.

"Excuse me, Madame," said The Comedian, speaking in an English accent. "I feel a wee 'bottom burp' coming on." He blew grotesquely loud raspberries and the entire group dissolved into a fit of raucous laughter.

Whoever thinks girls are the only ones who get silly and giggly has never been around a group of boys in the middle of the night, Gilda thought.

"Good night, Case Officer Zelda," said the boys, once they were back in their sleeping bags.

"Good night, boys. No more pranks, okay?"

"Okay."

Back in the movie theater, Gilda sat alone in the dark, watching, listening, and waiting. The museum had grown quiet; it seemed the entire building had gone to sleep.

As Gilda once again drifted into a sound sleep surrounded by posters of spy stories, the velvet curtains at the front of the movie theater opened.

37

Svetlana's Story: A Film

The setting: a small, sparsely furnished apartment with only a bed, a few chairs, a carpeted floor. A young woman whose elfin face has small, sharp features stands by the window, peering into a mirror.

"My name is Svetlana," she says. She opens a tiny perfume bottle and the room fills with the scent of roses and vanilla.

She closes her eyes and applies bright violet eye shadow, then outlines the rims of her eyes with a thin liquid line. Her dark, chalky makeup resembles that of a little girl dressing up for a pretend game.

Svetlana looks at her reflection and tries to smile, revealing one crooked tooth. The tooth is one of the most memorable and noticeable details of her face, but it is a detail she rarely shows.

"I am lucky," Svetlana says as she gets dressed. She wears a jacket with big shoulder pads and a voluminous skirt with a fitted waist, cinched with a vinyl belt. She puts on a pair of bright plastic earrings, then pulls on high-heeled red boots with pointy toes and a fox-fur hat.

"Most of my friends dress very nineteen-seventies even though it is nineteen-eighty-eight. I am more in fashion—because my boyfriend can get clothes from overseas.

"My boyfriend is a KGB officer. He has promised me marriage and a better life. He is also my spymaster.

"See? He gave me this beautiful red star brooch. And you see? It hides a tiny, secret camera." The layers of Svetlana's 1980s clothing conceal the thin cord that connects the camera shutter to a handheld control in the pocket of her full skirt.

Svetlana looks in the mirror, smiles, and squeezes the button in her pocket. The center of the brooch quickly opens to reveal a tiny camera lens, and she snaps her own picture.

Svetlana gasps. For a split second, another image flashes in the mirror—a black-and-white photograph of a dead woman with a gunshot wound on her head and a star brooch around her neck.

"My KGB boyfriend says he knows a man who's posing as a translator of Russian poetry—a man he suspects of being American spy. My boyfriend thinks I can do the job of entrapping this American spy much more easily than he can, so he gives me this job."

"'You go and meet him,' my boyfriend tells me. 'Say you are Moscow University student studying poetry. You go to café, flirt, make him like you. Make him tell you secrets—especially names of others who talk to him. See? A present for you. Spy jewelry.' My boyfriend pins the star brooch to my scarf.

"I don't mind spying for my boyfriend. I'm excited to do something different from waiting in line for cabbage or hanging wet laundry to dry in my apartment. *I am lucky,* I tell myself. With my boyfriend's help, I have my own apartment—my own television and refrigerator.

"But deep down, I don't believe the things I tell myself. I am not happy.

"I go and meet the American spy at a café, and we talk about poetry, especially poems of Anna Akhmatova, whose work he has translated. 'You look a little like Akhmatova,' the American tells me. I cannot help it; I truly like this man—the American spy I am supposed to trap. For the first time in ages, I show my crooked tooth when I smile.

"In fact, I like this man so much, I tell him who I really am—girlfriend of a KGB officer. I even remove my brooch and show him the hidden camera.

"The American spy is very pleased. 'You can help me,' he says. 'You can work for CIA.' He gives me fake CIA documents to photograph. These I take back to my boyfriend to throw him off-track—to make him think I am spying on the American. Meanwhile, the American tells me to visit my boyfriend's office and photograph documents from KGB files—lists of people, sketches of plans. Now I spy on my boyfriend and the KGB instead of the American.

"Some days I bring bread and sausage for my boyfriend's lunch, and while he eats, I take secret photographs of everything I see. I give these to the American man, who is very happy with me.

"My biggest secret: I fall in love with the American. I also have something more dangerous—hope that my life will finally change. 'I will help you leave soon,' the American tells me, 'but not yet.' He gives me an emergency signal to use, just in case we are discovered. 'If something goes wrong, leave this book of poetry in the window of the café—our usual meeting place,' he says. 'When I see the book I will know not to meet you, and then you will escape with me that night.'

"One evening, my boyfriend suspects my betrayal. He says nothing, but I see him watch me. Instead of going home to his wife, he stays at my apartment. He is a man trained to find secrets, and I believe that he can see through me.

"At the end, I will learn that he only knew my secret because of a man very far away—a man in Washington, D.C., who is a traitor against his own country.

"'I have a gift for you,' my boyfriend tells me. It looks like a gold tube of lipstick. 'See? It's a gun. Single shot.' He points this lipstick pistol at my head. 'Made special for you,' he says.

"'I don't understand,' I tell him.

"'Time for your first wet job.'

"'You want me to kill the American?'

"'He is dangerous and useless.' I sense my boyfriend is testing me. Will I kill the American to save myself? Will I be killed no matter what I do?

"'I can't,' I say. 'I'm not a murderer.'

"'Then find the best use for this.' And in his eyes I see a wolf who watches me with amusement before he kills. He wants me to suffer. He places this gun in my hand, and all I can think is how cold and heavy it feels.

"I remember the emergency signal: I have to leave the book of Anna Akhmatova's poems in the café window. If I can give the signal in time, I might escape. There might be time before my boyfriend's KGB colleagues get to the American—before they get to both of us.

"I walk quickly, but behind me, a black sedan approaches like a crocodile drifting through murky water. 'Get inside,' a KGB officer says, rolling down his window.

"I try to point the lipstick pistol at him, but he knocks it from my grip before I can shoot. He pushes me into the car.

"In the upstairs window of our apartment, I see my boyfriend closing the curtains. I know he will go home to his wife now—or maybe to a restaurant to drink vodka with another girlfriend. For him the show is over.

"They drive me to a secluded spot near the Moscow River, but before I take my last breath, I want to know something.

"'How did he know?' I ask these men. 'Did he have me followed?' I didn't want to learn that the American was someone my boyfriend hired to set me up. I want to know that the happiness I had in those last meetings was real.

"'The name of the man who betrayed you will mean nothing to you,' says the first man.

"'And what does it matter now?' says the second.

"Then they laugh as if this is the best joke they ever heard.

"'There is no harm in telling me who did this,' I say. But I also think how strange it is that I want to know the truth before I die—even when I will not be able to tell a single person. *Where will this truth go after I am dead?* I wonder. *What happens to a truth only a dead woman knows?*

"The first man tells me to get out of the car. He points the lipstick gun at me and I think how silly the gun looks with its tip painted red to resemble lipstick. *Foolish*, I think. *All of this is foolish*.

"'You want to know who betrayed you? It was a CIA mole—a man you have never seen in your life. His name is Loomis Trench. They call him *'the poet.'*

"And in my very last moment, I see something clearly—that this truth matters, and that I will somehow tell this truth after my life has ended."

Gilda awoke to find herself staring at the movie screen. As if emerging from a trance, she felt completely disoriented and couldn't account for the past few minutes.

That was so weird, she thought. *Was I awake or asleep just now? Was there really a movie playing in this theater, or was that all in my head?*

Gilda rummaged through her bag and pulled out her notebook to write an investigation note:

IDENTITY OF GHOST DISCOVERED THROUGH STRANGE
PSYCHIC "MOVIE"!
NAME: Svetlana.
Her boyfriend was a KGB officer, and she was killed by the
KGB. The CIA mole Loomis Trench revealed her identity to
the Soviets back in the 1980s.

WHAT SHE WANTS: Justice. I think she wants everyone to
know what really happened to her.

At the discovery of groundbreaking evidence of a new psychic contact, Gilda usually felt elated, but Svetlana's story left her feeling sad. The brightly colored posters of spy movies surrounding her in the theater now looked somber and lonely, darkened by shadows.

So many aspects of the spying life seem fun from a distance: pretending to be someone else, sneaking around, playing with gadgets and even secret weapons. But a story like Svetlana's makes me see a dark side: innocent people can get caught in the middle of "spy games."

Is it possible to be a spy who stays focused on exposing the truth rather than just telling lies and betraying people?

I guess that's something I'll have to think about if I decide to pursue the spying life. The CIA <u>should</u> be offering me a job when this is all over, but my guess is that they won't like the idea of a teenage girl discovering the mole they've failed to catch on their own. They'll want to keep that little detail quiet!

Still, if Balthazar and I can expose Loomis Trench and get him out of the CIA, that will at least be one dishonest spy out of the picture!

Gilda nearly jumped out of her skin at the sound of her cell phone ringing. She read a text message from Balthazar:

IT HAPPENS TOMORROW

Gilda immediately knew what he meant: he expected Loomis to make a last dead drop the next day.

38

Breakfast of Spies

On the morning after the Midnight Spy Slumber Party, the counselors looked bleary-eyed as they sipped their coffee. In contrast, their young recruits seemed energized by a night of spy games, pranks, and very little sleep. A few kids still wore the remnants of spy disguises from the previous evening's activities—games including leaving practice "dead drops" around the Spy Museum. Despite their silly and unkempt appearance (The Comedian, for example, seemed oblivious to the fake mustache stuck to his cheek, and Baby Boy wore Spider-Man pajamas with feet), Gilda noticed that the kids in her group seemed ever so slightly older and more experienced after their week at Spy Camp.

Feeling suddenly sentimental about saying good-bye to her team, Gilda stuck her arm up in the air like a playground supervisor to get the attention of her recruits. "Team Crypt! Last meeting over here!" She smiled as her recruits dutifully gathered around her.

"As you know, this is our last meeting together," she said. "When you first came here, you knew nothing; you were like mere toddlers who didn't know the difference between a Halloween costume and a real disguise."

"That's going a little far," said Stargirl.

"You didn't know the most basic life skills of a spy—how to take secret pictures or make your own lie detector or how to conduct surveillance on a building."

"I actually knew a lot of stuff about spying," countered The Misanthrope.

"You didn't know the difference between the CIA and the FBI, the KGB and the NBA. You thought the proper use of a wig was for playing indoor baseball."

"Wigball *rules*," said The Comedian.

"But now you leave here as true spies. And you also leave with the knowledge that you contributed to something important."

"What's that, Case Officer Zelda?"

Gilda gathered her recruits into a huddle. "This is top secret," she whispered, "but there's something important I want you all to know: you are the only team here who helped investigate not only a haunting in the museum, but also a current investigation of a real CIA mole."

"Really? Who is it?"

"Shh! Just know that when you finally hear about this story on the news, you'll know that you were right here in the middle of the action. And a special congratulations goes to Agent Moscow: if it hadn't been for her knowledge of a foreign language, we might not have been able to crack this case at all."

Team Crypt clapped for Agent Moscow, whose face turned pink.

"Now—let's do our Team Crypt chant one last time."

"We don't have a Team Crypt chant," said Stargirl.

"Then it's high time we made one up:

> *Who spies the best?*
> *Teeeeeeam Crypt!*
> *Who hides the best?*
> *Teeeeeam Crypt!*
> *The best decoders and dead-drop unloaders!*
> *TEEEEEEEEEEEEAM CRYPT!*

"Wait! I almost forgot something important, Team Crypt," said Gilda, regrouping her team as they began to walk away. "You won't have me around as your case officer to guide you anymore."

Gilda's recruits glanced around the room, showing signs of impatience with the good-bye speech.

"Anyway, I want you to promise me that you'll continue to use your spying skills for fun and for the cause of justice— never for evil."

The kids rolled their eyes but Baby Boy nodded very solemnly. "We promise, Case Officer Zelda!"

"To help you keep that promise, I'm sending you home with a letter to each of your parents, commending you for your performance here at Spy Camp and alerting them to some of the new skills you now have."

"You're tipping off our parents?! No fair!"

"I'm just trying to keep a level playing field," said Gilda. "If your parents don't have some awareness of your new skills, they might not know what hit them when you start conducting surveillance in your own home."

Gilda handed her recruits copies of the memo she had typed for their parents.

Dear Parents:

The child you are accepting back into your home may be a little different from the child you dropped off the first day at Spy Camp. "Different how," you ask?

On the positive side, your child may seem brighter--more intelligent, happy, and self-confident. While this is cause for celebration, you may also notice your child acting sneaky, elusive, and displaying a penchant for assembling odd gadgets with obscure purposes. In short, you may feel that your innocent little one is now "up to something."

In the interest of full disclosure, I am providing you with a checklist.

<u>YOUR CHILD HAS THE FOLLOWING SPY SKILLS:</u>

* Lie detection
* Homemade alarm construction skills
* Surveillance skills and surveillance evasion skills
* Disguise creation
* Decoding skills
* Knowledge of spy gadgets
* Ability to live undercover

The recruits fell silent for a moment as they read the list. Gilda noticed that Agent Moscow simply folded up the letter and stuck it in her pocket. *I guess her parents aren't going to see this note since she's in boarding school here all alone, even in the summer,* Gilda thought. She made a mental note to write a letter of recommendation for Agent Moscow to give to Jasper Clarke.

Gilda watched as her recruits walked away. Baby Boy practically jumped into his mother's arms as if he hadn't seen her in a month. The Misanthrope managed a tiny smile but cringed slightly as his mother flashed him an anxiety-laden megawatt smile.

At least he didn't act like he was about to pull out a weapon this time, Gilda thought, watching him leave.

"Bye, Hansen!" James Bond and The Comedian waved good-bye to The Misanthrope, who smiled and waved back.

"Are those your friends?" The Misanthrope's mom asked.

"Yeah," he replied, handing his mom Gilda's memo nonchalantly. "We had the best team."

Gilda saw The Misanthrope's mother blanch as she read the memo about her son's new spy skills.

Gilda glanced at her watch, wondering what might be happening in Oak Hill Cemetery. Would Loomis Trench make his move? Would he be arrested, now that Balthazar had alerted his contacts within the CIA and FBI?

39

The Last Dead Drop

Wearing his dark suit and bow tie in the hot sun, Loomis Trench carried a bouquet of daisies in one hand and a briefcase in the other. He walked quickly toward his familiar dead-drop location in Oak Hill Cemetery. His briefcase contained a classified report from a remote viewing session with Balthazar Frobenius completed just the day before.

Encoded within text from the poem "Song of the Last Meeting" by Anna Akhmatova, Loomis concealed his message:

> Dear Friends,
>
> I think you will find that the enclosed information is worth double our usual price.
>
> I will be out of contact now because I have a gut feeling that someone in the agency may be investigating me.
>
> As soon as I receive your payment, I will be taking a long vacation during the next few weeks.
>
> As always, The Poet

Loomis carefully placed the classified documents and his note inside the large, fake stone, replaced the concealment device in its usual spot along the path, and brushed the dust from his hands. He pulled a white handkerchief from his jacket pocket and wiped the sweat from his brow.

He glanced around, thinking for a moment that he heard a faint rustling sound in the surrounding trees. *Probably a rabbit or a deer*, he thought.

As he turned toward the tomb where Lincoln's son had once been buried, he caught his breath. In the partial shade of the mausoleum, a tall man sat in a chair. The man held his head in his hands, as if immobilized by some overwhelming grief. Then Loomis saw that the man wore unusual, old-fashioned clothes: high-waisted trousers with suspenders and boots. As Loomis moved closer, mesmerized, he saw that sunlight streamed through the man's translucent body.

Loomis froze. He had an urge to explain how he had gotten to this point, but he found he could not speak. As the bouquet he held in his hand fell to the ground, FBI agents popped out from the cover of surrounding trees and bushes to arrest him.

As they led Loomis from the cemetery in handcuffs, he glanced back at the tomb, but Lincoln's ghost had disappeared.

40

The Spy Party

Hey, Wendeeeeeeeee!

It's about 1:00 A.M., but I just had to write to tell you about this amazing spy party that Caitlin and I threw at our apartment!

Aren't you proud of me? I'm dying to call you, but I'm restraining myself for once! I had the phone in my hand, but instead of pushing the buttons and waking you up, I sat down to write a detailed letter. (There's no need to thank me.)

Just WRITE BACK IMMEDIATELY!!

For all I know, maybe you're still awake. Maybe you and my brother are out on a date, gazing into each other's eyes and whispering sweet nothings about obscure math equations and space robots. Pardon me while I quietly say:

"Eeew."

Anyway, about the spy party we threw to celebrate the fact that I helped solve a mystery of national significance. You heard me right—NATIONAL significance. The CIA and FBI are doing

their best to keep their own investigation under wraps, but it's only a matter of time before
you hear about this on the news. When the story
breaks, you'll know that I had something to do
with it!

When I'm back home I promise I'll give you all
the details. (WARNING: If you disclose classified
information to Stephen, I can't be held responsible for the consequences.)

Remember my roommate Caitlin? Did I tell you
how she wears nothing but black pantsuits or
workout clothes every day? Well, this morning we
went to a vintage clothing store in the city, and
we both found the most amazing spy minidresses!
You would love them. In fact, Caitlin liked
the concept so much, she also bought a clip-on
hairpiece and false eyelashes at the drugstore to
go with her dress. When we got home, I created
1960s spy-chic hairstyles for the two of us—
buns on top of our heads and the rest of our hair
curled with hot rollers. Then I showed Caitlin
how to wear eyeliner and false eyelashes to create
these mysterious-looking cat eyes. (Full disclosure:
Caitlin was a total baby about the eye makeup. She
said, "It looks like a couple little tarantulas
are trying to crawl out of my eyes.") She doesn't
yet have our experience with makeup and disguises:
we know that wearing little eyelash spiders feels
normal if you just give it time, right?

Next, Caitlin made nonalcoholic "mocktails" in pink plastic martini glasses for the party. I told her that she didn't have to make mocktails on my account: underage sleuths like me are used to being around inebriated intelligence officers who drown their sorrows in whiskey.

"No way," said Caitlin. "I'm your mom for the summer, and I insist we keep it to mocktails."

Lately Caitlin's been on this "I'm your mom for the summer" kick. If she is my mom, I'm one heck of a latchkey child, since she's hardly ever here.

But as I was saying, we made the drinks with ice cream, sherbet, soda, coconut flakes, pink food coloring, and maraschino cherries, and they were FABULOUS! I'll make you one when I get home. (But don't ask me to make one for Stephen. He'll just say it looks "too pink," and then it won't be fun anymore.)

PARTY ATTENDEES:

I invited everyone I work with at the Spy Museum and Caitlin invited all her friends and coworkers (about half of Washington, D.C., right there) along with an elevator full of people who live in our building.

Did I ever tell you about Roger, the guy who designs the exhibits and who first saw the Spy Museum ghost? Well, he brought us a compilation of spy music from movies, and even his own original

synthesizer composition called "Spy-Ghost Rock."
His wife came with him, and if you ask me, she
seemed a little annoyed at all the time Roger had
spent creating music for a museum intern's party.
She came to the party wearing a tiny sleeping
baby in a contraption strapped to her stomach.
You'd think a spy party would be too noisy for a
sleeping baby, but Roger said, "This is the first
nap he's taken all day. He likes it here." (To
be honest, I couldn't understand how such a tiny,
helpless infant could cause two grown people to
look so totally haggard and exhausted.)

A PROMISING MATCH OR AN IMPENDING DISASTER?

At one point during the party, I spotted Caitlin
standing in the corner talking to Matthew Morrow
(Spy Museum historian), who turned up wearing
spandex bike shorts and a huge T-shirt that said
BARENAKED LADIES. It's no wonder he doesn't get
invited to the more sophisticated Washington, D.C.,
soirees if that's his idea of party wear.

Get this: Caitlin and Matthew got in a huge argument about some obscure historical fact, and
after a few minutes, Caitlin flounced into the
kitchen, came up to me and whispered, "I really
like that guy you work with at the museum! I think
he might ask me out."

I glanced over at Matthew and if you ask me, he
looked more like someone who had just been hit by

a bulldozer than someone who was thinking about asking Caitlin on a date. Either Caitlin was totally deluded or Matthew had an odd way of demonstrating his interest in a girl. "I'll go see what I can find out," I said.

"Be subtle," said Caitlin.

"I'll be so subtle, he'll hardly know what I'm talking about." I moseyed over to Matthew, who was still standing by himself in the corner.

"Hi, Gilda."

"So what do you think of my roommate?" I hoped Caitlin couldn't hear my point-blank question.

"Your roommate?"

"You know. The girl you were just talking to. She's pretty cute, huh?"

Matthew blushed, which made me think that Caitlin might be right after all. "She's completely wrong about J. Edgar Hoover, that's for sure," he said.

"Who's J. Edgar Hoover?"

Matthew looked at me with contempt. "You've been working at the Spy Museum all this time and you don't even know who J. Edgar Hoover is?"

He sounded really familiar, but I wasn't sure.

Matthew sighed. "He was a very formative director of the FBI for no less than forty-eight years. He was pretty much responsible for giving the FBI an iconic status in American culture. Anyway, your roommate insists he actually went to work at the

FBI wearing women's clothing, and that's totally absurd."

"He worked at the FBI wearing women's clothing?"

"Of course not! The idea of him being a cross-dresser was a rumor started by the KGB. A very successful propaganda rumor, I might add."

"Oh."

"Try telling that to your roommate."

"Well, Caitlin just told me that she thinks you're cute and really smart."

Matthew was dumbstruck. "She did?" Suddenly he didn't care so much about J. Edgar Hoover's panty hose. His face lit up.

"Oh, yeah. She said you're the first guy she's ever met who didn't start crying during an argument." By now, I was feeling like a real CIA case officer, using somewhat manipulative tactics, "relationship building" from behind the scenes.

Out of the corner of my eye, I noticed my least favorite Spy Museum coworker, Janet, glaring at Caitlin from across the room as she pretended to examine a collection of CDs and books. (I'd better warn Caitlin that Janet may be out to get her soon.)

By the time the party ended, Caitlin and Matthew were making plans to train for a marathon together. If they end up running around the city arguing about J. Edgar Hoover's strapless gowns

and negligees, I guess it's partly my fault. Only
time will tell if my intervention falls into the
category of a helpful matchmaking strategy or ill-
advised CIA interference!

SPECIAL GUEST OF HONOR:
Balthazar Frobenius came to my spy party. You
heard right: BALTHAZAR FROBENIUS CAME TO MY PARTY.
A week ago, if you had told me I'd be able to
write that sentence, I'd never have believed it.

He turned up wearing a flowered shirt and flip-
flops, and everyone assumed he was just some guy
who lives in the building--maybe a computer pro-
grammer or a journalist. Nobody suspected that
here in the middle of our party was one of the
great psychics of our time.

Balthazar prefers it that way: in fact, when
he's at parties he tells people that he's a travel
writer. "Otherwise, I end up in the corner doing psychic readings and someone inevitably gets
mad when I tell them something they don't want to
hear."

ANOTHER SURPRISE OF THE EVENING: BALTHAZAR ENJOYED
TALKING TO JANET!
Go figure! Actually, I was relieved when Balthazar
went over to Janet and started talking to her
about ghosts in D.C., because I was worried that

she was going to attack someone if she didn't get
her mind off Matthew Morrow.

As it turns out, Janet and Balthazar are going
on a "ghost walk" through the nation's capital
tomorrow. I guess Janet can't be all bad if
Balthazar thinks she's okay, but she's still my
least favorite coworker.

NEWS ALERT:
I couldn't believe it. Standing right there in
the middle of our party was that spooky, grannyish
lady who has awakened me several times with the
lights going on and off in her apartment! What in
the world is she doing here? I wondered. "Take a
look at who turned up at our party," I said, grabbing Caitlin's arm.

Caitlin peeked into the crowd while mixing
mocktails in the blender. "Oh, yeah; I invited
her. She was standing on the elevator when I
told some other people about it. Believe me, I've
learned the hard way that you have to invite the
old ladies. Otherwise they hear the music and call
to complain when what they really want is just to
be invited."

Okay, I admit I never found evidence linking
Flashing Lights Lady to either the museum haunting
or the dead drop. Still, I couldn't help it; there
was just something freaky about her. "I still

think she's up to something weird in her apartment," I said.

"No better time than the present to find out,"
said Caitlin.

Caitlin walked over to "Lady Flash," handed her
a pink mocktail with a big maraschino cherry on
top, and introduced herself. I half expected Lady
Flash to do something bizarre, but the pink mocktail seemed to normalize her and within a couple
minutes, she and Caitlin were sitting on the couch
chatting like old friends.

"Okay--here's the deal," said Caitlin, returning
to the kitchen a few minutes later. "Her name is
Catherine. She seems to be independently wealthy
because she inherited a fortune from her parents.
They're dead, of course, and now she manages their
estate. She also has a part-time job in some government agency just to keep busy."

I had to admit it all sounded more normal than
I expected. I mean, the fact of her being a rich
old lady was a little surprising considering
the drab way she dresses, but it wasn't exactly
shocking. "But what about the flashing lights?" I
guessed there was no way Caitlin could find out
about that in less than fifteen minutes.

"I asked her about that, too, and she said
she's really sorry if it keeps you awake. She
told me she has this condition where she has a
compulsion to do things like turn off the lights

exactly seventy-two times before she goes to bed. And get this: if she doesn't do it exactly the right way or if she loses track, she has to start all over again; otherwise she can't sleep at all. She said she worries a lot about things happening here in the city, and I guess turning her lights off and on makes her feel safer or like she's controlling something, even though it makes no sense. I think that's why she acts so unfriendly --like she's always afraid of being attacked or something. Anyway, she said she's working on it, but in the meantime she'll try to remember to close her curtains. She's actually not quite as weird as we thought. I mean, her breath smells like old chickpeas, but after you get to know her, she's fairly nice. Satisfied?"

"I guess." Well, I felt kind of bad for being so suspicious after hearing this. After all, I had experienced firsthand how easy it is to be fearful in a city filled with intrigue and secrets. Who could really blame an old lady for turning her lights off and on in the middle of the night?

NOTE TO SELF--ADD THE FOLLOWING ITEM TO THE "MOSCOW RULES" FOR SPIES:

You learn a lot by peeking into people's windows. Sometimes you learn even more when you invite them to a big party and serve pink mocktails.

Entrenched in Lies:
The Revelation of CIA Mole Loomis Trench

By Matthew Morrow, Spy Museum historian

With his white shirt, briefcase, and careworn expression, Loomis Trench looked like any other middle-aged government employee walking down the street after work. He had a government job with a security clearance, a nice house in a nice neighborhood, a pretty wife, and two grown children attending reputable colleges. Only one detail of his appearance was slightly unusual: he wore a bow tie with his suit instead of a necktie. Loomis liked the notion that wearing bow ties would lead his colleagues to conclude that he adhered to quaint, formal traditions whereas the truth was that he broke the rules as often as possible.

If you observed him very closely (something his coworkers rarely did), you might notice a few tiny clues that he lived a lie: his eyes looked wary behind his rectangular, rimless glasses, and he stared and held his arms rigidly at his sides when he spoke to people, almost as if he wanted to avoid betraying himself with sudden gestures.

Later, when it was all over, his wife would remember odd details: the way he bragged about his children when other adults were around, but then ignored them entirely whenever they had a problem or failed at some pursuit; his delight in knowing obscure facts that nobody else in the office knew (and his willingness to argue for hours if contradicted); his penchant for reading everything he could find about Abraham Lincoln. "Lincoln was actually very misunderstood and unpopular during his own time," he would often repeat, as if striving to link his own existence with that of a great president.

Still, on the outside, he looked and acted pretty much like everyone else. Nobody suspected that on the inside, he was actually a criminal and a traitor.

During the 1980s, Loomis was a young reports officer working a CIA desk job when he became what the Soviets called a "walk-in"—a man or woman who literally walks into the Russian Embassy in Washington, D.C., with an offer to sell classified information. Trench's motivation was primarily financial: he needed to keep up with his friends by purchasing a big house in a nice neighborhood and a private-school education for his two young children. He had watched younger colleagues receive promotions and raises that eluded him. As his resentment grew, a solution formed in his mind: he would simply sell classified CIA information to the Soviet Union. As long as he ignored the fact that people could actually get killed as a result of his actions, selling American intelligence simply seemed like an easy way to leverage his opportunities to get ahead financially. *No risk, no reward*, he told himself.

"Besides," he wrote in a journal entry turned over to investigators, "if I can get away with it, it *proves* that I'm smarter than they are. If they had promoted me, I wouldn't be doing this. The agency deserves whatever happens."

Gradually, Loomis realized that it was not so much the money, but the *risk itself* that attracted him—the excitement of keeping a very dangerous secret from everyone in his life. When a feeling of malaise descended as he waited in line at Starbucks or sat in his office under fluorescent lights, he could instantly inject a rush of adrenaline into his workday by printing classified information, saving it in a secret pocket of his briefcase, and taking it with him when he left work.

Among his colleagues, Loomis Trench was regarded as a capable but argumentative man who was prone to complaining about coworkers and supervisors. "Loomis always had to be right," one of his colleagues commented. "If you disagreed with him, the friendship was basically over." Still, none of Trench's coworkers viewed him as the type of person who would actually smuggle secrets from the CIA and sell them to a foreign government.

Secretly, Trench knew he was very different from the person his colleagues knew at work. For one thing, none of them guessed at the deep loneliness that kept him looking forward to reading the letters that accompanied thousands of dollars in payment from his secret Russian contacts. "Sometimes I think it's really these notes more than the money that keep me going," he wrote. His journals depict the faceless KGB officers with whom he communicated through dead drops as "friends"— pen pals who appreciated him in a way none of his friends, acquaintances, or even family ever could. For Loomis, it was an ideal friendship—a friendship free of conflict, competition, and demands. His Soviet contacts were now his "true friends" and his coworkers at the CIA were the enemies who might discover his secret.

Loomis's feelings of alienation from the CIA increased

toward the end of the Cold War, when a young American case officer named Pete Biebow, who was undercover as a translator and academic, began to receive enthusiastic praise from Loomis's colleagues in the agency. Based in Moscow and occasionally joking with colleagues that he was independently running his own CIA operation code-named "project Romeo"—a reference to his penchant for accessing information by seducing Soviet women affiliated with the KGB—Biebow managed to cultivate a special relationship with the young, lonely girlfriend of a senior KGB officer—a woman named Svetlana (CIA code name "The Girlfriend"). Secretly in love with the American spy who listened to her, who gave her money, and who tempted her with the possibility of a visa to America and a new life, Svetlana disclosed essentially everything she could find out through her KGB boyfriend about the inner workings and intentions of the Soviet government, often using surveillance equipment obtained from her boyfriend to get photographs of secret documents. She became one of the best assets the CIA had.

Jealous of the CIA's praise for Biebow and deeply resentful of his amorous adventures, Loomis blew his colleague's cover to his Soviet contacts:

Dear Friends,
The information I am about to disclose is simple but incredibly valuable to you. I think you will see it is well worth the price we agreed upon.
Here it is:

A CIA case officer named Pete Biebow, who operates under the assumed name "David Brown" is currently in Moscow posing as an academic —a translator of Russian literature. He meets regularly with a woman named Svetlana—the girlfriend of one of your KGB colleagues. He even jokes that he's running a CIA project code-named Romeo.

Svetlana photographs KGB internal documents, including government organizational charts and other secret documents, which she gives to "Mr. Brown." I'm sure you will have no trouble finding this pair at cafés near the university in order to validate this information.

I can assure you that Mr. Brown (Pete Biebow) is a spy and an enemy of the Soviet Union.

Yours,
THE POET

As a direct result of Trench's note, Pete Biebow endured harsh interrogation by the KGB, after which he was expelled from the U.S.S.R. By now, Biebow may well have suspected the workings of a mole within the CIA, but upon his return to the relative safety of the United States, the intelligence officer met with a decidedly ironic death. Struck by a Metro bus while crossing a street near Dupont Circle, Biebow was fatally injured. Whatever suspicions he harbored were silenced, and for the time being, Trench's secret was safe.

Svetlana was found dead with a very unusual gun in her hand—a gold-plated "lipstick pistol" that she acquired from the KGB. Her death was reported in Moscow as a suicide, but the CIA speculated that she was more likely murdered by the KGB.

With the fall of the Soviet Union in 1991, Trench stopped selling secrets—at least for the time being. For one thing, the KGB was being absorbed into the new Russian government, and for another, Loomis had less need for excitement ever since he had been promoted to working with an exciting project in the CIA called Project STARGATE—a top-secret program to develop psychic spying techniques.

Colleagues speculate that Trench hoped to develop psychic skills for his own personal benefit, thinking that this would be a huge source of power. "He would have loved to perceive exactly what others were thinking before they spoke and to know if anyone had learned about his secret criminal activity," speculated Jasper Clarke, a retired CIA intelligence officer who previously worked with Loomis Trench.

But Trench's attempts to develop his own psychic skills failed miserably. As a result, he found himself clashing with the program's emphasis on routine, protocol, and the idea that "anybody can learn the technique" with the right basic aptitude and training and through diligent practice.

Relegated to the role of supervising and recording the ob-servations of other "remote viewers," Trench argued that the CIA needed to get some "real" psychics into the program, such as renowned psychic Balthazar Frobenius. "There are people that I believe have special genetic mutations that allow them to perceive information differently," he wrote in a memo to his supervisors. "If we study people such as Balthazar Frobenius, who has assisted in solving many state and federal crimes nationwide, we may eventually be able to develop a top secret military psychic pill or injection that would enable more ordinary intelligence officers to acquire the brain capability for psychic knowledge."

From Trench's perspective, the fact that the program was eventually exposed and even publicly ridiculed was a direct result of the failure of the CIA to take his advice and bring Balthazar Frobenius on board sooner. The official program folded, but Trench argued that he should be allowed to continue his work on psychic spying in secret.

Eventually, Trench received some limited funding to hire a handful of psychics, and he wasted no time in bringing Balthazar Frobenius on board. But it was clear that nobody who had aspirations for career growth in the CIA wanted to be connected with the program. The findings Trench put forward in memos identifying specific overseas targets were viewed with the utmost skepticism, regardless of their accuracy.

Infuriated and humiliated once again, Trench found himself strolling past the Russian Embassy on Wisconsin Avenue more frequently. His wife later remembered how he had compared America to a former friend who had betrayed and humiliated him, and who therefore deserved "some kind of payback." His journals describe feelings of nostalgia when he walked past his old signal sites—as if he were walking down memory lane, revisiting the favorite haunts of his youth. So far, he had gotten away with his activities as a CIA mole, but he couldn't resist a compulsion to sell secrets once again.

One day, a Russian diplomat approached Trench at a local park while he watched his teenage children playing soccer.

"I know who you are," she told him. She handed him a business card. The message was clear: either resume sending us some information or be prepared to have your past activities exposed. Be prepared to go to jail.

"But you don't understand," Trench protested. "The program I'm involved in now is different."

"What program?" The woman handed Trench a paperback book entitled *Surviving the Teen Years: A Parent's Guide*. He opened the cover and saw that the inner pages had been cut out, creating a little hole that contained money—a thick stack of hundred-dollar bills. "We are interested to know whatever you work on." Her smile was warm. She touched his hand, pressing the book into his palm.

"Something about her smile made me take the money," Trench wrote. "I miss feeling like someone believes I know something of value."

Trench agreed to leave copies of "remote viewing" reports in a secret location in Oak Hill Cemetery. "The Cold War may be over," Trench wrote, "but they're still just as eager to pay for my information." He made a point of choosing a location near a tomb where Abraham Lincoln's son was buried during the nineteenth century.

On a hot July afternoon, Trench parked his car illegally on Wisconsin Avenue, slung his suit jacket over his shoulder to reveal armpit sweat stains and a body that was somewhat pear-shaped due to lack of exercise, then headed toward his signal site—the Alley of the Russian Poets next to Guy Mason Park.

He had chosen the Alley of the Russian Poets for the simple reason that it was convenient—a short walk for his secret contacts at the Russian Embassy. His handlers could easily incorporate checking for his dead-drop signals as part of a casual outing—a stroll with a baby or a short walk on the way to a nearby restaurant.

An added benefit of this signal site was the flattery he received from his Russian contacts for his totally unintended tribute to Russian literature:

Your literary genius and sensitivity continues to impress us! So few Americans appreciate or even know anything about the Russian poets. But we have known for many years that you—the one we think of as THE POET—are different.

First, you introduce us to the lesser-known words of the eloquent Abraham Lincoln. Who but you would find a way to make a spy communication beautiful and educational as well as cryptic?

You continue to live up to your code name—THE POET.

We eagerly await hearing from you again.

Often, Trench's messages were encoded within poems or historical letters. The codes were childishly simple, but the literary references were slightly obscure—designed to impress his handlers. The Russian spies had been quick to notice how a few words of praise seemed to double the amount of valuable classified information Loomis provided, so they made sure they piled on the accolades in every correspondence. This flattery was very effective because Trench liked to think of himself as a literary person—someone who might one day write the Great American Novel during his retirement.

Little did Trench know that the letter encoded within an Anna Akhmatova poem would be his last communication with his Russian contacts. He apparently had some inkling that he was "being investigated," but he misjudged the urgency of the situation.

The CIA had received a tip from two undisclosed sources leading them directly to Oak Hill Cemetery, where Trench made his last information drop and was caught in the act. The authorities were there to meet him.

"We can't disclose the names of the individuals who led us to Oak Hill Cemetery," commented a CIA press agent, "but we have a *couple people outside the agency* to thank for helping us wrap up the case."

Gilda smiled as she read the article. When she reached the last paragraph she crossed out the words "a couple people outside the agency" and penciled in "GILDA JOYCE AND BALTHA-ZAR FROBENIUS!"

She clipped the article and taped it into her "Summer in D.C." scrapbook—a book that also contained several pictures of her and Caitlin wearing graphic-print minidresses, grinning broadly, and holding pink mocktails. Gilda looked forward to posting the photos in her school locker in the fall. She chuckled as she turned to a picture of the kids on her spy team. The Comedian, The Misanthrope, Agent Moscow, Baby Boy, James Bond, and Stargirl: all were in disguise, smiling into the camera with their agent files and fake passports in hand.

Also taped into Gilda's scrapbook were Polaroid photos of

Loomis Trench's dead-drop messages and the ghostly message that had appeared on the Spy Museum wall. Gilda knew that Loomis's original, handwritten messages were now preserved in plastic evidence bags at the CIA. Interestingly, the agency had rejected the opportunity to keep the photographs Gilda had taken as part of her own investigation.

"Aren't these relevant to the history of the case?" Gilda had asked the CIA intelligence officer who had questioned her about her involvement in the discovery of a mole.

"Sure," said the CIA officer, eyeing the photographs warily. "But just between you and me and the lamppost, it's kind of embarrassing to the agency when a teenage girl discovers a mole inside the CIA. It's not exactly the kind of public attention we want right now. And—I'm sorry to have to ask this, but we'd really appreciate it if you'd keep your involvement quiet."

"What's so embarrassing about help from a teenage girl?" Gilda persisted, taking issue with the derisive reference to "a teenage girl"—the implication that it was ridiculous to think that she might have something serious to offer.

"Look—it's just something we need to keep under wraps for now."

"I see." Gilda couldn't help feeling annoyed. While fantasies of newspaper headlines and television interviews celebrating her as a heroine might have been overblown, it still would have been nice to have some public recognition.

"Don't be too disappointed," said the CIA officer. "Rest assured, your talent and spy potential have been noted by people in the agency. Check back with us after college if you're interested, okay?"

"Sure," said Gilda, doing her best to hide her disappointment. "Unless you come to me for more help before then."

The CIA officer regarded her with an inscrutable expression. "Thanks," he said. "We'll keep the door open."

For the moment, Gilda was glad to be far away from spy games. She didn't even have her usual urge to put on a disguise and peek in her neighbors' windows. Instead, she wore her bathing suit because she and Wendy had decided to meet at a local swimming pool.

So far, Gilda had kept her promise; she had refrained from questioning Stephen about whether he *liked* Wendy as more than a friend. Although she hadn't yet had a chance to observe interactions between Wendy and Stephen (something she looked forward to doing), as far as Gilda could tell, there had been no significant developments in her brother and her best friend becoming a couple after math camp ended. *We'll see what happens when we're back in school,* Gilda thought.

Gilda grabbed her beach towel, suntan lotion, and city bus pass and tucked the "Summer in D.C." scrapbook under her arm, planning to share the pictures with Wendy. *I'm almost glad the CIA didn't offer me a job right away,* she thought. *If they had, I wouldn't be able to tell Wendy all my experiences without worrying that I'm giving away classified information.*

Gilda ran out the front door, simply looking forward to seeing an old friend who had known her for ages—a friend who preferred true stories to the "perfect cover."

Acknowledgments

While the story and characters in *The Dead Drop* are fictional, most of the historical details mentioned in the book are true. Most important, the setting depicted here is a very real and wonderful place: Washington, D.C.'s International Spy Museum. This novel wouldn't have been possible without the help of friends at the Spy Museum who shared their extensive knowledge and expertise, and who allowed me access to some of their outstanding programs for kids of all ages, including "Spy Camp." In particular, I would like to thank Youth Education Manager Jackie Eyl—a master of disguises, gadgets, and dead drops whose enthusiasm, creativity, and humor come through in every youth program she facilitates. I am immensely grateful to Spy Museum Historian Thomas Boghardt, who is a model of professionalism, objectivity, curiosity, and dedication in his approach to researching and writing about the "secret history" that so often influences the stories that end up in our history textbooks. Thomas expressed support for this book when it was just an idea. He generously shared his knowledge and expertise and contributed to Gilda's latest adventures by opening up a fascinating world of espionage history. Finally, I would like to thank Peter Earnest, the executive director of the International Spy Museum, who is indeed "a gentleman and a scholar" as well as a former spy. With a career that includes thirty-six years of distinguished service in the CIA, Peter has managed to do the impossible: he combines clandestine service to his country with telling true stories. His contribution to greater openness and to an educated, informed, and engaged public comes through in the Spy Museum's fascinating lectures, broadcasts, and book events that explore some of the most crucial and controversial events of our time. In short, I discovered that the International Spy Museum is more than a fun diversion during a family trip to D.C. (and it is immense fun!): it has an educational mission that greatly impressed me. Through my contacts with so many impressive and genuinely helpful people, I became all the more excited to give Gilda Joyce a chance to have her own adventure at the Spy Museum firsthand.

The Dead Drop was written during a year when I had three toddlers in the house, and I have to acknowledge that every time I took out my computer to write, Max, Marcus, and Gigi were more than eager to "help." Sometimes they just wanted to look at pictures of trucks and helicopters, but they also did their best to put their mark on Gilda's story. Because of this, I am also all the more grateful to my lovely editor, Maureen Sullivan, who is charming, patient, insightful, and always kind. Maureen always projects a sense of peace and calm that helped me almost as much as her great editorial suggestions did. Thanks also to my husband, Michael, who kept the household running and mostly kept his sense of humor during many hours when I was writing. And as always, I am indebted to my stellar agent and dear friend, Doug Stewart, who has an expert sense of what works in a good story and who has opened up so many opportunities for me to connect with the fabulous readers of the Gilda Joyce series. Julia Uspaskikh and her family contributed their knowledge of life in Russia to the story. Finally, I would like to thank my father, Professor Kenneth Brostrom, who contributed a beautiful translation of a poem by the Russian poet Anna Akhmatova to this story, with input from his colleague Dr. Laura Kline of Wayne State University in Detroit. Thank you, Dad, for always valuing the writing life.

GILDA JOYCE
Psychic Investigator

Read about Gilda's first adventure, as the girl psychic investigator helps her family in San Francisco uncover the terrible secret that has a tortured ghost stalking their home!

GILDA JOYCE
The Ladies of the Lake

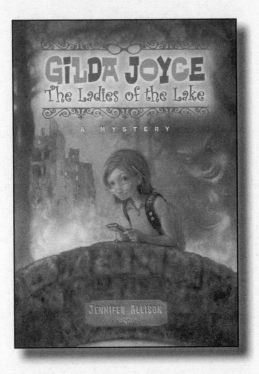

A mysterious death and a possible haunting at an
exclusive Catholic girls' school throws the student body
into an uproar, but Gilda Joyce is on the case!